A COUNTESS FROM MOSCOW

ALEX ALVIN

SASHKINA

Author: Alex Alvin
Cover Design: Damonza and Diego Catto Val
Editor: Kirsten Rees

•Website: sashkina.com
•Instagram: @alexalvinauthor
•Facebook: @AlexAlvinAuthor
•Email: alex@alexalvin.com

PART I

CHAPTER 1

November 1912

"Maman, how do I look?" Maria Suvorova tugged on one of her earrings, fidgeting in the seat of the carriage. She rolled down her gloves and stopped only when she felt her mother's firm grip around her wrist.

"Masha, please, be patient. We're almost there. And please remember, you must wear gloves at all times. Don't ever let a man kiss your hand ungloved." Her mother checked her watch and muttered under her breath, "Good, good, we'll just be a little late. The first ball of the season, and your very first ball, Masha!"

Masha.

Out of a myriad of nicknames, Masha was Maria's favorite. She could be called Mashenka, Marisha, Marusya, Mashulya. Her father called her Maria, and her governess, Antoinette, pronounced it the French way, rolling the 'r' for Marie.

"Oui, Maman." Maria sat back and looked out the window. "We're here!" She touched her hair, which she usually wore in braid but was now up in an intricate 'do that had taken hours, and squealed as the outlines of the Kutuzov estate appeared in front of them.

"Good, now, don't forget, we'll go upstairs to freshen up, and you have to slow down. Don't take your coat off yourself. Wait for the dressing lady to help you. And please, don't show your emotions, Masha. Stay calm. Remember where you come from. All eyes are on you tonight, Masha, a debutante of one the most prominent Moscow families." Her mother gave Maria a proud smile, reaching to tuck a loose strand of Maria's hair.

"Oui, Maman." Maria nodded, switching to French. She knitted her brow, trying to conceal her excitement. *My very first ball!*

Maria Suvorova had waited for this moment all of her life. All sixteen years of it. She looked down at the tiny bow that adorned the front of her off-white gown and retied it. The bow had been the topic of much debate, as it appeared in one of the latest fashion magazines, which, according to Maria's mother, disqualified it from being appropriate for a debutante's dress.

"It's too showy, darling, you don't want to look like you're trying too hard," Maria's mother insisted. "Your look has to be effortless, remember. It's the upstarts that follow the latest fashion, not people like us."

And so, Maria had to settle on a compromise – a small, barely noticeable bow.

"You look beautiful, Masha." The door of their carriage opened and they stepped out into the evening.

"Countess Zinaida Suvorova and her daughter," Maria heard the footman announce, and her heart leaped.

It's us! They're expecting us!

Until that moment, the ball was a vision, a dream she'd constructed after reading Pushkin. Only now did it start to feel very real, as she was blinded by the lights and followed her mother up the steps of the legendary mansion. With her mother by her side, Maria knew the evening would be perfect.

"This is my daughter, Maria," she heard her mother say, as if through a fog, taking in the glitter of the evening.

All chandeliers were lit and their light illuminated the bright hall of the mansion. Just as instructed, Maria followed her mother upstairs, into the dressing room, where they both took off their coats and adjusted their gowns. There were several other women in the room and Maria did her best not to openly gape at them. A diadem adorned one of the women's necks and Maria sighed, comparing it to her own miniature diamond earrings. They were small and under-stated, just like the bow on her dress. Another *unwritten rule*, according to her mother.

"We'll now be greeted by the hostess, Countess Irina Kutuzova," her mother whispered into Maria's ear as they descended the steps. Maria smiled with confidence, holding her head up straight. She knew what was expected of her. She needed to stand quietly next to her mother and say nothing.

Irina Kutuzova was a famous and very wealthy socialite, Maria had heard, the subject of much gossip in their circles.

Before she knew it, Maria was standing in front of the legendary Irina, who was even better in person than Maria had imagined. Extraordinarily beautiful and much shorter than Maria, the hostess had her blonde curly hair up in a puffy 'do. The woman wore a long gown of an ethereal green-gray celadon color that accentuated her large hazel eyes.

Doing her best not to gasp in adoration, Maria stood slightly behind her mother.

"Countess Suvorova, welcome." Irina smiled, and it was as if her whole face lit up.

"Thank you for hosting us. This is my daughter, Maria. It's her first ball." Zinaida Suvorova turned back to her daughter.

"Pleased to meet you." Maria stepped forward and blushed. Catching herself showing her emotions, she felt her cheeks redden even more. *This is harder than I thought.*

"Wonderful! I am so glad you chose my ball for your debut," Irina said.

Maria retreated behind her mother, expecting to walk away, but Irina continued speaking to her.

"So, my dear, how do you like it so far?"

Maria's heart started racing and her throat felt parched, as the eyes of the hostess fixed on her.

"Don't be anxious," Irina said. "I remember my very first ball as if it were yesterday." She stared at a distance. "Time goes by so fast, doesn't it?" She turned back to Maria's mother.

"How true." Countess Suvorova nodded.

Maria breathed a sigh of relief, now that the attention of the two women was no longer on her. She took a step back and almost bumped into a couple. Mortified, Maria slumped her shoulders, then immediately remembered her mother's instructions and straightened back up.

This is impossible! she thought. *The dances! The first dance is the polonaise,* Maria furrowed her brow, remembering the sequence of the ball, *then the waltz, then the mazurka.* She frowned, immediately recalling her dance instructor, a Frenchman, who had been recruited to get her ready for her first ball, and the endless rehearsals of the slow polonaise. Maria's body refused to slow down, to move gracefully and smoothly, as the instructor required her to do. She excelled in the fast dances, the ones that required her to be agile. She liked being constantly on the move.

"Masha," she heard her mother's voice and snapped out of her reverie. "Time to go into the ballroom."

"Oui, Maman." Maria nodded, moving alongside her mother into the glittering space.

"Now, Masha, remember, Count Nikolai will ask you for your first dance. We arranged it with the Yelagins." Maria's mother squeezed her daughter's hand. "But this is just the first dance. And then others will ask you to dance. Remember, one dance and you move on." Maria's mother gave her a reassuring smile. "You're going to do very well."

"Oui, Maman."

"I don't see him…" Countess Suvorova's voice trailed off. She surveyed the room, just as she'd taught Maria to do, slowly, casually, as if just looking around, but in reality scanning for a particular person. "But I am certain he'll be here any minute."

"Oui, Maman." Maria adjusted her bow, and immediately felt her mother's warning grip on her wrist.

"Masha, relax, you look fine. Try to enjoy yourself."

The ballroom was busy as more guests arrived, and the sound of voices intensified. Maria attempted to casually survey the room, but immediately caught the eye of an older general with a thick mustache and looked away in embarrassment. The ball wasn't going as she'd expected.

Count Nikolai. Maria thought of the solemn young man, who'd been appearing at their house with his parents nearly every Sunday for dinner ever since he'd finished the military academy in Saint Petersburg the summer prior. Count Nikolai's father, Corporal Yelagin, was a friend of Maria's father's, and the two men enjoyed spending time together. Nikolai Yelagin was in his mid-twenties, tall, had a receding hairline and bulgy eyes. Maria found him incredibly boring but wrote it off to their difference in age. He rarely spoke and spent most of the visits sitting in silence, the expression on his long face dignified, as if he pondered the futility of human existence.

"The Yelagin family is of the finest lineage, darling Masha." Maria's mother squeezed her hand. "And there he is now." Her mother, almost imperceptibly, darted her eyes to the farthest corner of the room.

Following her mother's gaze, Maria immediately identified the solemn figure moving through the crowd in their direction. With the distance closing between them fast, Maria tensed, preparing for her first dance.

"Masha, I'll go sit down. I'm not feeling well," her mother suddenly said.

Maria opened her mouth to react, but the next moment, her mother disappeared from view. The music started and, just as planned, Nikolai appeared in front of Maria. He was dressed in his officer's uniform, his hair slicked to the side.

"Permettez-vous?" he asked. The words she'd expected to hear.

The very first dance of her very first ball. She would remember this moment all of her life – so she'd been told. Everything was happening as if in a fairy tale. A tall man, an officer, the ball, and yet, instead of excitement, Maria felt a knot form in the pit of her stomach and something in her resisted accepting the dance.

She hesitated for a moment too long, and Nikolai must have noticed it, because he raised his eyebrows ever so slightly. Maria gave him one single nod. The next moment, she felt the count's hands on her gloved ones, as he swept her into the polonaise.

Dancing alongside Nikolai, Maria could hear her mother's voice in her head. "You can tell a lot about a man by how he dances. Don't trust the very good dancers, those are just out to get ahead in life. The social climbers. Some men have made a career out of it." Maria didn't know exactly what that meant, but she tried to assess Nikolai's skill as a dancer and compare it to her dance instructor's.

Nikolai's movements were slow, calculated. He knew the steps and led her through the dance with precision. And yet, she couldn't tell if the count was a good dancer. He was silent throughout, even though, Maria had been told, dancers made polite conversation. Maria knew she wasn't supposed to speak to him first, and the few minutes of the dance seemed like an eternity as other couples moved past them, and she and Nikolai danced the polonaise in silence. After the dance ended, the count led her back to the side of the room.

"Merci," he said, bowing slightly.

Maria also thanked him and glanced around the room, remembering too late she was supposed to do so casually and slowly. She didn't notice her mother, and was about to leave to look for her, but a waltz started. A young man materialized right in front of her, asking her to dance, and Maria accepted. She loved the waltz and eagerly joined the man in the fast dance, immediately forgetting about Count Nikolai and their awkward first dance.

The waltz was followed by another fast dance, the mazurka, which Maria danced with a very handsome young man, whose name she didn't retain, but who led her expertly through the dance and showered her with compliments, having learned it was her very first ball.

It wasn't until the fast dances were over, and Maria was completely out of breath, that she realized she hadn't seen her mother since the music had started.

Maman must be playing cards, Maria thought, walking away from the ballroom.

The sound of the music had faded into the background. She moved through the enfilade of rooms, deeper and deeper into the mansion. Each one filled with beautifully dressed guests, the atmosphere festive. Still no sight of her mother.

Panic rose in Maria's throat. This wasn't supposed to be happening. Her mother had promised to be by her side, to guide her through the ball. Having reached the back of the mansion, Maria was about to turn back, when she felt a firm tap on her shoulder.

"Countess Maria Suvorova?" It was one of the footmen, dressed in a gilded suit. "Your mother sent for you. Come with me, please."

"Yes," Maria responded, her lips feeling numb.

The man led her upstairs, to a room right next to the one where Maria and her mother had taken off their coats only an hour prior.

"Right through this door." He retreated and Maria entered. She found her mother reclined on a chaise. Zinaida Suvorova's face was pale, almost white, beads of sweat had formed on her forehead.

"Maman!" Maria yelped and kneeled beside her mother.

"My darling girl, I am so sorry. And at your very first ball." Her mother's lips barely moved, as Countess Suvorova squeezed out the words. "I think we better go home. Please ask for our carriage."

"Oui, Maman." Rising and rushing out of the room, Maria found the attendant waiting by the door and gave him the instructions. Minutes later, they walked down the steps, Maria holding her mother's hand, without saying goodbye to the hostess.

Once in the carriage, her mother closed her eyes and let out a wheezing sound that made Maria's blood run cold.

CHAPTER 2

"Just a little bit longer, we're almost home," Maria repeated over and over, like a prayer, as she held her mother's hand on the ride back.

It seemed to take forever as the carriage crossed the Moscow river, then navigated the winding streets of the Taganka neighborhood. At last, they turned onto Goncharnaya Street, where the Suvorov estate occupied half a block, and Maria saw the familiar outlines of her home. On summer days, its warm yellow made it seem especially welcoming, but now, in the darkness of the night, it looked almost sinister.

They pulled into the driveway, and immediately Potap, their butler, ran up to the carriage, his face bearing the usual, gruff expression. He twisted his thick mustache, as he opened the door.

"Maman isn't well," Maria managed to say and broke down in tears.

Immediately, Potap and two footmen helped Countess Suvorova inside the house.

"Go, call Dr. Petrovsky," Potap ordered, and one of the

footmen scurried away, as Maria followed the procession inside. To her relief, she saw her nanny standing at the door. Dunya had been Maria's nanny since Maria was born and had also cared for her father before that.

"Something is wrong with Maman!" Maria gripped her nanny's hands.

"I heard they are fetching the doctor. He will come soon. Come on, I'll put you to bed," Dunya said and headed upstairs, expecting Maria to follow. "I'll help you change."

When they were sitting in her room, Maria asked, "Shouldn't I do something? Maman might need me."

"Let the doctor examine your mother. Don't worry." Taking the pins out of Maria's hair, Dunya said, "Let's make sure you brush your hair before going to bed."

Maria's hair was long, to her waist, and every evening, Maria took extra care to brush it, running the comb through it at least fifty times, as per her mother's instructions.

"Thank you, Dunya. I just wish Papa was here," Maria said.

Her father, Count Suvorov, had gone away on business to survey their estate near Tula. He usually made the trip earlier in the fall, but this season had postponed it until November. He had been discussing selling the estate. Though Maria didn't know the details, she'd overheard her father speaking to her mother about the sale.

"Yes, yes." Dunya's voice was stern. "Now, let me get you some drops, so you can sleep." She pursed her lips.

"But Maman?" Maria tried to protest, but she knew arguing with her nanny was useless.

"You need to rest. The doctor will be here soon. He'll take care of her."

* * *

THE FOLLOWING MORNING, Maria woke up to a different reality. Hushed voices. The mirrors covered.

Her mother had died overnight.

It happened right around midnight; Maria was later told, shortly after Dr. Petrovsky had arrived and diagnosed acute heart failure. They had sent for the priest from their local church, who arrived just in time to administer the last rites.

In a daze, Maria spent the day wandering from room to room, accompanied by Dunya, who never left her side. Alternating from weeping to sitting by the window, she stared out at the cold November rain.

Maman is gone.

Maria refused to believe this. She didn't dare enter her mother's bedroom until the nanny took her there.

"Your mother died a saint's death. She looks so peaceful. Don't be afraid," Dunya told her, and Maria agreed to go in.

But she didn't really see her mother. The person laid out on her mother's bed was only a shell. Not the person Maria loved, who'd been by her side all of her life. Her mother was her best friend, and now there was a gaping void.

Count Suvorov arrived from Tula that evening. Maria had heard, through a fog of her grief, the sound of his carriage pulling up, Potap summoning the stable boys, giving them instructions.

"Masha, your father wants to see you," Dunya called her.

"Yes, okay," Maria responded listlessly. She put down the crocheting she'd been holding on her lap, though she couldn't concentrate on it, and was about to follow the nanny out of the bedroom when she heard a knock on the door. Her father always spoke to her in his study, and Maria looked up in surprise to find her French governess rushing in without waiting for a response.

"C'est terrible, quelle tragédie!!" The governess ran up to

her and took Maria's hands into her own. She spoke in rapid-fire French.

Maria pulled back. Antoinette had come recommended by a family friend and was hired earlier that year, after the previous governess had moved back to France. Having a native French speaker at home was a requirement in order to finesse Maria's pronunciation and grammar. Ever since Maria could remember, there was a French governess by her side. Although, she had been told, Antoinette was to be the last governess and would stay with the family until Maria turned eighteen or got married, whichever came first.

"I returned as soon as I heard. I was visiting my girlfriend and then I found out." Antoinette switched to her heavily accented Russian. "And I cannot imagine losing a mother. Oh, how sad. How sad!"

"We need to go." Dunya put her hands on her hips. "Your father is waiting." She spoke to Maria, ignoring the governess. Dunya never hid her dislike of the French governesses, whom she considered a nuisance, and always established her primacy over Maria's upbringing with them.

"Oh, poor girl," Antoinette rolled the 'r,' "I am zere for you. I vill support you."

"Merci, Antoinette." Maria breathed out, as the three of them went downstairs. Maria entered, then closed the door of the study firmly behind her, leaving Dunya and Antoinette outside.

"Have a seat." Her father pointed to a chair across from him. "Maria, life will be different now." He rubbed his neck.

"Yes, Papa…" Maria started to say, but stopped short, fighting back tears.

She'd never cried in front of her father, had been taught to contain her emotions so as not to upset him, but now struggled to do so. Her father was rarely around, but that, Maria had been told, was normal. Maria was always with her mother, couldn't imagine life without her. Couldn't understand how to go on.

"Maria, it's just you and me now," her father squeezed out. "We must be strong." Maria noticed red rims under his eyes, like he'd been crying. "We must be strong," he repeated again, and looked away.

* * *

HER MOTHER's funeral was on the third day after her death, at the Church of the Transfiguration of the Savior, atop the Taganka hill, right down the street from the Suvorov house. It was known as the Bolvanovka church and was legendary. Maria's mother had always told her the miraculous story, how, at the very place the church had stood, Russia threw off the Tatar-mongols in the fifteenth century after Tsar Ivan III refused to pay tribute to them.

Following the funeral procession uphill, each step made her mother's death more real. The bells tolled and Maria shuddered at the realization it was for her mother. The church was crowded, full of people Maria had met at one point or another in her life. But there were also some unfamiliar faces. Count Nikolai was there, accompanied by his parents, Corporal Yelagin and Countess Yelena Yelagina.

Dressed in all black, Maria stood next to her father, receiving condolences. It was an endless line of people, all of them encouraging Maria to stay strong and to trust her mother was in a better place. She dug her nails into the palms of her hands to stop herself from crying. At the very end of the procession, she noticed Irina Kutuzova.

The glamorous socialite looked completely different from how she appeared at the ball but was still incredibly beautiful. After expressing her condolences to Maria's father, Irina fixed her hazel eyes on Maria.

"Maria, losing a mother so young is a terrible thing," Irina Kutuzova said. Maria nodded, expecting Irina to continue with the same platitudes as the others, but instead she heard something else. "And nothing will bring her back. But you have to keep on living. Please remember that. When you're ready, please find me. I host a salon each Tuesday." Irina passed Maria a card.

Maria looked down at the tiny card now in her hand and stuffed it into her pocket. "Thank you," Maria mumbled, staring after the woman in confusion.

* * *

AFTER THE FUNERAL, Maria had taken to sitting in her bedroom, brooding, staring out the window. Everything reminded Maria of her mother, and she found herself unable to move on.

"Masha, Masha." Dunya shook her head. "It'll pass. It'll pass. The Lord is watching over you, Masha. Let me take you to church."

But going to church didn't help. Maria lit a candle for her mother, prayed for solace and peace, but none came. Instead, she felt as if she had a gaping hole in her heart.

Her mother's wake, done on the fortieth day after death, fell right before Christmas. A smaller crowd of mourners came to their home and Maria suffered through it, accepting condolences, while seated next to her father. He had become even more reserved and distant, spending most of his days in his study with the door closed.

"Papa, are we going to celebrate Christmas this year?" Maria asked him after the wake was over and the visitors left.

"Your mother is in charge of that," he mumbled absentmindedly, then, rubbing his tired eyes, looked up at Maria and sighed. "Oh. Yes. Of course."

Grateful for something to do, Maria took charge and asked the servants to set up the tree, just as they had done each year, decorating it and even sent for oranges. They always got oranges around Christmas. She walked into the living room to survey the decorations, proud of her efforts, and noticed the bowl filled with the fruit.

And then it hit her, the smell of citrus feeling like a gut punch.

Ignoring the servants, Maria bit her lip and ran into her room. She collapsed on her bed in tears, the memory of her mother and the celebration that was gone forever.

Nothing would bring her mother back.

CHAPTER 3

*M*aria found her life unraveled. Her education stopped completely after her mother's death. Before, private tutors appeared in succession, based on a well-organized schedule, teaching her English, dancing, literature, French and piano. But soon after her mother's death, all of her instructors quit one after another, either because her father stopped paying them or because their contracts weren't renewed. The only one who remained was Maria's governess, Antoinette, who announced she would be finishing her contract, before leaving for France.

In the Suvorov household, it was Maria's mother who was in charge of the social calls, the various outings, the museum openings, the galas, the receptions, and the balls. Soon, all of that, too, went away.

Letters arrived but sat unopened. Two months after her mother's death, Maria collected them and brought them to her father, padding into the dining room, trying to catch him at breakfast.

"Papa, we have these invitations." As she laid down the

thick stack, an image of her mother going over these religiously, twice a week, responding to each one, popped into her head.

"Maria, this isn't the right time." Her father looked at her, his eyes unfocused, and pushed his chair back. She watched in silence, as he withdrew into his study, the door closing behind him.

Count Suvorov ignored all social obligations, responded to no one and retreated into himself completely. Maria had no choice but to do the same.

By the time the year of mourning ended, most of their acquaintances and the social circle Maria's mother had cultivated over the years had nearly disappeared.

Maria now spent most of her days in Dunya's company. In her seventies, Dunya had first come to their house as a young girl, barely a teenager, and had dedicated her whole life to the Suvorov family. "I've taken care of babies since I myself was this big," Dunya liked to say, placing her hand two feet off the ground. Dunya was a short, stout woman, and, no matter the weather, wore wool shawls that she knitted herself, wrapping herself tightly in them.

Dunya was the one to make sure Maria remembered to eat, escorted her outside for walks, brushed her hair and put her to bed.

With time, the two of them took up needlework and crocheting. In the evenings, after Maria felt a little better, they told each other stories. Dunya told her fairy tales, tales of lore, about brave warriors, princesses, the far-away kingdoms with magical animals, dragons, and fairies. She told Maria stories of the domovoys, the elves who ran their house late at night and hid in their secret domains, under the cupboards, during the day. In turn, Maria read to Dunya out loud, because Dunya did not know how to read.

* * *

JANUARY 1914

Frost cracked into pretty lines on the glass panes, as Maria stared out the window from her favorite spot, with her needlework on her lap. Dunya sat next to her, knitting a shawl.

"Dunya, remember the story of Maria, the princess?" She straightened up the crocheting and examined it. "The one you'd tell me when I was little? You haven't told me that one in ages."

"And her husband, Andrei, the shooter? I sure do." Dunya's face took on a dreamy expression. "You used to like that story. You told me your husband would be named Andrei, just like Maria's in the story." Catching an incredulous expression on Maria's face, the nanny nodded. "Oh, yes, you did. You sure did."

"That's silly," Maria chuckled.

"Remember, how that story went? There was a tsar, and he had a shooter at his service named Andrei. The shooter went hunting one day, and he almost shot a beautiful turtledove. But the bird spoke to him and told Andrei to take her home. So he did, and it turned out to be a beautiful young princess."

"Yes, I remember." Maria shook her head. "It's funny how I wanted to be like that princess, right?"

"You used to tell me about your wedding, too." Dunya put the knitting down. "You knew exactly what your dress would look like."

"I don't remember that at all." Maria shrugged.

"Who knows, Masha, who knows?" Dunya's voice trailed off. "If you ever want to know the name of the man you'll marry, we can do a divination." Dunya, despite being deeply religious, believed in dreams, superstitions, predictions and signs, and shared her knowledge readily.

"How do you do that?" Maria straightened up.

"It's easy. For this particular divination, you go outside and then you ask the first man you meet his name. And whatever that name is, that's going to be the name of the man you'll marry."

"Just like that?"

"Yes. Well, it works better in a village. Not sure how you'd do that in a city, all of them, strangers, walking around." Dunya furrowed her brow. "But I suppose it'll work. You know what they say. You can't escape fate."

"Well, anyway, I'm not about to get married any time soon." Maria looked up at Dunya, "Why don't I read something to you?" She reached for a book.

"Oh, yes." Dunya nodded. "Maybe something short?"

"Alright." Maria surveyed the tomes of Dumas, Hugo, the novels by Dostoyevsky, and put them aside. At the bottom of the stack she saw the tome of Pushkin, which had been sitting, untouched, for over a year.

"How about some Pushkin?" Maria flipped the book open and a card fell out.

"Would you look at that!" Dunya stared at the card. "What is that Masha?"

"It's from this woman," Maria picked up the calling card, "Irina Kutuzova." She remembered the card the socialite had given to her at the funeral. The card was printed on thick, light mint paper, the letters of Irina's name relief stamped. In the corner there was an image of a bird sitting on a branch. The card was so delicate, beautiful, each detail so intricately done, it was a work of art in itself.

"How pretty. And the dove. Look, we were just speaking of a turtledove, and here it is," Dunya said.

"You're right." Maria stared at the card in amazement. "I guess it's a turtledove."

"Yes, just like in the fairy tale. What does it say?" Dunya asked.

"Just her name." Maria examined the card and noticed the text at the bottom of the card in tiny letters. "Salon on Tuesdays." Maria looked over at Dunya. And suddenly, an idea occurred to her, and she nearly jumped. "Do you think I should go there? To the salon? Is today Tuesday?"

"It is Tuesday." Dunya put aside her knitting and pushed her chair back. "You should definitely go, Masha. Sometimes angels make things happen that way. Look how you found this card on the exact day."

"But what do I wear?"

"I'll help you get ready. And we can let Potap know to get you dropped off." Dunya tilted her head.

Maria wasn't sure what one would expect at a salon, but, as she got ready with Dunya's assistance, she did her best to dress appropriately for a social occasion. It was the first time Maria would be out of mourning. She had gotten so used to dark colors, that she decided to wear a silk navy-blue dress, which the seamstress had made for her out of her mother's old gown.

An hour later, Maria was on the way to Irina Kutuzova's mansion.

I wonder if she still has the salon on Tuesdays, Maria thought.

She remembered what her mother had told her about Irina Kutuzova. Irina's husband, the wealthy Count Kutuzov, spent his winters in the French Riviera, giving Irina an unprecedented degree of freedom.

As soon as the stately red mansion on Ostozhenka Street popped into view, Maria's stomach flipped in anticipation. This was the place she last saw her mother well. Maria almost turned back home, unsure she could go through with her plan.

The Kutuzov mansion was enormous, even by the generous Moscow standards, its color a deep shade of red. It was designed by a famous Russian architect, Kekushev, in the medieval castle style. Kekushev's signature lion adorned one of the mansion's towers, looking up at the sky. The mansion was built in the daring, special style Muscovites adored and the residents of St. Petersburg, the capital city, considered to be bordering on outrageous. It was a well-established fact that the capital city looked down on the provincial Moscow, considered it lacking in beauty and class.

But Moscow was catching up to St. Petersburg fast, thanks to people like Irina, who also dedicated her spare time to philanthropy and supported museums and theaters, bringing the best European art to the second Russian city.

The building was just as Maria remembered it. The magnificent white lion, guarding the mansion from the tower, the portico decorated in the Neo-Grecian style. Hesitating for just a moment, Maria instructed the driver to wait for her and entered.

A tall doorman dressed in a gilded uniform opened the door and looked at her expectantly, raising his eyebrows ever so slightly. Maria understood he was waiting for her to present her calling card. But she'd never had them done, so Maria said simply, "Countess Maria Suvorova."

Had Maman been alive, she would have reminded me to print the cards, Maria thought and felt the edges of her lips droop.

The doorman bowed to her, and, immediately, another man popped into view, took her coat, and led her into the depths of the mansion. Maria heard voices, the clanking of glasses, and found herself in a brightly lit room, which she recognized as the ballroom. There were chairs arranged in five rows. In the center, a grand piano stood with three music stands next to it.

A quartet will perform, Maria guessed.

A group of men stood near the entrance, busy in conversation, and Maria moved past them, eyes wide, wondering what to do next. She was about to retreat into the corner of the room, when she felt a light tap on her shoulder.

"Well, hello, Countess Suvorova? You came to see me, at last."

Maria turned to find Irina Kutuzova standing in front of her. The woman was dressed in a dark green low-cut dress. Irina's hair was up, revealing her neck and shoulders. A long emerald necklace hung low, dropping into her cleavage.

"Hello, Countess Kutuzova," Maria said, blushing. She tugged at the sleeves of her dress, which seemed much too modest next to Irina's.

"Please, call me Irina. My dear, how lovely to see you. You look well." Irina gave her a kiss, and Maria's cheeks turned an even brighter shade of pink. "We have a wonderful program tonight. An opera singer will be performing."

"Thank you for having me," Maria squeezed out, mustering what she remembered of the instructions her mother had given her on small talk. "And for welcoming me into your beautiful home."

"Oh, my dear, please, no need to be so formal. I'm all about being modern and breaking society rules." Irina adjusted the necklace, so it ran exactly down the center, between her breasts. "We're living in the twentieth century, aren't we? And yet, and yet," she sighed, "Russia is so recalcitrant. It's like we're these dinosaurs, really. Are we ever going to catch up to Europe? Who knows?" Irina pouted.

Maria nodded politely, unsure of how to react.

"So I decided to break the mold, to shake things up." Irina winked. "Let's have some champagne. We must celebrate. I'm so glad to see you here." Irina called over a waiter, who immediately approached with a tray.

"Thank you." Maria took a glass, which felt cool to the touch.

"Now, darling, the musicians will be starting soon. I'll go check on the other guests. And break the mold, remember!" Irina blew a kiss and disappeared.

Break the mold, Maria repeated to herself, taking a seat in the back for an easy exit.

No one sat next to her, and, with the empty seats on either side, she felt as if she had a protective barrier around her. The musicians took their seats, and then the opera singer walked on stage. She was dressed in all red, the gown complementing her bright red hair, that rested in thick curls. The singer was busty, nearly bursting out of her dress. She pouted as she faced the audience, her expression defiant and yet vulnerable at the same time.

"Tatiana Orlovskaya," someone whispered.

Maria remembered hearing the name of the famous opera singer, who performed at the Bolshoi Theater, and stared at the woman in amazement.

This can't possibly be the one. Maria noticed a program on the seat next to hers, and saw the very singer's name printed on it. *This is incredible,* Maria thought, and straightened up in anticipation.

The concert started, and, as Maria listened to the renowned singer perform arias from 'Carmen' and 'La Dame aux Camelias', she reveled in the beauty of the evening. Just a few hours prior, she was at home, having spent over a year sequestered there. Now she was at a salon where incredible things were happening. It was as if a parallel, glamorous world, had opened up and welcomed her inside.

Before she knew it, intermission was announced, and Maria unfolded the program on her lap, preparing to wait.

"How was the first part?" she heard a man's voice speaking right into her ear.

Maria looked up to see a young man had taken a seat next to her, blocking her exit. Her first thought was to seek an escape, and she was about to ask him to get up, so she could leave, but then she looked at the stranger and froze.

Dark-gray, almost black eyes looked at her in wonder. Soft, chestnut hair fell against his chiseled cheekbones. Struck by his appearance, she did not speak.

Looking at her intently, the young man added, "I was late, and didn't want to walk in during the first part."

"It was lovely," Maria croaked.

"I wish I'd gotten here earlier. I love Tatiana's performances," the young man said. "I don't think we've met. Andrei Zurov."

"Maria Suvorova." She managed a smile. "It's my first time here."

"You'll like it here, of that I am certain. I hope you become a regular," Andrei said, and Maria felt her heart rate accelerate. Time stopped, and it was as if there was no one else around them. It was just Andrei, his gaze pulling her in, taking over her whole world.

"Thank you." Maria adjusted her hair, which she had braided and pinned with Dunya's help.

"Countess Kutuzova is incredible, and a great patron of the arts. We're so lucky to have her in Moscow," Andrei added after a pause.

"Are you speaking about me?" Irina walked up to them. Andrei leaped to his feet, and so did Maria, nearly bumping into him. The sudden closeness made her blush. He was much taller, broad-shouldered, with a strong physique.

"Glad the two of you have met. Andrei, you aren't boring Maria with your accomplishments, are you now?" Irina shook her finger at him in mock admonishment.

"I wouldn't dream of it." Andrei smiled and looked at Maria, who stood still, wide-eyed.

"Maria isn't aware!" Irina let out a giggle. "You haven't told her?"

"Told me what?" Maria asked.

"Andrei is a rising star at the Moscow Art Theater," Irina said.

"You're an actor?" Maria's mouth gaped open.

Andrei grinned. "Guilty as charged."

"Andrei, please, allow me. You shouldn't be so modest." Irina interrupted. "Stanislavsky himself loves Andrei. What was it the latest review of your performance said?"

"Oh, there is no need." Andrei raised his hand in protest, but Irina continued, tilting her head like a curious bird.

"Let's see. I believe they called your performance 'a triumph' and 'a spectacular achievement'. Was that it?"

"Thank you, Countess Kutuzova." Andrei turned red.

"Andrei, I beg of you. If you're to succeed in life, you must learn how to accept praise."

"I will try, Countess Kutuzova." He nodded.

"Now, I'll leave the two of you. I must check on my other guests." Irina floated away and left Maria and Andrei together.

"I've never met an actor before," Maria blurted out, and immediately regretted her words. They seemed much too forward.

"If you'd like to meet more actors, I can introduce you." Andrei pierced her with his gaze and Maria gulped. "Would you like to come to one of my performances?"

"Yes," Maria responded, realizing a second too late she'd just accepted an invitation from a near-stranger.

"Perfect, come this Friday. I'll be performing in *The Brothers Karamazov*," Andrei said, taking a step back.

"Countess Kutuzova will be there. She usually comes every Thursday and Friday."

"Thank you," Maria said.

Intermission ended and they took their seats. The opera singer started another aria, but Maria found she could not pay attention to the singing. She strained to keep her head fixed straight forward, feeling like she wanted to turn and smile at the handsome stranger sitting next to her.

Or, better yet, to go somewhere to talk more with Andrei instead of sitting in the salon that suddenly felt much too constrained.

CHAPTER 4

$\mathcal{M}$aria unhooked her dress and surveyed herself in the mirror, moving her head slightly to the right. She smiled at her reflection, still reveling in the glitter of the salon and the encounter with the charming actor.

"And how was your evening?" Dunya fluffed up the pillow on the bed in one quick, practiced motion.

"It went very well." Maria blushed, picturing Andrei's handsome face. Oblivious, the nanny had now moved to pulling off the bed covers. "I just realized something, Dunya. You know how we spoke of divinations before I left?" Maria tried to keep her voice even to conceal her excitement, but Dunya abruptly stopped what she was doing and turned to Maria, crossing her arms.

"Yes?"

"I met someone, and his name is Andrei. That's the first name I heard. Does this mean I'll marry a man by that name?" Unable to hold the nanny's gaze, Maria focused on pulling out her hairpins and setting them carefully on the vanity.

"Andrei? Maybe, maybe," Dunya mumbled. "But you

didn't do a proper divination, Masha. We'll try another time, alright?"

"Yes, please."

After she climbed into bed, Dunya fixed the covers over her. "You get yourself some sleep, Masha."

"Good night, Dunya."

The door closed behind her nanny. Maria stared into the darkness, trying to picture Andrei – his handsome face, so tall, so broad-shouldered, the sensation of being next to him – and felt her breath catch.

It was as if an almost physical need to be around Andrei suddenly emerged, and now she was powerless to resist it.

A part of her wanted the prediction to come true. Maria pictured herself in a wedding gown, standing next to the handsome actor at the altar. As she snuggled into the soft pillow filled with goose down, the fantasy dissipated and she stilled with the sudden realization: *I could never marry an actor.*

With her aristocratic lineage, she had been brought up to marry a descendant of one of the most prominent Russian families.

"I must marry an equal, someone from a family just like mine. I must do my duty," she whispered into the darkness.

* * *

ANDREI RARELY LEFT Maria's thoughts the next day.

As her curiosity to learn more about him got stronger, she grew impatient. Friday seemed very far away, and so, by Thursday morning, she had come up with an idea. The Moscow Art Theater building was just three blocks away from the Eliseyevsky market, the most famous grocery store in Moscow, if not all of Russia. Maria had not been there since her mother died, and now she had a plan.

I'll go to Eliseyevsky, and I'll stop by the Moscow Art Theater on the way back, Maria decided. *It's only to see the theater, nothing else*, she reassured herself, before giving instructions to Potap.

The Eliseyevsky market was just like she remembered it. As the footman opened the door and she stepped inside, the familiar smell hit her first.

Walking into the bakery section, the aroma of vanilla and chocolate filled the air, and Maria stared at the selection of desserts. Shelves filled with cakes, cookies, and baked goods, all intricately arranged. The market looked like a palace, with exquisite decor, gorgeous chandeliers, walnut wood panels, and an incredible selection of food. Even in the dead of winter, Eliseyevsky boasted tropical fruit. Its salespeople spoke fluent French in addition to perfect Russian and could advise on the best wine and cheese pairing, cold cuts and meat for any taste.

Hesitating for a moment, Maria walked up to the counter with the pastries and stalled in front of it, unable to decide. She'd never gone to the market alone, and now scrambled to remember the proper way to place an order.

"Mademoiselle," a salesman dressed in an immaculately pressed uniform, approached her, "how may I be of assistance?"

"I'd like to buy a dessert," Maria breathed out, wide-eyed. "And some chocolates!" She decided on the spot.

"Is there a particular dessert you would like? Cream-filled pastries, perhaps? May I suggest an eclair? Or perhaps the Napoleon?" The man pointed at the display.

"The Napoleon. Yes, please." Maria smiled in relief, remembering the mille-feuille cake she used to buy with her mother. "May I have two of them, please?" *Dunya will love these*, Maria thought, watching as the clerk placed the pastries into a box and tied it with a beautiful bow.

A few minutes later, she emerged from the market carrying the neatly wrapped treats.

The visit to Eliseyevsky boosted her confidence. As she instructed the driver to take her to the Moscow Art Theater next, Maria was filled with a sense of accomplishment.

Turning the corner from Tverskaya Street onto Kamergerskiy Lane, her carriage pulled up in front of the Moscow Art Theater building. It was a beautiful, recently reconstructed mansion, of a very light, greenish-gray color that occupied an almost entire block. She got out of the carriage and walked closer.

Right away, the poster for 'The Brothers Karamazov' caught her eye. And then she saw it. *Andrei Zurov as Alexei Karamazov* written in red letters.

It's true! He's really an actor, Maria gulped.

She threw another look at the poster, and, just as she was about to leave, a coach pulled up to the front of the theater. A tall, slim figure wearing a boiler hat emerged, and, immediately, a man, who'd been sitting on a bench in front of the theater, ran up to him.

"Please, please, another audition, please, another chance?"

"No." The slim-figured man shook his head and entered the building, as the second man dejectedly walked away.

Maria stared after him before returning to her carriage.

* * *

"Marie! You're back!" Antoinette greeted her by the door. "We've been waiting for you to come back." She knocked on the door of Count Suvorov's study.

"Antoinette, Papa doesn't like to be disturbed." Maria tried to stop the governess, but Antoinette opened the door without waiting for an answer.

"Oleg, Maria is here," she said in her accented Russian.

Oleg? Maria hadn't heard anyone call her father by his first name since her mother died. Before Maria could say anything, Antoinette emerged from her father's study once more and called her inside:

"Marie, your fazer would like to see you now."

"Merci, Antoinette." Maria walked in. She had always considered this room to be off-limits. It was her father's domain.

The massive desk that stood by the window, the bookcases with the thick tomes, the works of the likes of Voltaire and Aristotle, and the one-hundred volume encyclopedia, 'Brockhaus and Efron', her father had acquired, as it was being released, created a somber atmosphere.

Her father was sitting on the couch in the middle of his study. He indicated for Maria to sit on a chair across from him, and, as he did so, his eyes darted to the entrance, where Antoinette stood.

"Papa?" Maria opened her eyes wide. *Is he going to fire Antoinette?* She'd tried to calculate how much time was left in Antoinette's two-year contract.

The governess walked around the couch and stood behind the count, her hand on his shoulder.

"Maria," her father cleared his throat, "Antoinette and I have an announcement."

"An announcement?" Maria darted her eyes from her father's face to Antoinette's and back.

"You see, it has now been over a year since your mother's death."

"Yes, Papa." Maria felt a knot form in her stomach. *Did Papa find out about the salon? Maybe I wasn't supposed to go?*

"Sometimes life takes an unexpected turn," the count said and looked up at Antoinette who let out a giggle.

In that moment, Maria understood.

She watched, as if in slow motion, as her father reached

and squeezed Antoinette's hand. The white, plump hand of the governess in her father's with the massive ruby ring on his pinky finger.

"Antoinette and I, you see, Maria, have discovered we have feelings for each other. She has been a consolation to me in my time of grief." The two exchanged a look full of adoration and love.

"Papa?" Maria's throat suddenly felt parched, but it was as if her father didn't hear her speak. He continued, "But people talk. Society norms, they are stifling." Count Suvorov loosened his collar, as if invisible hands were strangling him at that very moment. "This summer, Antoinette and I will go to Nice to be together. Away from prying eyes."

"To France?" Maria gulped.

"Yes, to the French Riviera," Count Suvorov said. "Your mother and I went there right after we first got married. And of course, I've been there before, as a young man, to Monte Carlo." The Count paused. "Maria, we decided it's better for you to stay in Moscow." As he said this, he looked up at Antoinette and she nodded in approval.

"Have a seat," he told the governess, and Antoinette walked around, sitting next to Maria's father.

"Stay in Moscow," Maria muttered, struggling for words.

Two pairs of eyes stared back at her. The dispassionate expression on her father's face matched that of Antoinette's. There was an imperceptible similarity in the way they acted. The way their eyebrows moved and their noses scrunched in unison.

"Yes." Count Suvorov nodded, and Antoinette also moved her head, repeating after him.

"Very well." Maria got up to leave, eager for an escape. The thought that she should congratulate her father and Antoinette occurred to her too late.

"Maria, there is something else," her father said, a wounded expression on his face. "Please sit back down."

"Oui, Papa."

"Maria, you surely remember the Yelagins. Of course, the unfortunate events surrounding your mother's passing put everything on hold." Maria's father gave her a pointed stare, "But you will undoubtedly understand the urgency of deciding your fate."

"Urgency?" Maria's hands suddenly felt like icicles. A feeling of doom rushing over her.

"Dear girl, you're turning eighteen at the end of the month, Antoinette reminded me." Maria's father cleared his throat. "And with your mother gone, of course, these matters should be settled by women." Her father rubbed his neck, and Maria noticed his knuckles had turned white from pressure. "It had simply slipped my mind, Maria."

"Papa?" Maria noticed Antoinette fidgeting next to her father.

"You see… how can I put it?" Count Suvorov started again, but Antoinette placed her hand on his and interjected.

"Marie, what your fazer is trying to say is that you should be getting married."

"Married?" Maria's mouth gaped open. "To whom?"

"Well. Yes. I've checked with Corporal Yelagin, and they are still quite interested."

"Papa!"

"Surely you remember his son, Nikolai?" Marie's father scratched his head, and, turning to Antoinette, mumbled, "When was the last time they came over?"

"Count Nikolai? I haven't seen him since Maman's wake." Maria raised her hands in protest. "I barely even know him!"

The image of her first ball, the dance, the anticipation, and then, the solemn figure leading her into the polonaise appeared in her mind. Immediately followed by the image of her mother's face covered in cold sweat, the ride back, the funeral. All of it came flooding back.

"But I can't, Papa," Maria yelped.

"Maria, please be reasonable. If your mother were alive, it would been arranged with Nikolai's mother, but you must understand. I did what I could." Count Suvorov squeezed Antoinette's hand.

"Please, Papa," Maria protested again.

"Don't worry, I know how these things work. You will have time to get used to Nikolai. To get to know him." Maria's father nodded his head eagerly. "The Yelagins will be coming over this weekend, and we will discuss everything together."

"This weekend?" Maria repeated and saw Antoinette looking at her in eager anticipation.

"A Sunday dinner, like we used to have when your mother was alive." Her father rose from his seat as the cuckoo clock struck four.

CHAPTER 5

*H*er head pulsating, Maria rushed out of the study. The shock of learning about her father's relationship with Antoinette, the engagement to Count Nikolai, had thrown her into a state of shock. Antoinette's face, and that of her father, so alike, so in tune with each other. Maria felt like an outsider in her own home.

Only one person could make her feel better. Her nanny's bedroom was downstairs, next to the kitchen. When Maria was little, she would spend hours with Dunya in the tiny space. It was safe and familiar, the narrow bed pushed against the wall, the table in the corner, the chair. And on the other side of the room, the trunk that, she knew, housed all Dunya's earthly possessions and had been a gift she received after serving the Suvorov family for twenty years.

"Dunya." Maria knocked on her door. Immediately, there was the shuffling of footsteps and Dunya opened the door.

"What is it, Masha?" Seeing her face, the nanny gasped.

"Can I come in? Please. Something terrible just happened."

"Oh, yes." Dunya stepped back, letting Maria inside.

Struggling to speak, Maria choked out her words, "Papa just told me…"

Dunya put her arms around her. "Don't be upset, Masha."

"But he, he said," Maria continued and again, could not finish her sentence.

"Your father and the madam. It's just the way of the world." Dunya sucked her lip and huffed.

"You knew?"

"I knew him and the madam were an item." Dunya sighed.

"How long have you known? Why didn't you tell me?"

"It's your daddy's affairs, Masha. None of my business." Dunya straightened up her dress. "But I can tell you, this ain't nothing new."

"But they're leaving for France, before Easter. And Papa said I must get engaged."

"Engaged? You?" It was now Dunya's turn to look surprised.

"To Count Nikolai Yelagin. I can't even remember what he looks like."

"Is he the military man who used to come over here with his parents?"

"Yes. I haven't seen him in over a year." Panic constricted Maria's voice. "I don't want to marry him!"

"Engaged doesn't mean you'll be getting married." Dunya scratched her head. "Let's go have some tea. How about it? And on Sunday we'll go to church and pray, let the Lord guide the way."

"Very well." Maria acquiesced. She didn't quite share Dunya's firm belief in God but speaking to her nanny and sharing the news made Maria feel better. "Dunya! I just remembered, I got you some cake. Napoleon, like Maman used to buy." Maria leaped to her feet. "I think Potap took it to the kitchen."

"Oh, yes, Napoleon. That guy was no good. Burned

Moscow. But our city was protected by God himself." She crossed herself. "I don't know why they'd name a dessert after that villain." The nanny shuffled out of her room with Maria following.

The kitchen was the domain of their cook, Fekla, a plump woman with ruddy cheeks in her mid-thirties.

"Hello, Fekla," Dunya greeted the cook as they entered the kitchen, but Fekla scowled at the nanny. Then, turning to Maria, the cook plastered an eager smile on her face and adjusted her bright headscarf.

"Hello, Miss." Fekla lingered on Maria's face. "I'm just starting a soup." She pointed to the table where vegetables had been arranged on the cutting board. "A little later today, miss, the grocer's delivery was delayed."

"Of course, thank you, Fekla," Maria said.

"Fekla, we're going to have some tea. I'll start the samovar," Dunya announced, dignified.

"Oh, yes, yes. I'll leave you to it." Fekla sauntered out of the kitchen, and Dunya took over. In the hierarchy among the staff who served the Suvorovs, it was Dunya who had utmost seniority, rivaled only by Potap.

Potap Filimonovich Konopatov was a tall, burly man with a figure of someone who was used to regular physical labor. He had been with the Suvorov family for over twenty years, having moved to Moscow to work for the family after completing military service, where he learned to read and write. Potap's responsibilities at the mansion extended from being a butler to maintenance to bookkeeping. He was indispensable to the functioning of the mansion. The man could fix most things, and if he didn't know how to do it himself, he would find someone who did.

He had a bushy mustache that he twirled between his thick fingers when lost in thought. Potap had a family, or, as he called them, 'his people', back home, in a village near

Ryazan. There were never any specifics, and Maria suspected that this family didn't really exist, couldn't exist really, because there had never been a time when Potap wasn't around.

Dunya and Maria had started drinking tea together the previous summer, and it grew into a daily ritual. Maria loved watching her nanny heat the water and prepare the samovar. Dunya liked her tea strong and drank it with sugar cubes she picked up with special tongs. She crunched on them, while sipping her tea, letting the sugar dissolve gradually.

Dunya tried to entice her on a few occasions, but Maria preferred her tea without sugar. Both loved dessert and were in full agreement that having cookies or cake with their tea made it so much better.

It wasn't until the two of them sat across from each other, the servings of Napoleon in front of them, that Dunya spoke.

"Don't you worry, child, we'll go and pray, go and pray together. Let the Lord guide the way."

"Yes," Maria said vaguely. She felt her lower lip tremble, remembering the conversation with her father and Antoinette's new status. "If Maman were alive, none of this would have happened. But now, I can't even ask anyone about Count Nikolai. Maman always told me, there are things to find out before marriage..."

"I never been married myself. I so wish I could help you." Dunya hesitantly took a bite of the Napoleon, then, savoring it, opened her eyes wide. "Isn't it something?"

Maria put a forkful into her mouth. "You're right. It's so delicious. The cream is incredible." She furrowed her brow, pausing in contemplation.

"What is it, Masha? I just saw that look on your face." Dunya shook her head.

"I think I just got an idea." Maria pushed the plate aside. "I will tell Irina Kutuzova about the engagement. I think she can help."

"Is that the woman with the turtledove?"

"Yes. That's the one. I'll go see her tonight." Maria fidgeted in her seat. After the conversation with her father, she'd nearly forgotten about the planned outing to the Moscow Art Theater. But now Maria felt eager to act.

"You'll go to her house so soon?"

"I can see her at the Moscow Art Theater." Maria jumped up. "I should get ready. Dunya, thank you, thank you. This is a great idea."

She pecked Dunya on the cheek and ran out of the kitchen.

* * *

POTAP TOOK her request in stride, and just an hour later, Maria was on her way to the Moscow Art Theater for the second time that day. This time, the street in front of the theater was filled with coaches, the theater crowd gathering for the performance. Several groups stood together, engaged in conversation, and Maria adjusted her hat and raised her head up high, trying to project a look of self-confidence.

She gave the driver instructions on where to wait for her and walked to the box office. Suddenly, her plan to see Irina at the Theater appeared much more difficult to execute than she had imagined.

Where would I even find Irina here? Maria wondered and was about to take her place in line to the box office, when she noticed Irina strutting towards her.

"Maria! Is that you?" Irina Kutuzova wore a sable coat over an elegant shimmering dress, a tiny hat pinned to her blonde curls. "My dear, I am so glad to see you."

"Good evening, Countess Kutuzova. I mean, Irina."

"I didn't expect to see you here." Irina took her by the arm. "Let's go in, shall we?" They walked into the theater vestibule.

"Andrei invited me." Maria blushed, only then remembering she had come to the theater a day early. "But I've come to see you. Andrei said you'd be here," she added, her voice hurried.

"Yes, I come every Thursday and Friday." Irina leaned closely, and as she did so, Maria caught a whiff of the woman's sweet perfume. She whispered, "Andrei is quite charming, isn't he?"

"Yes." Maria tried to give her voice a tone of worldliness. "I suppose so."

"But is everything alright, my dear? You look a little pale this evening," Irina asked as they were handing their coats to an attendant. "By the way, is this your first time here?"

"Oh, yes. I mean. It's my first time here, but not everything is alright," Maria blurted out.

"Whatever happened?"

"I just learned I'll be getting engaged." Maria's voice faltered.

"Getting engaged? It's quite sudden, isn't it?" Irina raised her eyebrows. "Who is the young man?"

"Count Nikolai. Yelagin."

"I know the Yelagins." A slight furrow of the brow followed. "They are a decent family. The mother is a busybody, but she is harmless, really."

Maria nodded, biting her lip. She'd expected more, a solution, a way out, and now hoped disappointment didn't show on her face.

"I guess I have no choice but to take you under my wing." Irina reached and brushed her gloved hand against Maria's cheek. "You're such a sweet girl. Listen, if you follow my advice, getting married just might be your way to freedom."

Irina winked at her imperceptibly. "It is a woman who holds all the power in a relationship, don't you know?"

Maria shook her head, opening her eyes wide. Now she badly wished to hear what else Irina had to say on the topic, but they heard the first bell.

"Let's go in, shall we?" Irina led her inside. "Stanislavsky demands everyone be in their seats by the third bell, so the performance doesn't get disrupted."

"But I don't have a ticket."

"My dear, you're with me." Irina flashed a confident smile. "I'm one of the founding members of this place."

Following Irina inside, Maria took in the theater hall, the crowd, the noise, the anticipation of the play about to begin, but as soon as they took their seats, the swirl of thoughts of the events of the day overpowered her. Her father's announcement, Antoinette's smug face, her own imminent engagement to Count Nikolai, all made it nearly impossible to focus on the play.

"This theater is like nothing you've seen before. It redefines acting," Irina whispered into her ear. "And this play is a gem. I've seen it a dozen times, and Andrei is incredible. Such talent."

Maria nodded and did her best to make sense of what was happening on stage, but she hadn't read the novel by Dostoyevsky and now felt decidedly confused. She sat in silence, her mind wandering from her engagement, to Antoinette, to her father's departure for Nice, to Irina's words about marriage which contained a promise. A secret that held the key to her future. Unsure how she would get through the next hour, Maria prepared to politely suffer until the intermission.

All until Andrei Zurov appeared on stage.

Her body reacted to Andrei before her mind did and she jerked upright. Maria's heart started beating so fast, she wondered if Irina could hear it. Andrei Zurov moved on stage deliberately, his gestures smooth. It no longer mattered to her if she didn't follow the plot. She just wanted to watch Andrei.

He spoke, and it was as if he were speaking right to her, confiding in her. His voice was melodic and deep, his eyes sparkled.

Maria's mouth gaped open as she stared at the actor from the safety of the box. She assumed Andrei couldn't see her, but then he looked over at the audience and paused. It was as if his gaze burned right through her.

"How do you like it?" She heard Irina's purr, which reached her ears as if through a thick fog.

"It's lovely," Maria croaked. She felt both hot and cold but couldn't look away.

The scene ended and Andrei left the stage, and only then could she catch her breath. She wanted him back. She winced, noticing Irina looking over at her, a victorious smile on the woman's face. The bell rang for intermission, and Irina rose from her seat.

"We can go backstage now. You can say hello to Andrei. He'll like that," Irina noted casually.

"We're allowed backstage?"

"Oh, yes, my dear." Irina put her hand over Maria's reassuringly. "We are. Ready?"

Maria barely paid attention to where they were going and followed Irina, who confidently led her through one of the doors down a long corridor. It was like a maze, busy, full of people, shuffling back and forth, carrying things, exchanging words and instructions Maria didn't catch. It was like they spoke a language she didn't understand, but everyone else backstage did.

Someone said hello to Irina, she responded, and then they stood in front of a door with the number five on it. Irina knocked softly, but the door opened on its own and a man emerged. Maria recognized the same slim figure she'd seen enter the theater earlier that day. Only now the man wasn't wearing a hat or a coat but was dressed in a fully buttoned suit.

"Countess," he acknowledged Irina with a half-smile. "Always a pleasure."

"Monsieur Stanislavsky." Irina tilted her head playfully. "We're just checking on our favorite actor."

"Of course. I see. Well." Stanislavsky raised his eyebrows ever so slightly and his eyes fell on Maria. The realization that it was the legendary director himself she'd seen earlier that day struck her and she blushed.

This was the man who had singlehandedly revolutionized theater in Russia, had reimagined it, had rebuilt it from scratch to make it more accessible to all people. He had introduced the concept of a theater director, of method acting – the genius who had taken art to the highest degree. Maria had heard her mother speak of him many times, of how symbolic he was to Moscow, having picked not the capital city, but the second Russian city for his theater.

"How silly of me!" Irina exclaimed in fake bewilderment, as her eyebrows leaped up. "You've never met our youngest theater lover?"

"I have not had the honor." Stanislavsky was staring right at Maria, and she extended her hand for a kiss. Her fingers trembled as the famous director pressed his lips ever so slightly to her hand and nodded. "Enchanté, mademoiselle," he murmured and nodded at Irina. "I must leave you now."

Then, tilting his head to the dressing room, he called, "Andrei, please remember what I said. Your arm shouldn't stay glued to your body. Put your hand in your pocket. It looks more natural that way."

"Yes," Andrei replied.

At that moment Maria bulked, realizing Andrei must have been watching their entire interaction from inside the dressing room. He was wearing a suit, the same one she'd seen him wear on stage, but the collar of his shirt had been loosened, revealing his muscular neck.

"We just stopped by to say hello," Irina said. "I'm showing Maria around."

"Thank you for coming by." Andrei rose from his seat and walked towards them. Maria took a step back, as if standing close to Andrei would put her entire being at risk.

"I am sorry we interrupted your conversation." Irina shrugged in a way that made it clear she wasn't actually excusing herself but said it as a mere formality.

"It's always a pleasure to see you, Countess. And Stanislavsky loves to make adjustments, so you practically saved me!" Andrei smiled. "Hello, Maria." His eyes fixed on her; she had no choice but to meet his gaze.

"Good evening, Andrei," Maria said. His name felt soft against her lips, like a prayer.

Time stopped. Maria smiled at Andrei and felt a current run through her body. And though it lasted for only a moment, she felt a sudden certainty that Andrei could feel it too.

The bell rang and broke the spell, spurring them into action.

"Please come by on Tuesday, Andrei. I've prepared a nice surprise for our next salon," Irina said.

"Thank you, Countess," Andrei said, buttoning his collar. "I trust Maria will be there as well?"

Both of them were turned to her, and Maria read curiosity in Irina's eyes and definite interest in Andrei's.

"Yes," Maria said. "I will most certainly be at the salon on Tuesday."

Andrei. Maria thought of the actor on her way home. The look in his eyes, the hint of his interest in her, the promise of seeing him at Irina's salon. She pictured him – so tall, handsome, talented – and blushed.

The second she got inside, Maria rushed to her bedroom to examine herself in the mirror, eager to see how she'd appeared to Andrei. She always wore her light brown hair up but had let it down so it fell below her shoulders. Her eyes were a dark shade of brown and Maria tried to bat her eyelashes the same way she'd seen Irina do. When Irina did it, the socialite looked flirtatious and adorable, but Maria could not get the expression right.

"Masha, you're back." Dunya walked into her room. "Did you speak with that woman?"

"Yes, I did. She told me the Yelagins are a nice family." Maria scratched her head, "And marriage would be a way to freedom?" She frowned, trying to remember Irina's words that had been so quickly displaced by Andrei.

"Trust the Lord, Masha, trust the Lord. I'm glad she made you feel better. Now, go to bed. It's late. The morning is wiser than the evening." Dunya cited her favorite proverb, as she lifted the covers off Maria's bed. "Come on, come on."

"Yes, Dunya."

* * *

THE OUTING to the theater and the conversation with Irina had served their purpose, having assuaged Maria's concerns over the impending engagement. The following morning, when her father, the look on his face solemn, asked her to prepare for the Sunday dinner with the Yelagins, Maria was calm and collected.

"Papa," she noted casually. "I have thought about what you said and I agree with you. Count Nikolai is a suitable candidate."

"You do?" Her father stared at Maria in bewilderment. Then, clearing his throat, corrected himself. "But yes, I am very glad. Very glad indeed. And Antoinette was absolutely correct to suggest this."

"Of course, Papa." Maria narrowed her eyes ever so slightly but did not otherwise react, so certain she was of her own bright future ahead.

"Now, Maria, because of the delicate situation, perhaps at dinner you wouldn't mention Antoinette's new role. I count on your discretion."

"Of course, Papa," Maria said again, feeling sorry for Antoinette and the need to hide her in fine society. There was no need to clarify the issue any further, given the unwritten code, where a liaison between an aristocrat and a governess would not be paraded to another noble family.

While getting ready for the Yelagin family visit, Maria went over the events of the previous evening in her mind again and again. *Andrei is quite charming!* Maria recalled Irina's characterization of Andrei. *Charming!* She daydreamed, recalling him as Alexei Karamazov, their conversation backstage, and the promise of seeing him again on Tuesday put her in a pleasant mood, which lasted until Sunday, when Count Nikolai arrived for dinner with his parents, Corporal Yelagin and Countess Yelena Yelagina, the very woman Irina Kutuzova called a 'busybody.'

The elder Yelagin was a quiet man, who spent most of the evening grunting and drumming his fingers on the table, while Yelena Yelagina dominated the conversation, covering all topics, from summer weather to managing estates. And closer to the end, hearts and fates that were meant to be together. This not-so-subtle reference to her son and Maria was well-received by Maria's father.

Count Nikolai, like his father, was a man of few words. Maria examined Nikolai, taking in his distinct equine features and his eyes, large, bulgy, and a strange shade of a murky green. She tried to picture herself being married to him. But her imagination failed her, and so, seated across from him, instead she let her mind wander.

And so, while Nikolai ate his meal in silence, Maria spent the dinner dreaming about how Andrei's touch felt on her hand and the promise the actor's gaze held.

She would have continued savoring the memory until they finished eating, were it not for the sudden realization the table had fallen into a strained silence. Expectation thick in the air.

Maria's confusion lasted for only a moment, because right away, Count Nikolai cleared his throat and pushed his chair back.

"Mother." Count Nikolai bowed to Yelena, then turned to Maria's father. "It is my honor to ask for your daughter's hand in marriage."

"Granted." Count Suvorov chuckled. "Just a formality, of

course. So, it is settled, then. We shall announce the engagement right away."

Maria sat in stunned silence. No one, not Nikolai, who was now officially her fiancé, nor his parents, not even her own father, had asked her whether she accepted the engagement.

What did Irina mean exactly about having more freedom? Maria wondered, as she observed as a mere spectator, as if the conversation did not directly impact her future. *I guess I'll learn more once I'm married,* Maria concluded.

"Yes, yes, we must hurry, so that we do so before Lent." Yelena nodded. "All propriety must be observed. And the wedding can be this summer," she added after a pause. "Of course, not in May. That's inauspicious. In April, right after Easter is the best. July is also a good month for a wedding." Yelena tapped her fingers impatiently on the table.

"Could it not wait until September?" Maria's father asked.

"September? Why so long?" Yelena raised her eyebrows, throwing a look of concern Maria's way. As if her future daughter-in-law could vanish at any moment and had to be contained.

"It's just that I have planned a business trip to France. I'll be leaving in April, as soon as the weather clears, and I expect to come back at the end of summer."

"But then, I suppose we don't have much of a choice. We must wait. Though it's not ideal, it's not the end of the world," Yelena noted, a look of disappointment on her eager face.

"So, it's settled then. I must confess, I am touched. It's an honor to have our families unite through our children." Count Suvorov extended his hand to Corporal Yelagin, who shook it earnestly.

As they walked out of the dining room, out of the corner

of her eye, Maria caught Antoinette's silhouette moving in the shadows.

As soon as the Yelagins left, the governess ran up to her, and, speaking in rapid-fire Russian with French words inter-mixed, whispered, "Félicitations! Nikolai is so tall and impos-ing. And how he looks at you, with such reverence. That's exactly how a man should look at his *amoureuse.*" Antoinette finished the last word with a conspiratorial hoarseness in her voice.

Maria's father walked up to them.

"A September wedding. Why not, why not?" He scratched his chin, then put his arm around Antoinette, and the two retreated into his study.

CHAPTER 7

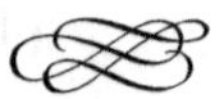

"*D*unya, I just got engaged," Maria shared with her nanny later that evening. The two of them were in Maria's bedroom. "Did you see Count Nikolai? Antoinette says he likes me."

"I did, I did, Masha." Dunya narrowed her eyes slightly. "When is the wedding?"

"I guess in September. After Papa comes back from France."

"A September wedding? It's a good month. Akulina got married in September. She's been married a long time now." Akulina, Maria knew, was Dunya's closest friend.

"So, I think I'll go back to see Irina," Maria noted after a pause. She had just taken down her hair and was running a brush through it. "I want to tell her about the wedding." Maria turned to Dunya to see her reaction.

"You mean the theater again?"

"No, the salon. I'm thinking I'll go on Tuesday again this week."

"Yes, yes. The turtledove. That little card sure was pretty." Dunya nodded in approval. "So pretty."

"So, do you think it's okay for me to go? Since I'm engaged now…" Maria's voice trailed off.

"I don't see why not, Masha. You still got time before the wedding."

Maria noticed a glint in Dunya's eyes.

"Dunya, I was just thinking, I guess the divination really doesn't work." Maria shrugged. "I got the name Andrei just the other day, but I'm going to marry a Nikolai!"

Instead of an answer, Dunya let out a sigh and shook her head.

* * *

I'm now an engaged woman. Maria straightened up in the seat of the carriage, which was taking her to Irina's salon. *I'll be Countess Yelagina. Maria Yelagina,* she repeated. Then said her own name. *Maria Suvorova has more ring to it.*

Looking over at the Moscow river, Maria twisted the beads on the skirt of her dress, an embroidered gown that used to belong to her mother, and her thoughts turned to her mother's wedding dress. Maria found both dresses while going through her mother's closet the day prior. Her mother's wedding dress hung in the closet, beautiful, delicate.

Maria sighed, remembering how her mother had let her touch the dress years ago, and told her the story of her own wedding. *I wish Maman was here.*

The carriage pulled up to Irina's mansion, and Maria got out. She walked up the steps, a bounce in her step from the anticipation of seeing Andrei. But as soon as she walked inside, Maria remembered what Irina had said about a 'surprise.'

Instead of a glamorous, glittery crowd, a haggard-looking man approached. He was dressed in a gray overcoat that had seen better days. The man extended his hand to her, and

53

Maria noticed his nails. They were long and dirty, with the right pinky nail yellowing at the end.

The man gave her a curious look. "Ivan Afanasievich Engelghart."

"Countess Maria Olegovna Suvorova." She extended her hand for a kiss, hesitating ever so slightly. Maria wasn't sure why she stated her full name and title, including the patronymic, but as she did so, she noticed the man's eyebrows arch upwards.

Ivan gave her a haunted look and shook her hand instead.

"I will give a speech tonight," he muttered.

"How lovely? What kind of speech?"

"About social justice." Ivan straightened his shoulders back. With his head held high, he stood just a little taller than Maria.

"I'm Andrei Zurov." She heard from behind, and her heart fluttered. Maria snapped back and saw Andrei. He extended his hand to Ivan first, then acknowledged Maria and she gulped. His eyes burned through her, and it was as if the whole world had faded away.

"Hello, Maria." Andrei turned to her. "I managed to get here on time tonight. Rehearsal ended early."

"How nice." She nodded.

"How did you like the performance?" Andrei leaned closer in, his cheeks blushing slightly.

"It was lovely. Really great."

"I'm Ivan Afanasievich Engelghart." Ivan cleared his throat. "I'll speak tonight about Russia's fate in the world. About social justice."

"Ah! I see you've already met Ivan." Irina fluttered to them in a beige dress, a delicate pearl necklace around her neck. "We should be ready to start in a minute. And since we'll be covering serious topics, let's be merry now," she proposed, and immediately a waiter materialized next to them, with a tray of flutes filled with champagne.

The four of them took the glasses.

"It's an honor." Ivan bowed while holding his flute up. "Thank you for hosting me tonight."

"Of course, of course, Ivan. My pleasure." Irina lifted her glass.

"A toast!" Andrei said. "To friendship."

"Yes, to friends and comrades," Ivan added.

They clinked their glasses.

"The best French invention," Irina noted, examining her glass with satisfaction. "I make sure I get only the Louis Roederer brand. Now, we should get started." Irina surveyed the room, then raised her eyebrows at Ivan.

"Of course, Irina." Engelghart nodded.

Maria wondered why Ivan didn't address Irina properly, by her title. As she followed the hostess into the brightly lit room she saw, like the last time, chairs had been arranged in rows. But in the center, next to the grand piano, stood just one chair.

Ivan walked confidently to the lone chair and stood, leaning on it, examining the crowd.

"Let's sit together," Andrei said to Maria, and she followed, the idea of being next to him filling her with excitement. He led her to the last row, and they took their seats in the back of the salon, like the week prior.

"What do you think of Ivan?"

"I'm not sure." Maria shrugged.

"I heard he's a big-time revolutionary," Andrei whispered. As he did so, he leaned close, and she felt his breath on her ear.

"A revolutionary?" She turned to face Andrei. His face was right next to hers. Just a little closer, and his lips would be on hers.

"Friends," Irina's voice broke the spell between them, "many of you have been coming to my salon for years. And you know my love for the arts. Tonight, however, I decided to try something different." A murmur ran through the room.

"I invited a special guest, Ivan Afanasievich Engelghart, here to speak to you about social justice. This is a topic that is very important to us all. It is about Russia's future and our place in the world. Please, over to you, Ivan." Irina turned to the speaker, who cleared his throat and produced a piece of crumpled paper out of his pocket.

The room grew very quiet. Irina took a seat in the first row, the noise of her chair scraping the floor slightly the only sound in the room.

"Comrades!" Ivan said, throwing his head slightly back. It was as if he had grown in size, and his shabby appearance no longer mattered. "Russia's future is in our hands! Together, we can change history. But first, let me tell you what's happening in our country."

Ivan continued to speak, describing the dismal conditions at the factory where he worked. He spoke of students who had nothing to eat, of peasants who did not know how to read, of the urban poor who drank themselves to death, of the ignorance and darkness of the Russian countryside, of the lazy landowners who exploited the peasants, of the misery that surrounded them, but went unnoticed.

By the end of his speech, Maria was so moved, she felt tears well up in her eyes at the injustice and at the need to help the underprivileged.

Listening to Ivan, Maria thought of her mother, who had collected donations at Christmas for a local orphanage each year. A tradition Maria had completely forgotten until that instant. *I should have collected funds for the children,* she thought ruefully, but at that moment Ivan raised his voice.

"Comrades, we must act!" Ivan appealed to the room. "It is now or never."

"I think he's on to something," Andrei whispered into her ear.

"I call on you to use your resources to transform Russia. What are you doing with your time? The world is changing. France went through a revolution over a hundred years ago. Russia is way behind. We must advocate for change. We must join the proletariat!" Ivan pumped his fist in the air. His face was flushed, beads of sweat forming on his forehead, as he stared at the audience in triumph.

"Thank you for your attention," he said and stuffed the crumpled paper back into his pocket.

Irina got up from her seat and clapped. Others in the salon also started clapping, hesitantly at first, and then someone in the front row stood up, and others followed. The whole room gave Ivan a standing ovation.

"Join the proletariat!" someone called out, and others repeated, "Join the proletariat!"

"Vive la révolution!"

"Vive la révolution!" Andrei repeated, turning to her. "Maria, this is an incredible day! We're part of history. I feel it, I really do." He took her hand.

"Yes." Maria nodded, blushing in excitement. "What an incredible evening, indeed."

Following the speech, the guests surrounded Ivan, asking him questions, offering their support, showering him with compliments. Andrei joined the crowd, while Maria quietly slipped away, mindful of the time.

When Maria got home, and was hanging up the dress in her mother's closet, she noticed her mother's wedding gown. It was only then that she remembered she hadn't shared the news about her engagement and wedding with Irina.

CHAPTER 8

$\mathcal{E}$xactly one week after the engagement, Nikolai Yelagin called on Maria. He came by himself, appearing at the Suvorov mansion on a cold Sunday afternoon. Maria had been expecting his visit and led him to the drawing room, where he sat across from her. They left the door open to ensure propriety.

"Maria," Nikolai said. "Thank you for accepting my hand in marriage." He cleared his throat, and, not waiting for her to speak, continued, "I want to use this opportunity to get to know you."

"Of course." Maria averted her eyes.

"Once married, you and I will move to the Yelagin estate, away from Moscow. I believe living on the land is important."

"Away from Moscow?" Maria's voice faltered.

"Yes, away from the city. From its corrupt influence." Nikolai scratched his forehead and Maria noticed his receding hairline. "We must live in the purity of the land, the traditional way. Morality, first and foremost, especially for the children." Nikolai's eyes bulged slightly. "Our children," he added for emphasis.

"Yes." Maria nodded, feeling a knot form in her stomach.

"I am glad you've been brought up the traditional way, Maria. It is refreshing to meet someone pure and unspoiled by society." Nikolai twisted his lips in a half-a-smile. "You see, I am responsible for the land my ancestors have owned for generations. I am the sole heir of the Yelagin dynasty and must procreate." His eyes glazed over. "You understand, Maria, what this means?" He paused. "Once married, we'll have an obligation to produce male heirs. I have looked into your bloodline, and I must say, it's the best Russian stock there is."

"Thank you," Maria said, unsure if she should feel flattered or revolted by his words.

Count Nikolai continued speaking, as Maria sat in stunned silence, listening to his views about morality, destiny, and responsibility to his glorious ancestors. Nikolai spoke of purebred horses and dogs, and how some people paid more attention to their lineage than to their own.

"It's a pity, Maria, a real pity. Russia cannot afford to lose its best. But I've made it my mission in life to contribute to the Russian aristocratic stock. With you by my side," he said triumphantly and rose to leave.

"So, what do you think?" Dunya asked after the visit, running a brush through Maria's hair.

Maria stared blankly at her reflection.

"Nikolai wants to move away from Moscow, to live on his estate, once we are married." Maria bit her lip, deciding to omit the part of the conversation where Nikolai lectured her on the importance of producing male heirs and the purity of Russian aristocracy.

"Well, if that's the case, I'm coming with you," Dunya announced, dropping the brush.

"After I get married? You will do that?"

"Absolutely, Masha." The nanny put her hands on her hips.

"Thank you, Dunya, I don't know what I'd do without you." Maria jumped up and gave her nanny a hug.

* * *

AFTER NIKOLAI'S VISIT, Maria suspected he would not approve of her visits to Irina's salon. But, after giving it some thought, she decided to continue going. *We're not married yet,* she told herself, as she got ready to go to the red mansion for the third week in a row.

To Maria's surprise, she found Ivan at the salon again, but this time, he brought with him several other young men. They spoke excitedly of the need to reform Russia to keep up with the West. Like Ivan, they spoke of the injustice that existed in Russia, of the oppression of the classes, of the ruling class that was living in the past and trying to hang on to power while exploiting the hard-working proletarians.

They called to raise funds to support reform, because the future of the whole country was at stake. Maria sat next to Andrei, listening to their speeches with interest. And the week after that she returned, eager to hear more. Maria paid close attention, enthralled by almost every word.

Despite the conversation at the salon becoming focused on politics and fundraising, Maria and Andrei still found time to speak together. Over several weeks, bit by bit, she got to know Andrei, also sharing details of her life. She savored their interactions and had managed to learn a lot about the actor.

His father worked as an accounts manager for a prominent timber merchant in Kazan. Andrei was the oldest son and was expected to follow in his father's footsteps but broke with his family tradition and became an actor. His decision had sent the Zurov family into a frenzy.

She was shocked to learn that when Andrei was accepted to attend the best drama college in the country, the Higher Theater School in Moscow, his family disowned him. Andrei had graduated with honors, but they did not know of his success.

"I have not spoken to my parents in over five years," he told Maria one evening. "One day, maybe they'll see my name on a poster and will come to see my performance. But I doubt it will ever happen. I'm on my own in this world." He ran his hand through his soft curls.

"Just like that?" She paused. "Come to think of it. I'm also alone in this world. My father is about to marry my governess."

"And your mother?"

"She died," Maria shared. "It was unexpected. One evening, she didn't feel well." With a sigh, Maria took a look around Irina's salon and added. "It actually happened right here. After my first ball."

"I'm so sorry." Andrei looked at her with compassion. "Here I am, talking about myself, and you've had such tragedy in your life."

"Tragedy?" Maria paused. "I guess so. But maybe you can reach out to your parents?" Maria asked, wishing to change the subject. "Make up with them?"

Andrei shook his head. "That will never happen. I'd always loved acting. Even when I was little, I put on plays for the family. I could never be anything else. And the only way for them to accept me again would be if I became an accountant," Andrei noted ruefully. "And besides, I would not want to give up the life I have now. Here, in Moscow. The friends I've met here." His eyes lit up as he looked at her, and Maria felt a current run through her body.

He means me, she thought and the idea made her jittery with excitement.

A bond between the two of them had formed and was growing stronger with every visit.

* * *

"Ouch," Maria yelped.

Rushing to finish a crochet project, she scratched her finger with the hook. She remembered one of Dunya's favorite sayings, 'easy does it,' and put the nearly completed throw aside.

Staring out the window, Maria noticed the first signs of spring were in the air. The snow had started to melt, and the tiniest buds popped up on tree branches. Several days prior, Count Suvorov left Moscow to finalize the sale of the Tula estate before leaving for France.

Because of her father's absence, they would not be receiving the Yelagins that day, though it was Sunday, and Maria smiled. A knock on the door snapped Maria out of her reverie.

Dunya walked in, her face flushed.

"Masha, Count Nikolai is here to see you," Dunya breathed out.

"Nikolai? With his parents?" Maria checked the time, wondering if the Yelagins had not been informed of her father's absence.

"He is alone. Come now, Masha. He says it's urgent."

Maria rushed downstairs to find Count Nikolai pacing in the hallway. His hair, usually slicked to the side, was out of place and, as he saw her, he hastily buttoned his collar, which had come undone. She walked over, expecting Nikolai to greet her as he usually did, by kissing her hand.

But instead, he knitted his brow, and, darting his eyes Dunya, said, "Maria. I needed to see you alone."

"What is it?" Maria stepped back, leading Nikolai to the drawing room. "Did something happen?"

"It's a delicate matter, Maria," Nikolai uttered.

They took their seats across from each other. Nikolai sat on the edge of the chair, crossed and uncrossed his legs, looked at Maria, and, struggling to speak, drummed his fingers on the side table. Maria waited in silence.

At last, the count squeezed out, "I've been informed of your association." His face contorted in anger.

"Count Nikolai? I don't understand."

He must know about Andrei. But how? She'd become a regular at Irina's salon and hadn't missed one in nearly two months, but had never mentioned this to Nikolai.

"I've been informed. You must immediately stop." Red blotches popped on the count's face.

"Stop what?" Maria muttered.

"Your association compromises your good reputation," Nikolai said. "I only pray that Mother doesn't find out." He raised his hands in frustration. "This is why I came to see you now. I gave you the benefit of the doubt. I realize you're still young and naïve. Surely, she took advantage of you." He stared at Maria as if seeing her for the first time. "Surely, this can't be true." Nikolai's nostrils flared.

Maria gulped, scrambling to stay calm. *She?*

"I don't understand." She blinked fast.

"Have you ever been to Irina Kutuzova's salon?" Nikolai jumped up and approached. As he hovered over her, she felt an almost paralyzing terror. "I've been told that you were seen there. Is that true?"

"What?" Maria's lips felt numb.

"My bride visits a salon that houses subversive elements. Associated with the woman who conspires to overthrow the

Tsar!!! The Tsar!!! Who has been ordained by God himself to rule Russia." He was gesticulating wildly. "Do you have any idea what kind of people she brings together?" Nikolai's eyes looked like they would pop out of their sockets.

"But this isn't true," Maria mumbled.

"So you've been there! Oh!" Count Nikolai paced the room.

"Yes. But Irina is my friend. She's very kind. She supports the arts." Maria crossed her arms.

"The arts?" Nikolai sneered. "Do you realize the secret police, the *okhranka*, is after her?"

"What?" Maria opened her eyes wide. "But we only speak of the poor. That's all."

"Maria, you are a naïve girl. I don't expect you to understand what you have done." Nikolai furrowed his brow. "Yes, just a naïve girl. When I saw your name on their list, I thought it must be a mistake. A good friend from the military academy works at the *okhranka*, it's just by chance I found out. I heard Martynov himself is personally supervising Irina Kutuzova's case. Promise me you will never go back there." He had completed his circle and hovered over Maria once more.

"Of course, I won't go back." Maria swallowed hard, looking up at Nikolai. "But I promise you, it's nothing like that. It's some kind of misunderstanding."

"She is really taking her freedom too far, that woman! Her salon is like a festering boil." Nikolai spouted out. "And my young bride, contaminated by those people. I pray it isn't too late." He glared at Maria.

As a tiny bit of his spit hit her cheek, she subtly wiped it away. Maria realized her entire world would soon be limited to this man and his family.

CHAPTER 9

As soon as Count Nikolai left, Maria ran to her room. She sat at her vanity and took her hair down. Brushing her hair always helped her think, and, as Maria ran a comb through her locks, she pondered what to do. A knot had formed at the very end and, as she jerked, it tugged and she cried out in pain.

"Masha, what's wrong?" Dunya walked in at the very moment.

"Dunya, everything. I really miss Maman." Maria fought back tears. "Nikolai told me I can't go to the salon. He told me the secret police are after Irina."

"Oh, dear. But Masha, this sounds dangerous." Dunya scratched her head. "You better do what Count Nikolai says. He'll be your husband soon." The nanny crossed herself. "Trust in God to show you the way."

That night in bed, Maria tossed and turned, unable to fall asleep, then sat up with one thought. *Andrei. Andrei could be in danger!* The realization pierced her imagination. *If the secret police are watching Irina's salon, then they must have Andrei's name on their list.* Maria gasped. *I must warn him. And he can warn Irina! Of course!* Maria checked the time.

It was just after eleven, and if she hurried, she could make it to the Moscow Art Theater in time to see Andrei. The Moscow Art Theater actors, Maria knew, stayed at the theater after each performance to chat with Stanislavsky and get his feedback, which the theater director liked to provide right away.

Maria hastily put her hair up, got dressed, and ran downstairs. Noticing the closed door to Dunya's room, Maria rushed outside to the carriage house to get Potap.

"Potap, please, can you take me to the Moscow Art Theater now? It'll be quick. I have to see someone."

"Yes, yes, of course." Potap rubbed his eyes. He gave her a curious look but said nothing. Years of service had taught him not to ask questions. "It'll be just a few minutes."

On the way to the theater, Maria stared out of the coach at the Moscow streets. The snow had almost entirely melted during the day, but the air felt crisp, and she pulled her coat around herself tightly. She got to the theater to see the last coach pull away. Maria confidently walked in. She remembered the side entrance leading to the dressing rooms and headed straight to the door. Navigating the corridor, she almost reached door number five, when Andrei materialized in front of her just as she was about to pull on the handle.

"Maria!" He breathed hard.

"Andrei, I came to see you." She could feel her cheeks flush a crimson shade of red and hoped the dim lighting concealed it.

"I wanted to speak to you, too," Andrei said.

"Really?" Maria looked up at him, so tall, so strong. Her heart beat faster.

"Yes, maybe we can speak in my dressing room." Andrei turned to the door.

"Of course." She followed him inside. The door closed and it was just her and Andrei now.

He sat down. Andrei hadn't changed and was still dressed as Alexei Karamazov. He tugged at his collar, hurriedly loosening the top button and rolled his neck in relief.

"Maria." He looked directly at her. "I need to tell you something. But you go first."

"It's Irina's salon. I am not supposed to go there anymore," she said, averting her eyes.

"Why is that?"

"I think it's because of Ivan. The *okhranka* is watching it." Maria swallowed hard. Saying the words out loud made them sound sinister, ominous, and only then did the full impact of the news hit her.

"The *okhranka*?" Andrei lowered his voice and darted his eyes to the door as if the secret police could hear him. "We must warn Irina. Have you told her?"

"I can't go there anymore. I was told not to see her anymore. But I know the *okhranka* has all of us on their list."

"You were told by whom? Masha, I don't understand." *Masha.* It was the first time Andrei had called her that.

"I came here to warn you. Someone told me." Maria bit her lip. She had not mentioned her engagement to Andrei. The omission wasn't deliberate at first, but then, as their friendship deepened, she had kept this information from the actor. It never seemed like the right time, but now she felt as if she'd been caught in a lie.

"Was it your fiancé?" Andrei asked, his voice even. He looked at her intently.

"Yes." Maria stepped back. "It was."

"Irina told me you were engaged." Andrei pierced her with his look, and, unable to hold his gaze, Maria averted her eyes. "I was waiting for you to tell me yourself." He let out a deep breath. "At first, I hoped it wasn't true."

"It wasn't like that—"

"Then, I thought maybe I was wrong. I shouldn't have assumed. And what could I expect?" Andrei was speaking faster now as if rushing to get his words out. "What could you possibly want with someone like me?"

"It's not like that," Maria repeated.

"Irina told me, your fiancé is a count. Comes from a prominent aristocratic family." Andrei rose from his seat.

"Andrei, please." Maria shook her head.

"And I'm just an actor. So, there was no point."

"No point?" Maria opened her eyes wide. "No point to what?"

"To us." Andrei stepped closer and took her face into his hands. Maria felt as if she were being burned by fire. "To this."

Andrei brushed his hand on her cheek, gently, and this time Maria held his gaze.

"Masha," he whispered. "Masha. I love you. I've loved you since the moment I first saw you." Andrei took a deep breath. "I know I wasn't imagining it. All this time, I thought myself insane. I half couldn't stand being around you. I would come to the salon, waiting for you, thinking about you, living just for that moment, so I could sit next to you. Just so I could see you, even for a second."

"Andrei, I love you, too," she said.

"I love you." He put his arms around her waist and she put hers on his shoulders, as if for a dance. The gesture felt so natural as if she'd done it all her life. "I love you," Andrei repeated, gently pressing his lips onto hers. As his lips parted hers, she felt a yearning, a desire for him so deep, she felt all consumed by it.

A kiss. One long kiss that absorbed her entirely. She submitted to it, feeling his lips, firm, yet gentle, his hands that caressed her.

"Masha," he whispered again and pulled back. "I'm sorry. I'll always remember you."

Maria could not speak. She was aching to feel his lips on hers again. To press against his body. Strong. Powerful. The sensation of having Andrei's hands on hers, the protective gesture, gave her the feeling of security she'd been seeking.

"Andrei," she croaked. She pressed against him again, but he shook his head, gently but firmly pushing her away.

"I'm sorry," Andrei said. "You're engaged, Masha. No one must ever know of this, or you'll be ruined. I know enough about your world to understand this."

Maria stared at him in stunned silence. She wanted to protest but was too weak. None of what was happening seemed real. Not the sudden closeness, not the pulling away.

"Maybe one day we'll meet again. In a different life."

"A different life?" she repeated. "But I don't love *him*. I don't want to marry him, Andrei." She now knew this to be true, just as she knew she loved Andrei. Had loved him from the very first moment she saw him, just as he had admitted to her too.

"It's the right thing to do. I'll walk you out," he added after a pause, opened the door of the dressing room and she followed him out. They walked in silence through the corridor, into the theater foyer. "Thank you for warning me about the *okhranka*. I'll let the others know."

His parting words to her cut like a knife.

CHAPTER 10

Leaving the theater, Maria was in a daze. The lights had been turned off, and Maria was glad of it. She could barely contain her tears. Emotions flooded over her. Her first kiss. Andrei's arms. The connection, the feeling of closeness, the desire and passion for him. His feelings for her.

It was like a fairy tale, except for the terrible ending. Over before it even started.

In a different life.

Maria dreamed of him that night. *Andrei,* she called his name. He took her hand and they embraced. A kiss. He appeared in her dream as Alexei Karamazov and spoke about morality and doing the right thing.

'I'm sorry. In a different life,' Andrei said, fading into the background.

"Masha," she heard Dunya's voice. "Time to wake up." A second later, she felt Dunya's hand on her forehead. "But would you look at that? You're burning up!" her nanny murmured. "Potap said you went out last night." Dunya put her hands on her hips. "Why didn't you wake me up?"

"Dunya, I had to warn someone," Maria breathed out.

"Was it Andrei? You were calling his name just now."

"I was?" Maria's lips were parched. "Water? Do you have water?"

"Here, Masha, drink. What did he do to you?"

"Nothing, Dunya, nothing." Maria closed her eyes, her only wish to drift back to sleep. "It was just a dream."

"It's the nerves, Masha. My poor girl."

Dunya brought over tea so hot it burned Maria's throat, with honey and a mix of dandelion and raspberry leaves to 'strengthen the nerves'.

"I shouldn't have left you alone with the count yesterday. What was it he said to you?"

"He warned me. He's right, Dunya." Maria squeezed out. The image of the grimace on Nikolai's face as he sneered at her floated in front of her eyes. "We're engaged." As Maria said those words, she felt a lump form in her throat.

"Engaged or not. It's indecent, a young girl alone with a man. But I wasn't fast enough. Who does he think he is, pushing me out of the drawing room?" Dunya shook her head in indignation.

"It's okay, Dunya, don't worry," Maria mumbled. Her eyelids felt as if they were closing on their own accord.

As she drifted off to sleep, she heard Dunya muttering, "It's my job to worry about you, Masha. All I know, once he left, you were not the same. I should have been there; I should have paid attention. It's all my fault. Engaged or not, whoever hurts my Masha will pay."

At Dunya's insistence, Potap sent for the family doctor, and Dr. Petrovsky arrived later that day, carrying his black case. He was a tall man who, over the years of examining patients shorter than himself, had gotten used to slouching ever so slightly. He had small, intelligent eyes that reminded Maria of an elephant she'd once seen at the Moscow Zoo.

As he examined her, Maria was transported to the time when she was a young child. The doctor's visits back then meant she would stay in bed and have her mother's undivided attention. Except now, her mother was gone, and the bitter-sweet memory gnawed at Maria.

"It's not serious," Dr. Petrovsky concluded at the end of his visit. "But Maria needs full rest."

"Should we send for Count Suvorov?" Dunya asked. "He is due to return at the end of the week."

"No need, no need." Dr. Petrovsky shook his head. He turned to the patient, who was propped up on the pillows. "You take good care of yourself, Maria."

"I will." Maria managed a smile.

"I see you have a nice library here." Dr. Petrovsky pointed to the stack of books on Maria's shelf. "Always good to read some classics."

"Oh yes, good idea."

Following the doctor's orders, Maria turned to reading Pushkin. She opened the *Belkin Tales*, expecting to be carried away by the smooth, immaculate prose of the great Russian author. She read *The Stationmaster*, and right away compared herself to the girl in the story, seduced and dishonored by the 'slim young hussar'.

I let him touch me, let him kiss me, I am no better, Maria thought of her encounter with Andrei and their passionate kiss.

She pictured Andrei as a treacherous cavalry officer, whisking her away, just as Pushkin's hussar took the girl away forever and slammed the book shut in disappointment. Maria decided to turn to another one of Pushkin's works, *Dubrovsky*.

She'd read the story of the Russian Robin Hood before with her mother and remembered it as poignant and romantic. But now found the parallels in the book to be unsettling, starting from the name of the heroine, Masha, to the father's romance with a French governess, alluded to in the story.

Just like Papa.

Maria slammed the book shut in frustration. She told herself that her own situation wasn't as bad, that her own father did not have a child with the governess, and tried to focus on the main character, Vladimir Dubrovsky, instead. Immediately, she imagined Andrei as the romantic hero, the outlaw, and then wondered whether he was safe.

But, Maria knew, she would not see Andrei again. She had been dangerously close to the edge. She knew that, if Andrei had asked her, she would have gone with him that night. Would have run away and thrown everything to the wind. And that knowledge terrified her.

The encounter with Andrei had nearly ruined her. Maria would not take the risk another time.

* * *

As soon as she felt better, she threw herself into wedding preparations and brought out her mother's wedding gown to get it tailored. She would wear it to her own wedding, Maria decided, as a tribute to her mother.

"You look lovely, Masha." Dunya helped her try it on. "But we've got to take in the waist. You're not eating enough, so skinny."

"Oh, Dunya." Maria smiled, turning left and right in front of the mirror. The excitement of dressing up for the wedding made her forget her worries. "And the veil, I love the veil!" Maria threw it over her face and peeked out from underneath it.

"Is this the dress?" she heard her father's voice. He had come back from Tula the previous evening.

"Yes, I'll get Maman's dress tailored," Maria noted. "For the wedding."

"Very good, very good." Her father noted absentmindedly. "Maria, let's speak in my study."

"Yes, Papa, I'll just change out of the dress," Maria said.

Once wearing her everyday clothes, she was sitting across from her father in his study. The cuckoo clock struck four and she jerked, remembering their last conversation in the study.

"I sold the Tula estate last week. I wanted to let you know. Antoinette and I are leaving for France at the end of the month and you'll be left in charge," her father said.

"Okay, Papa." Maria stared at her father, wide-eyed. She'd never discussed business matters with him, and the new responsibility was unexpected. "I'll miss Tula," she added, trying to keep her voice even.

All through her childhood, Maria had spent winters in Moscow and summers at the Tula estate.

"Of course, you've got Potap, who'll take care of managing the property, and if you need anything, just send me a letter," her father added, clearing his throat. "So, it's really more of a formality. But you'll need to manage the staff."

Maria thought of the twelve people they employed, the cook, the stable boys, the two maids, the two footmen, and Dunya. And Potap, who performed all functions around the house, from repairs, to running the stable, to supervising the provisions.

"How do I do that?" Maria's mouth gaped open.

"Just listen to Potap. Of course, Potap doesn't need much supervision, and you've got Dunya," Count Suvorov waved his hand vaguely. "I suppose you and Potap will be managing everything together." Her father scratched his chin.

"Yes, Papa. And it's only for a few months."

"Of course."

* * *

THE YELAGINS CAME over one last time, right before Count Suvorov left for France. As they were about to sit down for dinner, Count Nikolai pulled Maria aside,

"I am sorry for speaking to you the way I did." He pushed his chin up. "It was only because I felt you were in danger. I did not want to offend you," he continued. "But, the *okhranka*. And your reputation."

"Thank you," Maria said. "I will not go back." She looked up at Nikolai, taking in the dignified expression on his face, his hair carefully slicked into place. She read the concerned expression in his eyes as kindness.

I almost threw my future away, Maria thought. *It would have been a terrible mistake.*

After the Yelagins' visit, her ex-governess approached Maria. Antoinette's cheeks were bright red, and she fanned herself with her hand and spoke in a conspiratorial whisper. "Your fiancé, the two of you, you're ze perfect match!"

"Ah now, what's going on?" Maria's father approached.

"I was telling Marie how great she and Count Nikolai look next to each other." Antoinette let out a giggle.

"Oh. Yes, indeed." Count Suvorov nodded.

"I so wish I was here to help with the preparations," the former governess croaked.

"What preparations?" Maria gave Antoinette an absent-minded look.

"For the *marriage*, bien sûr." Antoinette pronounced the word the French way, emphasizing the last syllable.

"There will still be plenty of time after we get back." Count Suvorov threw an adoring look at his future wife.

"Of course, chéri."

Her father took Antoinette by the hand and the couple walked away, leaving Maria standing alone in the hallway.

* * *

"IL FAIT TROP CHAUD." Antoinette fanned herself while overseeing Potap's struggle with all of their luggage.

A stack of suitcases formed outside to be loaded onto the carriage, which would take Count Suvorov and the former governess to the train station. From there, they would board a train for St. Petersburg, then change for the luxurious Nord-Express, which would bring them directly to Paris.

"You're now in charge." Those were Count Suvorov's parting words to his daughter. "We'll be back before you know it."

CHAPTER 11

Following her father's departure, the house seemed unusually empty, and it took Maria several days to get used to her new role. But then it was Easter, and Maria spent the holiday with her future in-laws. She attended Easter service with them the night before and visited them during the Bright week festivities. And once that concluded, her future mother-in-law announced, it was time to plan the wedding, so that they could put in place most of the arrangements before the Yelagins' departure for their summer estate.

Maria found herself firmly at the hands of Yelena, who came over several times a week to discuss the wedding. Never had Maria imagined how tedious and time-consuming planning a wedding would be. There was the guest list to consider, the venue, and the seating arrangements. And also, it seemed, the dress.

"I'm not sure it is a good idea to wear your mother's old dress." Yelena glared at Maria, who had tried it on for her future mother-in-law one afternoon.

"I had it taken in." Maria gulped, wondering whether the dress had made her seem too thin.

"No, no, it's not that, I'm thinking it'll be bad luck." Yelena sighed. "You shouldn't be wearing an old dress to a wedding."

"But as a memory of my mother?" Maria protested meekly.

"I think you should wear a new dress. Why don't you ask your father to bring you one from France?" Yelena suggested. "Nikolai's wedding should be perfect. He's my only son, you see." She stared at Maria, her words a thinly veiled threat.

"Yes, of course." Maria nodded. "I will write to Papa."

"And your mother's dress could be a backup, in case the new dress your father brings doesn't work out." Yelena acquiesced. "And this is another reason a September wedding is so challenging. Everything needs to be prepared before the summer."

Maria nodded. She'd been going along with whatever Yelena said, agreeing to everything.

The Yelagins departed for their summer estate in Tver in early June, 'later than usual', as Yelena pointed out, 'so that wedding arrangements are in place'.

It wasn't until after the Yelagins had left, that Maria wondered whether she should have been invited to join them at their estate, but, in the end, she was glad the invitation never came. Maria didn't want to leave Moscow that summer, thinking it was her last summer in her childhood home.

And so, she stayed, the long June days merging into one in their monotony. There was nowhere to go, no one to see.

The aristocratic families never stayed in Moscow in the summer, and, before her mother's death, the Suvorovs were no different. Each year, they would set out for Tula, accompanied by Dunya and two maids, usually at the end of May.

Maria's mother ordered the whole house to be packed up,

which took over a week. The servants took special care in preparing their summer wardrobes, and they would spend a Saturday afternoon on the road, to arrive at the country estate in the early hours of the evening. Maria loved that first day, which marked the beginning of a summer holiday. She cherished the anticipation, the excitement, the chatter, and, most of all, the first steps she would take in the countryside, opening the windows of their country home and welcoming the fresh air into the rooms. The servants would dust the furniture, take the protective cloth off the piano, and her mother would play a bit of Chopin. And then, they sat around the veranda table and would have their evening tea – a tradition that lasted through the summer.

All of that had gone away with her mother, and now even the estate was sold, the memory of her mother fading.

That June, it was only her and Dunya, and the occasional interactions with Potap.

From time to time, Maria wondered what had happened to Andrei. Her thoughts would turn to him, but her recollection of the actor, as days turned into weeks, faded. She'd gotten used to her solitude and even enjoyed it. She spent her days crocheting and reading. With her upcoming nuptials to Nikolai still three months away, Maria had reached a state of melancholy equilibrium.

With her father gone, Fekla cooked very little, and Maria and Dunya spent more and more time in the kitchen together. Dunya brewed the two of them tea and they had it with sugar and cookies. But when the Apostles' fast ended and they could include animal products in the diet, Maria remembered Eliseyevsky and its delicious, creamy Napoleon pastries and immediately went to the market.

From then onwards, Maria went to the Eliseyevsky market twice a week, arriving home with the dessert, which she and Dunya consumed together. They chatted about everything in the world. Dunya mused about God and the meaning of life, and how God was their great protector, and lectured Maria on being firm in that belief.

"Always trust the Lord to show you the way," Dunya would say.

"Of course, Dunya," Maria agreed.

Dunya would cross herself and then cross Maria. "God is great. He watches over you. When I'm no longer around, Masha, don't forget this."

"Dunya, don't say that. And you'll be coming with me after I get married."

"Yes, yes, but I'm an old woman. One day I won't be there. God is love, Masha. Pure love."

* * *

"WOULD you look at the sky? Not a cloud in sight." Dunya wiped the beads of sweat that had formed on her forehead. "And you know what the best thing is on a hot day like this?" The nanny placed the steaming samovar on the kitchen table. "Hot tea."

Though the kitchen faced the wooded part of the estate and was in the shade, the Moscow August heat seeped through the house.

They had just taken their seats next to each other around the kitchen table, and both stared out the window at the greenery.

Dunya reached for the cookies. Because the Dormition August fast had just begun, they had to abandon animal products and the Napoleon cake with its delicate cream. "Aren't these tasty, Masha?" She smiled at Maria. "You've really spoiled me."

Maria was about to respond, but there was the unmistakable noise of someone arriving, a rider dismounting. A greeting. They'd had no guests in several weeks, and Maria gave Dunya a curious stare.

"Who could it be?" she asked.

"I don't know, Masha. But I had a terrible dream last night. I didn't want to tell you, but now, I just have this feeling." Dunya crossed herself.

"I'll go check." Maria pushed her chair back and walked out of the kitchen. She found Count Nikolai standing in the hallway, dressed in his officer's uniform.

"Have you heard?" His face, normally expressionless, was flushed red and his eyes bulged more than usual. "I came as soon as I heard. Maria." He started, but stopped, seeing Dunya emerge from the kitchen. He didn't acknowledge the nanny's presence.

Taking Maria by the hand, Nikolai pulled her aside and said, the tone of his voice urgent. "Maria, please, we must speak now."

He turned confidently to the drawing room and Maria followed right behind.

"Masha," Dunya called softly. "I should be in the room."

Nikolai stopped abruptly and Maria nearly bumped into him.

"Oh, yes." Nikolai glared at the nanny; his irritation palpable. "I suppose so, though we are nearly married."

Maria nodded, remembering Dunya's promise to supervise Nikolai's visits. The trio walked into the drawing room together. Maria and Nikolai sat across from each other, and Dunya sat down last, on a chair by the entrance.

"Maria, the reason I came here today is to share something very important." Nikolai gave Maria a pointed stare. "We're at war with the Germans."

Dunya gasped, putting her hand over her mouth.

"War?" Maria repeated. "Russia is at war?"

"Yes, it was quite expected. I won't explain, it's too

complex to understand." Nikolai cleared his throat. "But we must support Serbia. France and Russia are united against Germany, Maria."

"France? France is at war as well? But Papa," Maria felt the tips of her fingers grow cold, "is Papa okay?"

"Your Papa. Of course, of course, he is in France. I hadn't thought of that. I came to tell you I am called to the front, Maria." Count Nikolai raised his head.

"The front? I see. So, this is why," she gestured at him, "the uniform."

"Maria, I know Mother has arranged everything for September 15th, but we don't have much time, and I must depart immediately." Nikolai straightened his uniform. "And for this reason, Maria," Nikolai said, "I came to ask you to wed me this week."

"This week? But Papa won't be back in time. And the arrangements. And my dress. Papa is bringing my wedding dress." Maria shook her head.

"Don't worry, Maria. I will speak to Mother. And I already asked my superiors for a continuance on the occasion of our nuptials." Nikolai curved his lips in a barely perceptible smile. "My command has granted me one extra week."

Maria fidgeted in her seat.

"But who will give me away?" she asked. "There is so much to do." Her voice trailed off.

"I'd like to unite our fates before leaving for war."

"Masha…" Maria heard her nanny's voice. She turned back to see Dunya gesticulating for her to come over.

"Please excuse me," Maria said to Nikolai and walked over to Dunya, eager for a break in the conversation.

"Masha, the fast. The Dormition Fast is this week," Dunya whispered into her ear. "No one gets married during this time. It's a sure way to hell."

Maria nodded at Dunya but said nothing. She walked back to Nikolai.

Taking a deep breath, she sat down across from him and said, "It's the Dormition fast."

"The fast?" Nikolai raised his eyebrows.

"Yes, honoring the Virgin Mary. No priest will wed us now." Maria shook her head. "I'm sorry."

"I had not thought of this complication. I will consult with Mother. Perhaps we can find a priest to grant us permission," he started to say, but Maria shook her head.

"I cannot. It would doom our marriage from the start." She rose from her seat. "I am sorry, Nikolai."

"I see. But you're right." He also got up. "I suppose this is it. We'll have to wait until I come back for leave."

"Do you think you'll be able to come back on September 15th?" Maria asked.

"Maria," Nikolai curled his upper lip. "Now, I don't expect you to understand how these things work. But no one would grant me permission to leave the front so quickly. However, I trust you will come to bid me farewell. Mother is arriving from Tver tonight, and I was planning on discussing with her the new date for our wedding. But seeing as we aren't going to wed yet, I will likely leave before the end of the week."

"Yes, I will come to the farewell. Of course," Maria said.

Nikolai nodded curtly and took his leave.

After he left, Maria and Dunya reconvened in the kitchen.

"It was as if God himself instructed me to be there," Dunya said. "Imagine! Getting married during the Dormition Fast. And without your Papa there? What an idea?" She shook her head indignantly and crossed herself.

"Do you think it would have been so bad?"

"Of course, Masha, the worst."

It was as if the two of them, without ever discussing it, had agreed to sabotage the wedding, and now, having jumped on the opportunity as soon as it presented itself, Maria felt giddy with relief.

Dunya had always instructed her to be obedient, and now Maria wondered whether her nanny had secretly disapproved of Nikolai. She thought this was worth probing. Wringing her hands, Maria stepped closer to her nanny.

"How do you find Nikolai?"

"It's not my place–"

"Please, tell me, I don't have anyone else who can tell me the truth."

"Nikolai," the nanny mumbled, "no, I can't, I can't. It's not my place to say anything."

"So you don't like him, do you?"

"I think it's too soon for you to get married." Dunya crossed herself. "Trust in God, Masha. Trust in the Lord to show you the way."

"I see." Maria was about to leave the kitchen but then stopped. "Is that why you said you'll be moving with me after I get married?"

"Not my place, Masha, not my place. Come on, it's done now. God is watching over you, Masha, God is on your side, dear girl." The nanny followed her out of the kitchen.

CHAPTER 12

The gravity of what Maria had done, her effective refusal of Nikolai, was delayed, because immediately after Nikolai left, Potap also got news of the war and informed the other staff.

By that evening, everyone at the Suvorov mansion spoke of nothing else and all the work stopped. They speculated whether there would be a draft and planned for food shortages, urging Maria to prepare for the worst. It was the same with the rest of Moscow, and, when Maria sent for the papers, she found the front pages abuzz with news about the war.

Potap would share the recap of the latest news with Maria, and so did the others at the mansion. All staff, no matter how hazy an understanding they had about geography, became instant experts in European politics and alliances.

All agreed that Serbia must be helped and disliked the alliance with the French, whom many mistrusted, recalling Napoleon and the burning of Moscow just a hundred years prior. Some predicted the end of the world, with the war being the first sign of the end of humanity and quoted the Bible.

Potap, ever practical and organized, immediately sent to buy provisions and stocked the mansion with flour, salt, and sugar.

He called Maria aside to tell her about this decision. "Maria, I am informing you, as it is my duty."

"Thank you, Potap. I will write to Papa to let him know," Maria said, her voice quivering.

"And do not worry, I am too old for the draft. I've paid my dues to the military." Potap curled his mustache. "So, I won't be going anywhere."

"I had not thought of that possibility." Maria frowned.

"There is talk of full mobilization," Potap noted gravely. "I suppose the stable boys will all be gone within a few months."

"Is that so?" Maria gulped. "I wish Papa would come back soon." She had not received any letters from her father for several weeks, and anxiety started to creep in. "Maybe he can help get an exemption for them to stay? They are so young."

"Young or not young, when the tsar calls to serve the country, there's not much choice, Maria."

With tears in her eyes, Maria nodded, knowing deep down Potap was right.

* * *

LATER THAT WEEK, Maria went to the Yelagins' residence for Nikolai's farewell. She found his home filled with visitors, none of whom seemed to know who she was. Maria wandered the crowded hallways until she found Count Nikolai standing next to his mother in the dining room.

"My dear boy," Yelena repeated, staring at her son in adulation.

"Mother," Nikolai noted somberly. Nikolai's father sat in the corner, observing, drumming his fingers on the table in near silence.

Noticing Maria, Yelena remarked, "I knew, I knew a September wedding would be inauspicious. And you could have been the couple of the year! Maria, we must stick together now. You're family now. Please, call me Mother," she added, pursing her lips.

"Yes, I will. Thank you," Maria said.

"Of course, I imagine we could have gotten a waiver from the priest." Yelena Yelagina narrowed her eyes ever so slightly. "But what can I say? I suppose It's important to have principles."

"My Papa will be back soon. And then we can schedule a new date for the wedding. And he'll bring the dress," Maria added, unable, hard as she tried, to ignore the feeling of a rift that had formed between her and Yelena.

"Of course, of course, my dear." Yelena wrinkled her nose. "Now, I must check on the other guests." She called her husband and the two walked out of the dining room.

"Maria," Nikolai said after his parents left the room, "I'd like you to meet my cousin, Sergei."

Maria turned to see a young man of about sixteen or seventeen, not much taller than her, with a broad, open face and very clever, slightly slanted eyes.

"Sergei Chegodaev." He smiled, a nice, open smile, and Maria noticed his high cheekbones. "Pleased to meet you."

"I'm Maria Suvorova." His hand, as he reached to kiss hers, felt pleasantly firm.

"Sergei will be staying with my parents in Moscow," Nikolai said, patting the young man on the back.

"How nice." Maria nodded.

"And I asked him to keep an eye on you while I'm gone." Nikolai smirked.

"On me?" The memory of Andrei flashed in Maria's mind. *The kiss,* she thought and blushed ever so slightly, but enough for Nikolai to notice.

"I thought you could use some company. Sergei is in Moscow for his studies. Too young to go to the front," Nikolai continued, with regret in his voice. "Russia needs its men to fight for it."

"A few more years before I qualify for the draft," Sergei said, his eyes lighting up.

"Well, no one expects the war to last too long," Nikolai chuckled. "I'm thinking six months at most."

"How very true," Maria chimed in. "I read in the papers, it should be over by November."

"Maria, dear, let the men handle this topic. Really, women shouldn't be speaking about war. It's unnatural." Nikolai curled his lips in what may have been a smile. Only his eyes remained cold. "I think Mother is calling me," he said and walked off, leaving Maria standing next to Sergei.

"So, you'll be marrying into the family," Sergei noted once his cousin was out of earshot, a tint of sarcasm in his voice.

"Yes." Maria raised her eyebrows.

"I'll be staying with the Yelagins for the foreseeable future," the young man said. "So I suppose we'll be seeing each other."

"Yes, of course. And please do come by. It will be a pleasure to see you."

"The pleasure will be all mine." The clever eyes that looked back at Maria seemed almost out of place on his youthful face.

"I should be going n–"

"Don't let him get to you," he said. "Nikolai has a kind heart. He just isn't very good at expressing himself."

"Oh yes, of course." Maria blushed. The conversation was bordering on improper, and she felt the urge to stop it before it got out of hand, but something about the young man, the way he looked at her, the inflection in his voice, made her want to continue speaking with Sergei. "Thank you for saying that," she added.

"Nikolai is a distant cousin. My family fell on hard times," Sergei said, "So that's the real reason I'm here, you see. I wanted to go to the front, but they won't take me. Not until I'm twenty-one. So, here I am. In a kind of exile."

"You want to go to the front? But aren't you afraid?" Maria opened her eyes wide. She hadn't dared ask Nikolai this question, but with Sergei, she felt like she could be more open. The young man was closer to her in age, and his admission of a somewhat lower economic status made him more approachable.

"No. Well, yes, of course I'm afraid. But I want to see how it feels. I want to experience war. It's important for every man to go through that."

* * *

Nikolai departed Moscow three days later. Maria felt relief mixed with guilt over his departure, second-guessing her decision to postpone the wedding.

I could have been a married woman now, she thought ruefully, opening Nikolai's letters that arrived regularly, at least once a week.

His letters were written on the Yelagin family stationery and were precisely three pages each. He called Maria 'my sweetheart' then dutifully accounted for the events of each week and signed off with 'your loving Nikolai'.

Maria responded, trying her best to keep her letters entertaining, all the while anxiously awaiting news of her father. She had not heard from Count Suvorov since early

August, after writing to him with the news of the wedding being postponed.

At first, Maria assumed her father was already on his way back to Moscow, but then, the first week of September came and went, and then the date of Maria's wedding did as well, and there was still no news.

Despite the victory of the French army in the Battle of the Marne, which had stopped the Germans from marching on Paris, Maria felt uneasy. Images of her father being stuck on the frontlines popped into her mind more and more often.

Sitting in her bedroom one afternoon, Maria stared at the stack of letters from Nikolai. She'd been struggling to respond to her future husband, while worry over her father gnawed at her.

"Dunya, what if something terrible happened to Papa?" Maria asked, unable to hide her anxiety any longer.

"Masha, my dear girl, your papa is fine. Trust in God, Our Savior."

"What if he was traveling back, and then… why doesn't he respond? And I read in the papers, train service with France is about to be suspended."

"Masha, patience, please." Dunya took Maria's hand into hers and patted it, like she'd done for years, the gesture calming and reassuring.

CHAPTER 13

It wasn't until the middle of November that the long-awaited letter from Count Suvorov arrived. Sealed in a thick envelope and embossed with the Suvorov family crest.

"You see, Masha, you just needed a little patience." Dunya smiled, when Maria brought the letter, so they could read it together. "Now, go ahead, open it."

The two of them sat next to each other at the kitchen table, in their usual configuration, and Dunya propped her head up with her hand, preparing to listen.

"Papa wrote a lot! What a relief to finally have his news." Maria's hands trembled, as she ripped the envelope open. The first few pages were folded together, wrapped around a thick card. "What do you think this is?" Maria held it up.

"It looks very nice, whatever it is," Dunya said.

"I think it's an invitation." Maria ran her finger along the edge of the card. It was light blue, embossed with golden letters. "It's a baptism invitation!" Maria gasped. "But whose baby is it?" She stared at Dunya in confusion.

"I would guess the madam's." Dunya waved her hand. "I should have known."

"Antoinette's?"

"Yes, her. I saw her huffin' and puffin'. I'm guessin' that's why your Papa done leave for France when he did. To get the madam to have the baby over there. In France." Dunya crossed herself.

"Konstantin Olegovich Suvorov," Maria mouthed, reading the card. "Born on the 1st of August. So, Papa now has a baby. But that means I have a little brother. A brother!"

"It sure does." Dunya nodded. "It sure does. A blessing, a blessing it is."

"Dunya, but I just don't understand. Papa has a baby?" Suddenly, Maria remembered Dubrovsky. "Just like in the Pushkin story," she mumbled.

"But what else does your Papa say? Read the letter, Masha." Dunya tapped the letter. "He must be coming back soon now."

"Alright." Maria straightened the papers on her lap, preparing to read. Sitting next to her, Dunya fumbled with the edges of her shawl, folding and unfolding them over her chest. Maria cleared her throat and read, struggling her best to keep her voice from quivering.

My dear daughter,

Please excuse the long delay and the way I am sharing the blessed news with you. Your brother Konstantin was born on August 1st, 1914. He was baptized at the St. Nicholas Orthodox Church in Nice last month.

I received the news of the postponement of your wedding to Nikolai Yelagin due to his departure to the front. With your wedding now postponed, I urge you to remain in Moscow and to pray for Count Yelagin's safety.

I will remain in Nice to take care of Antoinette and baby Konstantin until train service is restored and it is safe for the three of us to travel back to Moscow.

Antoinette sends her regards.

Your Papa

P.S. Please pass the enclosed instructions to Potap.

The expression on the nanny's face was focused, and she hung to Maria's every word. "Is that it?" Dunya asked.

"I think so." Maria flipped the page over, but nothing was written on the back. She checked the other papers. "I guess these are for Potap." The long list of instructions, all written in her father's neat, slanted cursive, were references to payments, supplies, and securing the place for the winter.

"Oh, what news, what news." Dunya shook her head.

"It doesn't say when Papa is coming back," Maria tensed, "and I really want to meet my little brother. I don't understand why Papa didn't tell me earlier. Because he must have known Antoinette was expecting when they left for France. Why would he hide it from me?"

A suspicion of something terrible happening, a premonition, was so strong that Maria rose, unable to stay seated, and paced the kitchen.

"Oh, trust in God, trust in God," Dunya mumbled, also pushing her chair back. The nanny crossed herself, then crossed Maria. Shaking her head, the nanny shuffled out of the kitchen. Maria let out a deep breath and followed Dunya. She needed to pass the instructions to Potap, and she'd think of the implications later.

Paying a visit to the Yelagins was also on her mind. Maria had seen her future in-laws a handful of times since Nikolai's departure. These visits were somber affairs, with Yelena expressing her worry and concern over her son's well-being, while Corporal Yelagin sat in silence, observing, and Maria nodded politely. Despite the promise to 'watch over her', she hadn't seen Sergei Chegodaev, Nikolai's young cousin, since meeting him on the day of Nikolai's farewell.

It was a cold November day when Maria set out for her future husband's residence. The Yelagins lived on the other side of Moscow, in the Gruzinka. The driver took a new route, and, as they navigated the city streets, Maria stared out of the window in awe, noticing the changes for the first time. In the three months since the war had been declared, Moscow had lost most of its luster. Passersby looked shabbier, the expressions on their faces somber and bleak. The streets were dirty, and the cold November rain fell in a steady stream, promising to soon turn into sleet.

The coach pulled up to the front of the Yelagin residence, and Maria alighted, taking care not to step into a large puddle at the front door.

"Countess Suvorova," Maria heard the footman say and straightened up. Hearing her title out loud was like a call to arms, an obligation. Maria remembered her mother's instructions to maintain proper posture, which was a sign of respect for yourself. And then it hit her.

It was November 14th, the day of her mother's death.

Maman.

It had been two years since Zinaida Suvorova had passed away. Walking into the Yelagin residence, Maria glanced at her watch. It was after eleven, and Maria decided to go to church right after the visit, to light a candle in the memory of her mother.

"My dear, it's so good to see you." Yelena descended the stairs. She bared her teeth as she embraced Maria. "The corporal is out," Yelena noted, as she walked to the drawing room, inviting Maria to follow.

Yelena was proud of her preference for the traditional style rather than modern accouterments. The Yelagin mansion was decorated in a style that mimicked the royal palaces of the late eighteenth century, in burgundy and gold, a combination that, Yelena insisted, was timeless. Maria waited for the hostess to sit down before taking a seat opposite on a sofa upholstered in burgundy silk with gold thread.

"Countess Yelagina, I heard from Papa." Maria cleared her throat. "He doesn't know when he'll be coming back to Moscow. Not yet. So, I don't know when he would be able to give me away."

"Yes, what a terrible situation with the trains. But my dear, tell me, I've heard from a family friend who is in Nice, I take it congratulations are in order." Yelena wrinkled her nose.

"Yes." Maria flinched. Suddenly, the good news she was about to share felt almost shameful. "Papa had a son. Baby Konstantin," Maria said.

"So, it's true." The expression on Yelena's face turned predatory, and she looked like a hound on a trail. "And is the baby legitimate?"

Maria flinched at the words. "Of course. Papa remarried."

"And to whom, may I ask?" Yelena stared at Maria in bemusement.

"To Antoinette. She's French." Maria averted her eyes. "She was my governess."

"A governess? How unoriginal," Yelena said. "And how

upsetting, really. To throw it all away. The generations of the Suvorov dynasty gone in a flash." Yelena snapped her fingers.

Maria fidgeted in her seat, forcing herself to stay put, despite the desire to run away and disappear.

"I haven't yet written to Nikolai to let him know. But I will do so," Maria said.

"Don't worry, dear, you must have a lot on your mind. I will let Nikolai know myself." Yelena tilted her head and stared at Maria for a moment, like a curious bird. "Maria, dear, please tell me. Is it true that your father has sold the Suvorov estate?"

"Yes. Papa sold it this spring," Maria blurted out. Suddenly, she felt as if she'd just divulged a deep secret.

"I see, of course, that all makes sense now," Yelena said, as if to herself. She threw a curious look Maria's way. A servant appeared silently at Yelena's side and enquired about whether she would like some tea.

"Thank you, but Maria is in a rush. No tea this time." Turning to Maria, Yelena gave her a cold smile. "Such terrible weather. I suppose you're in a hurry to get home."

"Really, it's not so–" Catching a cold stare from Yelena stopped her short.

Maria understood at once.

She was no longer welcome at the Yelagins. And her engagement to Count Nikolai was over.

PART II

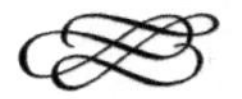

CHAPTER 14

aria had no one to counsel her on the proper way to address a broken engagement. For the first few weeks after the visit to the Yelagins, Maria hoped she had misread the signals, and waited for a letter from Nikolai, but none came. There were no explanations, no announcement.

After a few months, she deduced her father and Corporal Yelagin must have had an understanding, for in his letters, her father abruptly stopped mentioning the wedding and no longer told Maria to pray for Nikolai's safe return home. Once, her father alluded to 'addressing her situation' as soon as he returned to Moscow but provided no other details.

The rejection stung.

Maria gnawed at herself for not agreeing to advance the date of the wedding before Count Nikolai departed for the front. Going from a young bride with a promising future to an outcast was hurtful. Maria pictured Yelena Yelagina snapping her fingers, indicating, how the purity of the Suvorov family was gone 'in a flash' and shuddered.

"Dunya, I just don't get it," Maria shared this with her nanny one evening. "Just because of baby Konstantin?"

"Oh, Masha, don't worry about those people. Terrible sort, just terrible." Dunya shook her head. "I never liked that Nikolai. A mean man, that's what he is. And going back on his word, breaking an engagement. And his mother!"

"But you told me I had to obey him since he would be my husband," Maria protested.

"I still never liked him. Never. And the way he spoke to me, oh no. We're all God's creatures." Dunya opened her arms wide, as if to embrace the world. "Your family knows that. The Suvorovs are always kind and polite to everyone. And his mother, rejecting you. Whoever heard of such a thing?"

Though Dunya was speaking out of solidarity, her words did little to assuage Maria's anxiety. The Yelagins were a prominent family, and, Maria suspected, a broken engagement would leave a dark mark on her reputation, limiting her marriage prospects. Other aristocratic families would wonder whether something was wrong with her, and sorting through the maze of social implications was a daunting prospect.

"But what will happen to me now? Who will marry me, Dunya?" Maria threw her hands up in the air.

"Don't you worry about that. God shapes the back for the burden," Dunya cited another of her favorite proverbs. "The right man will come along." She crossed Maria. "Or you can be like me. I'm just fine without a man."

"But I want to marry, Dunya. I always have. And I thought I'd have a nice wedding. Wear Maman's dress," Maria pleaded, tears in her eyes. "If only Maman were alive."

"If your mama was alive, none of this would have happened," Dunya noted wisely.

"And I can't even go back to Irina's salon." Maria sighed.

"Irina probably thinks me so rude. I never checked on her, I just stopped going after Nikolai told me to stop."

If only I hadn't listened to Nikolai, I could have been going to Irina's salon now. At that thought, Maria blushed, remembering Andrei.

There was nothing to prevent her from seeing him now. No engagement. No Nikolai.

Immediately, she dismissed the thought. Connecting herself with an actor, and so soon after a broken engagement with a count, would surely throw her even further down the social ladder, a prospect she found terrifying.

She counted down the days to her father's return, expecting him to fix all of her problems. In her mind, Maria had set the deadline of Easter 1915, which would mark exactly one year since Count Suvorov's departure.

Her life had fallen into a rhythm. Potap managed the household, as per her father's instructions, Fekla reluctantly ran the kitchen, and Maria spent most of her days in Dunya's company. To pass the time, Maria read, crocheted, and twice a week took a ride to the Eliseyevsky market to get the Napoleon pastries. On Sundays, she went to church with her nanny.

One Sunday afternoon, Maria walked into the kitchen to find Dunya deep in conversation with Potap over tea.

"The woman's got no shame. Stealing in broad daylight," Dunya was saying. "Don't bite the hand that feeds you, isn't that what they say?"

"Avdotiya Timofeevna." Potap picked up the saucer with his thick fingers and sipped the tea from it. "Better the devil you know. If we get someone else, it'll be even worse. At least it's the same amount every week. No surprises there."

"Are you speaking about Fekla?" Maria guessed.

Fekla was the only one of the staff who didn't stay at the mansion full time. Her family lived on the outskirts of

Moscow, near Kuzminki, and every weekend Fekla traveled home to see her husband and children. Fekla always carried a bag, and, watching the cook's figure disappear into the night on Friday afternoons, Dunya would shake her head in disapproval.

"Yes," Dunya and Potap responded in unison.

* * *

IN LATE MARCH, a thick envelope arrived from her father. Maria ran into the kitchen to read the letter to Dunya.

"Good news! I think Papa is coming back soon." Maria tore open the envelope. "And this must be for Potap," Maria put aside the instructions for the butler, settling in at the kitchen table. The nanny sat down next to her, propping her head, preparing to listen.

> My dear daughter,
> I have taken the difficult decision not to return to Moscow for the time being. The trains are not running and the situation is too unstable to travel through Constantinople.
> Seeing as it has now been almost a year since I was last in Moscow, I would like to have you gain a better understanding of how to run the household. I have taken the decision to have you be my eyes and ears on the ground. Until things stabilize and I can return to Russia, I ask of you to learn from Potap and to manage the household.

"Dunya, Papa isn't coming back just yet," Maria muttered, turning to her nanny. "And does this mean I must now think of everything?"

"Does he say anything else?" Dunya asked, pointing to the letter. "Read the rest, Masha."

> Seeing as the Tula estate had been sold, your responsibilities will be solely with the Moscow mansion. Please have Potap show you the books. He keeps excellent accounts and can explain everything. I have sent him detailed instructions regarding what he has to do. Keep me updated on your progress.

Maria finished reading the letter and folded it in her lap.

"A great man. Count Suvorov is a great man." Dunya nodded. "He has such foresight. Such wisdom."

"But Dunya, I don't think I can do this!" Maria threw her hands up in the air. "How would I even begin to understand what I have to do? And without Papa here?"

"Your Papa believes in you. Oh yes, he does. He sure does."

"This is nothing like what I thought my life would be like, Dunya." Maria sighed. "I don't even know when I'll see my father again. And now I have to manage all this?" Maria took a look around the kitchen.

"The Lord gives and the Lord takes away." The nanny put her hand over Maria's. The familiar, protective gesture was reassuring.

"I suppose I don't have much of a choice." Maria took a deep breath, folded the letter and put it back into the envelope. "I'll go see Potap now," she said and rose from the table.

Aside from running the mansion, Potap had a network of people who helped him ensure the safety of the estate. The Taganka area, where the Suvorov mansion was located, was just across the river from the dangerous Khitrovka neighborhood, which was full of slums notorious for attracting the worst of the Moscow population. Thieves, runaway convicts, and other bottom-feeders of the Russian society lived in the Khitrovka. To protect the Suvorov mansion from them, Potap had formed a friendship with the local police captain. At least once a month, Potap visited the man at the police station for a friendly chat over a glass of vodka. The mansion staff knew about these visits and referred to them with reverence.

"Potap is over with the captain," they would say. "Keeping us safe."

Maria crossed the yard over to the carriage house where Potap stayed, enjoying a high degree of autonomy. The butler kept two pets: Volk, his German shepherd, raised to protect the mansion, and an old, large turtle. Potap claimed the turtle was three hundred years old, and, for all Maria knew, it may have been true. The turtle loved Potap. In the summer, Potap brought it out to the yard, and fed it cabbage leaves, while petting its bold reptilian head, while Volk sat next to them, panting in the summer heat.

Now over ten years old, the dog wasn't as fast as in his prime, but his bark was no less menacing, and he barked at Maria as she approached. But then came to sniff her and, as she pet him between his ears, licked her hand.

"Quiet now, Volk," Potap said to the dog, coming out from the carriage house to greet Maria, but looked at Volk in approval, as he did when the dog ran along the fence, barking at an occasional passerby.

Dunya, though she held Potap in high esteem and called him Potap Filimonovich, referring to him by his patronymic, did not extend her regard to his two pets. Dunya considered the turtle to be akin to a snake, an animal who, in Dunya's eyes, was the epitome of all evil. And Volk, according to the nanny, 'was just taking up space'.

Mulling her father's request over, Maria passed the instructions to the butler with some trepidation. She watched, as Potap unsealed the instructions and sat at his desk to read the letter.

"Let's see, let's see," Potap mumbled, while Maria stood in silence, waiting for his reaction. After he was done reading, he rubbed his forehead and cleared his throat.

"Alright, Maria. I'll bring the books over this afternoon, like your father asked." Seeing the confused look on Maria's face, he added, "The accounting books. I write everything down."

"Of course, I see." Maria nodded.

"I've been waiting for this moment. A Suvorov estate should be run by one of its own. Not someone like me. At your service, Maria."

That afternoon Potap arrived in her father's study with three thick leather-bound books. At first, Maria suggested they go over them elsewhere, but Potap insisted the study had the best set-up for 'serious matters', as he put it. He was wearing a clean long overcoat, pressed for the occasion.

"These are the books I've been keeping," he noted, opening one of them to show to Maria. He sat down at the desk, and Maria pulled up a chair next to him. "This one is for the mansion. I write down everything about repairs, firewood purchases, food provisions, things like that." The butler ran his thick finger along the columns.

"But where did you learn how to do bookkeeping?" Maria stared at Potap in surprise.

"In the military, that's where I got done getting all my schooling. I was always good at adding and subtracting."

Potap folded and unfolded his thick fingers to show the mathematical function.

"I see. And what's this book right here?" She pointed to the second thick volume.

"This book right here is for day-to-day things. This is where I keep the receivables." Potap gave her a careful stare. "That's the money that's coming in. Like when your father sends us funds."

"I see."

"Your father had everything set up right. Or in the past, when we got funds from the Tula estate. Your father had taken me over there a few times. I've seen it with my own eyes. A great estate it was." Potap nodded. "The farm, the two mills, an orchard. I tried to talk your father out of the sale, but he wouldn't hear any of it."

"I haven't been there since Maman passed away," Maria said. "I never knew it was so great." The memory of Tula, her childhood summers, was like a dull ache, the thought of something idyllic and beautiful, now in the past.

CHAPTER 15

"But where would it go?" Maria opened her eyes wide.

"You have to check everything, doing inventory they call it." Potap tapped on the bag of flour. "Count the bags, verify, Maria."

In the last few months, Maria had learned as much as she could from Potap. They went over the accounting books, the supplies, the repairs.

"You never know, you just never do. Now, remember, Maria, flour is the most important thing. Bread." Potap would point to the sacs. "Without bread, I don't know what we'll do."

Though Fekla did little cooking, she still baked bread for them daily during the work week, and Maria nodded in understanding.

"Salt. Also important." The look on Potap's face was serious as he pointed to another shelf. "Very important. For pickling. To make sauerkraut from the cabbage we used to get from the Tula estate." Potap scratched his forehead. "But now I found someone to sell it to us, got a farm outside of Moscow. And don't forget. The sugar. To make jam."

Maria took a jar of raspberry jam off the shelf and turned it in her hands, the memory of her childhood suddenly fresh in her mind. "This is the kind Maman always gave me when I had a fever."

"Yes, the very one. But we've also got strawberry and blueberry. Avdotiya Timofeyevna likes those sweets." Potap smirked.

Training with Potap had kept Maria busy, and the visits to their fully stocked pantry created the impression of abundance. It wasn't until right before Christmas, that Maria realized life in Moscow had changed for the worse.

It hit her one day, when she went to the Eliseyevsky market to buy her usual, slices of the Napoleon dessert, and found the market had closed early on the account of a lack of customers and concerns for safety. And when she went back the following morning, she found the buttery cream of the Napoleon had none of its usual thickness.

For Christmas, Maria had planned to get Dunya chocolates from Eliseyevsky, and now wondered whether they would be of the same quality, but, knowing how much Dunya loved chocolate treats, she decided to continue with her plan, doing her best to keep the gift a surprise.

Maria picked the perfect time for her outing: Dunya's best friend, Akulina, was coming over and would keep Dunya distracted for several hours. The two women had known each other for years. Originally, Akulina was from a village outside of Moscow, but she'd married a Moscow man and moved with him to the city. Her husband owned a hardware store, and they had raised four children, all of them successful. Akulina and Dunya attended the same church and shared a mutual love for the occult. They believed in signs, dreams, premonitions, and divinations. Occasionally, they did card spreads for each other, verifying information, and shared dreams with each other, arguing over their meanings and interpretations.

"Dunya, I'll just pop over to the Eliseyevsky," Maria said, trying to sound casual, tucking into her pocket the extra bag she'd prepared, which would allow her to sneak the chocolates into the house unnoticed later.

"Akulina's daughter, the youngest one, poor thing, can't find anyone, might just end up a spinster." Dunya sighed. "Twenty-one already. All those men at war, fighting. Tough times."

"So, she's like me?" Maria, who would turn twenty in a few months, raised her eyebrows.

"Don't you compare yourself," Dunya started to say but then paused. "You know what? Akulina's daughter will be doing a divination on Christmas Eve. Why don't you do one, too?"

"A divination? With the name?" Maria recalled the last time she'd tried it when she'd first met Andrei. "But that doesn't work, Dunya. I'm not marrying anyone named Andrei."

"You didn't marry Nikolai, did you?" Dunya noted casually. "But we can try a different one."

"Alright, I guess it won't hurt," Maria said. Faced with an uncertain future and no prospects, a divination seemed like a good distraction.

"Now, let me just find out what type of divination Akulina is going to do for her daughter and we'll do the same thing. The best predictions are done on Christmas Eve, so we've got time."

Deep in thought, Maria headed to the Eliseyevsky market. The conversation with Dunya reminded her of Andrei, and during the ride, Maria considered walking over to the Moscow Art Theater but immediately dismissed the idea. The coach parked in front of the store, and Maria instructed the driver to wait for her. It was just after four in the afternoon, but already dark, the streetlights illuminating the way. As usual, Tverskaya Street was crowded, the noise of conversation mixing with the haggling of the drivers and the horses' neighs.

Light snow was falling, and Maria paused, doing her best to navigate the way across the sidewalk and into the store. As she did so, Maria noticed a figure that seemed vaguely familiar. She squinted, trying to place the silhouette. He approached, slouching, looking incongruous in his old and worn coat, too light for the weather. Despite the freezing cold, he wasn't wearing a hat and Marie noticed his bright red ears. *Ivan.*

Maria called after him, "Ivan Afanasievich," trying to be heard over the noise of the street. The man stopped cold in his tracks, then put his hands into his pockets and sunk in his head, turned and scurried off. "Ivan, it's me, Maria Suvorova." She ran after him.

He quickened his pace, but something pushed Maria to continue her pursuit. She caught up with him and he stopped and whispered right into her ear.

"Follow me just down the street. The best place to hide is in the middle of the action. Just down and to the left."

The directions indicated by Ivan were how one would get to the Moscow Art Theater, and Maria winced, but followed Ivan anyway, keeping a safe distance between them. To her relief, he turned on Glinishchenskiy Lane, several blocks before the street that led to the Moscow Art Theater and stopped halfway down the unlit street.

"Maria, what a surprise." He turned to face her and she noticed his cheeks were unusually red, strikingly so on his pale face. "But how did you recognize me?"

"I don't know. But I have a good eye, I guess." Maria

shrugged. She'd been told this before, her ability to see and remember the smallest detail.

"With this skill, you'd be indispensable for the revolution." Ivan gave her a pointed stare.

"Oh, yes," Maria responded vaguely, recalling Ivan's lectures at Irina's salon.

"I have to say, thank you for warning us back then. I managed to get out of the city right in time."

"So, the *okhranka*, it was true?" Maria said, but Ivan pressed his finger to his lips, indicating for her to lower her voice.

"Andrei told me right after you came to see him. And that you'd risked everything for us. For people you barely even knew. I'll never forget what you did for us," he whispered. "The revolution will remember you!" he added emphatically.

"Andrei told you?" Maria clutched to the mention of Andrei with a zeal that surprised her.

"Yes, of course. That very night, he came to warn me of the *okhranka* and I left Moscow. I got arrested anyway, but not in Moscow. I should have known to lie low, but it's not my style." Ivan chuckled. "So I was shipped off to Siberia, but I ran away. Pulled a Houdini."

"You ran away from prison?" Maria gasped.

"Shh!" Ivan put a hand to his mouth again. "Yes. I've got powerful friends. I bet those guards are still wondering how I managed it. The revolutionary movement will not be held back." He smiled, a crooked smile, and she noticed one of his front teeth was missing. "We're strong!" He pumped a fist in the air, and Maria recognized the gesture from Irina's salon.

For a moment, Maria was transported to the glitter of the red mansion's living room, the piano, the bright lights, the champagne, Ivan's speeches about equality and justice. And Andrei, their conversations, the promise of something incredible between the two of them.

"It seems like that time was ages ago, doesn't it?" Maria said, her lower lip quivering. She felt a sudden hopelessness, the glitter of the salon in the past, and she, still young, and yet so alone.

"Maria?" Ivan looked at her in surprise. "Remember, we need to fight." Ivan was suddenly consumed by a bout of coughing. He pulled out a crumpled, dirty handkerchief and wiped his mouth. "I'm sick," he said nonchalantly. "As you can see. Prison didn't agree with me."

"Ivan Afanasievich, let me help you, please," Maria offered. "Do you need a place to stay? I've got spare rooms in my house. And they would never look for you there."

"Thank you, Maria, I'm quite alright. I've got a place to stay. Friends of the revolution." Ivan waved vaguely into the night. "And besides, it's just for a few more days. Before I set out for St. Petersburg."

"Why there?"

"The capital awaits. That's where we'll attack the capitalist hydra. And once done, the party of the people will triumph, Maria. Mark my words."

"I will." Maria nodded.

Ivan's words sounded fantastical, akin to the ravings of a lunatic, but she remembered his ability to captivate a full salon for hours and paid close attention.

"Goodbye, Maria," Ivan said. "You have a kind heart. I don't believe in God, but may he protect you anyway, as they say."

"Ivan, wait." Maria suddenly had an idea. She reached into her purse and pulled out the money she'd set aside for shopping that day. "Here, please. It's not much, but I want to help."

"Maria, I couldn't." Ivan stepped back.

"It's for the revolutionary movement." Maria stuffed the money into Ivan's hand and, before he could protest, she rushed off into the bustle of Tverskaya Street.

"Thank you!" She heard Ivan's voice as she turned the corner.

The encounter left Maria in a state of confusion. She'd forgotten all about Eliseyevsky, the pastries, the chocolates she had planned on getting for Dunya, and didn't remember the Christmas gift until returning home to find the kitchen door closed. Hushed voices filtered through from behind the door.

Maybe doing a divination is a good idea, Maria thought, going up to her room. *I'll ask Dunya after she and Akulina are done.*

Maria sat down in front of her vanity and let her hair down. It was straight and very thick, with her braid now all the way to her waist. She checked her face, pale in the reflection. Maria never thought of herself as particularly pretty, but now, looking at her dark brown eyes, her high cheekbones, her straight nose, she was happy with what she saw.

Maria thought back to the encounter with Ivan. *What are the chances? And Andrei.* She remembered the handsome actor. Their last encounter, that kiss nearly two years prior. *Things could have been different now.* Maria sighed, running the comb through her hair. And then an idea occurred to her.

She remembered a simple divination, which involved placing a comb under the pillow after brushing one's hair and asking the groom to appear in a dream.

And why not? This way, I don't have to wait until Christmas to do the divination.

Maria loved to act fast and found the idea so pleasing that she smiled at her reflection, brushing her hair with a newfound zeal. Having completed all of her brushing, she put the comb under her pillow.

She didn't tell Dunya about the divination, and, by the time she climbed into bed hours later, had almost forgotten about the comb. But that night, Maria dreamed of a man in uniform. He was a soldier, an officer. She didn't know the ranks well enough to tell. She didn't see his face, but the man in her dream was not Nikolai. Of that, she was certain. Maria remembered asking the man to turn, to show his face, and his refusal to do so. Instead, the figure in uniform guffawed, responding, 'all will be revealed,' as he faded into the night.

"Dunya!" Maria yelled and rushed downstairs in the morning, holding the comb in her hand, as if it were evidence of the supernatural creeping into her life. "I saw him."

"What is it, Masha?" The nanny stepped out of her bedroom, rubbing her eyes. "It's just after six, still dark out." She pointed to the windows, and only then did Maria realize she'd gotten up much earlier than usual.

"I did the divination. With the comb. Last night." Maria took her nanny by the hand, leading her to the kitchen. Fekla was already there, pots and pans clanking, about to bake bread. The cook looked askance at Maria, mumbled 'good morning', and went on baking, her whole figure demonstrating a person too busy to be distracted.

"Alright, I guess we can speak elsewhere," Maria mumbled and they went into Dunya's room. "I saw him. The man," Maria said, closing the door tightly behind them.

"You did it by yourself? But why didn't you tell me? And you should have waited until Christmas Eve." Dunya shook her head.

"I just thought, why not? You were busy. And it was easy. I brushed my hair and put the comb under my pillow. But I saw a man in uniform." Maria raised her head up. "Not Nikolai!" she yelped, seeing the nanny's furrowed brows.

"Did you do it right before going to bed?"

"No. Does it matter?" Maria shrugged.

"Of course, it matters. You didn't follow the rules, Masha. So do you know who the man was?"

"He wouldn't tell me his name."

"He spoke to you? Oh, Lord Jesus." Dunya crossed herself. "Lord Jesus," she shook her head, "oh, may Lord Jesus protect you from harm." She crossed Maria. Then added, "I don't think we should do another divination right now. But after Akulina goes to the fortune-teller with her daughter, we'll see."

CHAPTER 16

*M*aria walked into the kitchen to find Dunya and Potap sitting at the kitchen table, chatting.

"The Lord will save us. Trust in God," Dunya said, and Maria sighed and silently shook her head. She'd been hearing the nanny repeat this very phrase more and more often, as the war approached its third year.

"God helps those who help themselves," Potap countered. "Gotta be ready for the end of the world."

"Potap, let's go over the books now." Maria interrupted the conversation.

"Yes, of course, everything is ready." Potap scratched his head and immediately got up from the table.

Several minutes later, Maria and Potap were seated in Count Suvorov's study.

Maria opened the books. The neat rows of numbers that had once seemed so confusing, now made perfect sense to her. She could tell right away which column referred to payments owed and noticed her expenses at the Eliseyevsky market.

"I've noticed it's gotten more expensive," Maria said. "I get the same thing every time." She averted her eyes, remembering the recent encounter with Ivan, and the money she'd given to the escaped convict. "And yet, look." Maria pointed to the column.

"Yes, almost twice as much." Potap shook his head. "Tough times, tough times. I wish your father knew what we are going through here."

"Papa must know. I keep him updated in my letters."

"So do I, but the prices keep on rising. Changes every week now." Potap let out a deep breath. "No stoppin'."

"I don't think Papa is coming back just yet." Maria sighed. "Train service hasn't been restored." In response, Potap grunted but did not react.

"I suppose I could ask Papa to increase the transfers?" Maria added after a pause.

"That might be a good idea." Potap nodded. "Though we're saving on the salaries, aren't we?"

All of their male staff, except for Potap and an older footman, had been conscripted. Then, two maids quit over low salaries, the footman failed to return from extended leave, and they were down to just three staff, Potap, Dunya, and Fekla.

"We sure are." Maria nodded. "I think we can keep things running with just the three of you."

"Just gotta watch over Fekla." Potap shook his head in disapproval. "That woman."

"But we need her, don't we?" Maria noted, and Potap nodded in agreement.

"That we do, that we do." Potap twisted his mustache. "I hear there are bread shortages in Moscow. Better keep her on to make it for us. Safer that way."

* * *

THE FOLLOWING MORNING, Maria arrived at the Eliseyevsky market to find a long queue snaking all along down Tverskaya Street, turning into Gnezdnikovsky Lane. Maria stared at the line of people, whose faces bore focused, angry expressions.

"What do you want?" An older woman narrowed her eyes at Maria.

"Excuse me, please, are you trying to get into Eliseyevsky?"

"No, lining up for the Filippovsky bakery," the woman hissed. "Bread."

"Bread, bread." The crowd murmured.

"Bread?" Maria opened her eyes wide.

"Where have you been?" The woman put her hands on her hips. "There is no bread."

"No bread?" Maria took a step back.

"Gotta get in line," someone said. Another person poked Maria in the ribs and she winced.

"What are you doing?" She turned to confront the offender, but the line started moving, leaving Maria standing on the sidewalk in befuddlement.

"Bread, bread, they are bringing out bread," someone yelled. The queue jerked forward.

A man emerged from the store, a tray with a few loaves extended on his arm high up above the crowd. Greedy hands reached onto the tray, pushing and shoving.

"One each, one each!" he yelled.

No more than thirty seconds later, the loaves disappeared. The lucky customers at the front of the line left, stuffing the loaves into their bags, while the rest of the crowd, grumbling, prepared to wait for the next tray.

Maria saw an opening in the queue, and, without waiting, breathing out in relief, entered the doors of the Eliseyevsky market, rushing all the way to the dessert counter. It wasn't until she was standing in front of it that she noticed something was amiss. The smell. The familiar smell of a mix of cinnamon, vanilla, and sugar that filled this particular corner of the Eliseyevsky, was gone. And then she noticed the counter. It was completely empty.

The stacks of cookies, pastries, cakes that had previously filled it had vanished. Not one single crumb remained. There was no Napoleon, no eclairs, no marmalades, nor chocolates.

"Countess," she heard and turned around. It was François, a salesclerk she'd gotten to know well over the years. He was a Frenchman, who had settled in Russia years ago and had worked at the Eliseyevsky since the day the store opened. The expression on François' face was impenetrable. Years of working in sales had taught him to reveal little of his emotions, but Maria noticed a slight downturn in his mouth, a sign of regret.

"What's happening?"

"They passed a law today prohibiting the baking of sweets."

"What? You can't possibly be serious."

"Oh, yes, there is a flour shortage in Moscow. It's a supply issue. So, in all of Moscow, we're not to waste flour on pastries. Only bread." François shrugged.

"Now I get it. I was barely able to make it inside." Maria pointed to the line of people blocking the entrance.

"Yes, it's been like that since the early morning. No Napoleon today, Countess. Or for the foreseeable future."

For the first time in her life, Maria stepped out of the Eliseyevsky market empty-handed. She maneuvered around the line and rushed home, anxious to share the news with Potap and Dunya.

"Potap," Maria ran into the mansion, "the flour!" she yelped, almost bumping into the butler, who looked just as out of breath as she was.

"There you are!" he said.

"I heard there is a shortage of flour everywhere. No bread in the whole city, it's a disaster."

"I knew it." Potap smacked his head. "I knew it."

"What is it? But we're okay, right? I just checked last night; we have three bags left." Maria stared at him in confusion.

"No. The flour is gone."

"What do you mean, gone?

"She took the flour, Maria. Stole it."

"Who?"

"Fekla did."

"All of it?" Maria swallowed hard. A feeling of more bad news weighed on her. "The three bags?"

"What's happening?" Dunya came out of her room. She was standing, wrapped in her shawl, eyebrows knitted.

"Fekla ran off and took all of our flour with her," Potap said.

"But how did she manage?" Dunya's mouth gaped open. "I sleep right by the kitchen, and I didn't hear a thing."

"The tea!" Potap's mouth gaped open. "She must have done slipped something in the tea last night. "And Volk didn't even wake up. She must have planned the whole thing. I'm an old fool. I've failed you, Maria."

"No, no, Potap, it's not your fault," Maria said, straightening up, at that moment remembering her mother's words about posture and how a countess always maintained composure, no matter how shocking the news. "I'm sure we'll find a solution. We'll figure something out. And besides, we don't need bread."

Potap shook his head in consternation.

"I should have locked up our supplies. Should have known better. But I didn't think she'd go that far, that Fekla woman."

"No wonder I saw a snake in my dream last night. Bad times." Dunya frowned.

"I'll go after her. I'll go to Kuzminki, find out where she lives, and get her to return the flour." Potap jerked forward.

"Potap Filimonovich, it's too dangerous." Dunya raised her hands up in protest. "Who knows what she's capable of."

"Potap, please, don't do that," Maria said. "We'll be fine."

"The Lord's justice will catch up with her. Oh yes, it will. Lord Jesus sees everything," Dunya said, staring at a distance. "Yes, he sure does." She was mumbling to herself now, ignoring Potap and Maria, who exchanged glances.

"I'll go see the police captain," Potap concluded. "See what Zakhar Nikodimovich says about the situation."

"Maybe the police will go after her." Maria said, her voice quivering.

"Some people are just rotten to the core," Dunya noted and Potap nodded in agreement.

CHAPTER 17

The information Potap brought with him from the police station was nothing like they expected.

"The tsar is about to abdicate," the butler said, walking into the mansion.

"What? But that's impossible." Maria's mouth gaped open.

"Zakhar has his sources. He's always right." Potap furrowed his brow. "Maria, I've been thinking all the way back here. You need to go to your father. To France."

"I can't leave you. And Dunya." Maria turned to her nanny, who was sitting at the kitchen table, a dejected expression on her face.

"It's not safe here, Maria." Potap shook his head. "Look at what's happening?"

"But Papa needs me to watch over the estate." Maria shrugged. "And what would I do in France, anyway?" She remembered a recent photo she'd received from her father. He was sitting next to Antoinette, with baby Konstantin, now two years old, on his mother's lap. The family looked complete without her.

"Join your father," Potap repeated, but Maria shook her head.

"I'm fine right here, Potap. And you've taught me so much. And besides, it might be good for Russia to modernize," Maria said, suddenly recalling Alexei's speeches. "I read in the papers the other day, an opinion piece, they said we can become a republic. We'll be like France."

"A republic? Russia?" Potap chuckled. "With everyone stealing? At least with the tsar, we know God is on our side."

"Alright, then. But why would I want to leave my home?" Maria ran her fingers down the wall. "I love this house. Can't imagine living anywhere else."

* * *

THE POLICE CAPTAIN WAS RIGHT, and Tsar Nicholas II abdicated just two days later. Hearing the news, Dunya broke into tears.

"How could he abandon us? How could this happen?" she cried out.

"The temporary government is now in charge, we'll be fine, Dunya," Maria said.

"No, no, we're doomed, doomed."

"You gotta have a strong leader in Russia. This is bad news." Potap grunted, twisting his mustache. "War is still dragging on, the country is on its knees, without a tsar showing us the way we'll be ruined."

"Yes, and the prices. And no one takes money anymore." Dunya chimed in. "Akulina told me she'd traded earrings the other day for potatoes. And with Fekla gone, who is going to buy food for us? Who will go to the bazaar?"

"Dunya, why don't I do it?" Maria suggested, immediately picturing the outing as an adventure, walking around and trading a piece of jewelry for food.

"Go to the bazaar? Not without me! All those bad people out there. You could get mugged." Dunya narrowed her eyes. "Or worse!"

"I'll go," Potap offered.

"No, Potap, better let women deal with this." Dunya shook her head. "I'll go get dressed right away."

"Dunya, Potap, please, let me do this on my own. I've been going to the Eliseyevsky for years now, and I'm just fine. I know what I'm doing."

"Masha." Potap shook his head. "This is different. There are riots near Presnia."

"Oh, yes, and the bad people runnin' around. The other day, these people stole Akulina's friend's bag, right in broad daylight."

"You never told me any of this." Maria looked at Dunya, then Potap.

"We were trying to protect you. Don't want you worryin'." Potap grumbled.

"I see." Maria sighed, wondering what else the two of them were hiding from her.

"Oh, yes, they all get together, these troublemakers. They come from the factories and instead of working, like us, like honest folks should be doing, they get up there and march around, demanding things," Dunya continued.

Maria immediately pictured Ivan, his eager face, marching alongside the factory workers.

"Some say they're even protesting near the Arbat!" Potap added, raising his hand up for effect.

"Well, the Arbat is far. We should be safe in Taganka," Maria noted casually.

"Yes, the cadets are fighting back," Dunya added solemnly. "But I'm still coming to the bazaar with you."

Thirty minutes later, Maria came downstairs dressed the same way she'd dressed to go to Eliseyevsky market: in a long black skirt and a simple coat. Maria was just zipping up her boots when Potap walked up to her.

The butler surveyed Maria critically. "You can't go like this. Not to the bazaar."

"And would you look at your gloves?" Dunya added. She'd just walked out of her room, wrapped in a warm shearling coat.

"My gloves? What's wrong with my gloves?"

"Dunya is right. Those gloves of yours are too expensive."

"Once the bad people see your fancy gloves, they'll jack up their prices. Or worse!" Dunya rounded her eyes. "Right, Potap?"

"You know what? I just thought of something. The bazaar can wait. We need to hide your jewelry, Maria. All the valuables you got in the house. In case the bad people come and take it," Potap said.

"But the police captain? Isn't he protecting us?" Maria stared at him in bewilderment. "And we've got Volk."

"Volk is useless," Dunya said, and Potap nodded in agreement.

"Volk's too old now. Let Fekla take off in the middle of the night," Potap said ruefully. "And the bad people can show up at any moment. Zakhar warned me just now."

"And I had a bad dream last night. I saw a broken mirror, and you were looking into it. And it was on a Friday night, when dreams come true." Dunya took off her coat. As soon as Dunya mentioned her dream, Maria knew there was no point arguing.

"Alright, let's put away the jewelry then," Maria agreed. "But right after we're done, we're going to the bazaar."

"I'll go get the silver." Potap headed to the dining room.

"We can be like those people in Stevenson's books! Remember, Dunya, *Treasure Island*? Maria clapped. "We can hide the gold and then make a map to figure out where to look for it. It will be fun! I'll go get Maman's jewelry box."

"How are you plannin' to dig with all the snow?" Dunya pointed outside. "Potap!" she called, walking away from Maria. "The ground is frozen. Where are we goin' to hide all the stuff?"

"Let me show you." Potap walked to the corner of the house, behind the stairs. "Remember the mouse we had last year?"

"Yes, the one that had eaten a hole under the floorboards," Maria said.

"When I did the repair, it was like I knew we would need it." Potap grunted as he got on his knees. "I think it's right over here." He tried pulling the floorboard to the side. The wood made a cracking sound but stayed put.

"It's so dark here," Maria said. "Let me take a look." She squinted and felt the floor with her hands. "I think it's this one." She pointed to a floorboard that was slightly lighter than the others.

"Let's try." Potap reached and pulled, and, right away, an empty space appeared underneath. "What a good eye you got!" he exclaimed.

Potap brought over the silver, and Maria and Dunya collected the jewelry. They wrapped it all in a thick cotton cloth and placed the items into the hiding spot. Potap affixed the floorboard on top and tapped it into place.

"Now. You should be all set." He looked at Maria. "Even if the bad people do come, they'll leave with nothin'!"

* * *

Later that day, as Maria and Dunya walked from the bazaar together, Maria felt giddy with excitement.

"You see, Dunya, it wasn't so bad!" Maria said.

"I suppose not. And we got all that we need to make soup. I'll show you how to cook that meat bone, so the soup will be nice and thick."

"Thank you, Dunya, I hope I can learn from you quickly, so I can also help out."

"If that good-for-nothin' Fekla could do it…" Dunya started to say, but then sighed. "Never you mind. We'll make it with the sauerkraut and can add some onions and carrots, there's not much to it at all."

When they sat down to eat later that evening, Maria stared at her plate in awe, while Potap sighed holding up his spoon.

"Would you look at that, a countess making dinner for herself. The world is truly upside down."

"I am so glad I've learned how to make soup." Maria smiled. "Thank you, Potap and Dunya. I'm grateful to have you in my life."

Dunya wiped a tear, while Potap grunted.

* * *

A MONTH LATER, on Thursday afternoon, Potap walked into the study where Maria was waiting for him, expecting to review the accounting books together.

"Maria, I have thought about it." He swallowed hard. Maria noticed Potap was wearing his traveling clothes. He placed the cage with his pet turtle next to him. He bowed his head, wrinkling a cap in his huge hands.

"I've got to go check on my folks back home. And help with the harvest," he grumbled.

"Back home, alright," Maria said. "So, when are you coming back?" But on seeing the expression on Potap's face, she knitted her brow.

"I've gotta go, Maria. I'm sorry to leave you with no man

around. I've spoken to the police captain. He'll come around to check on you and Avdotiya Timofeyevna." Potap cleared his throat. "And Volk, he's old now. I'm taking him with me. He's not much help to you anyway. I gotta see to him. Don't want him to be a burden on you."

"You aren't coming back, are you?" Maria flinched, feeling a familiar, gnawing feeling. No one came back. Not her father, not the footmen, not the maids. Certainly not Fekla.

"I'm not sure, Maria. I don't want to mislead you. Maybe in the fall, after the harvest."

"Thank you for telling me. Thank you for everything," Maria said, getting up from her seat. "You've taught me so much."

"You take care of yourself, Maria. And remember what I told you about going to France to join your father."

"If I leave, who will take care of the house?"

"As you wish. I've chopped some wood for you. It's over in the shed. You'll need it for the winter." He pointed outside.

"Yes, thank you, Potap," Maria nodded absentmindedly.

The winter was far away, and she had to attend to more pressing matters.

CHAPTER 18

It wasn't until the first night after Potap's departure that Maria realized their predicament.

"Good night, Dunya," she said to her nanny, and was about to head upstairs, when Dunya stopped her.

"Masha, we need to bolt the front door."

"Oh, yes, of course." Maria rushed and moved the bolt into position. Potap had always locked the front door before leaving through the side entrance, and Maria had never paid much attention to this safety precaution before. Had taken it completely for granted her entire life. But now, moving the bar into position, she felt a knot in form in her stomach.

"Dunya, I'm scared," she said, suddenly feeling exposed in the large mansion. "What if something happens to us?"

"Don't you worry, Masha. Pray to the Lord."

That night, as Maria tossed and turned in her soft bed, clutching the goose-down-filled blankets for safety. The familiar, silky sheets did not offer any comfort. The dark bedroom felt sinister, danger lurking just outside. Dunya, who was downstairs, seemed too far away.

I should have asked Potap to introduce me to the police captain before he left, Maria thought. But it was too late.

After struggling to fall asleep, she sat up in bed and reached to flick on the lamp. The realization she was on her own hit her. Maria's fingertips felt icicles. If anything happened, it was up to her to defend herself. A loud thump made her jump.

She got up, moving silently to the door of her bedroom to investigate the danger, only to realize it was a tome of Pushkin that had fallen from the shelf.

Maria picked up the book, then, with a sigh, pushed a chair against the door as a precaution. Only then was she able to fall asleep.

The following morning, she and Dunya headed to the bazaar. Maria no longer saw the outing as an adventure. Now, she dreaded going there, and found the haggling, the half-rotten vegetables, the stale meat, depressing.

As they walked down the stalls, Maria tried her best to not show her disgust, in part out of fear of offending the sellers, and in part to not appear to be any different from the others who were scouring the market for decent quality food. Instead of money, which had no street value because of inflation, she had two silver spoons in her purse. Knowing what a silver spoon was worth took time, and Maria and Dunya walked around the bazaar several times, bargaining, trying to figure out how much they could get, and hoping to get the best deal.

"How much will we get this time?" she whispered to Dunya, who was wrapped in a heavy woolen shawl, despite the warm day.

"Let me do the talking," Dunya responded.

That day, they emerged from the bazaar exhausted, but victorious, carrying several bags of provisions.

"Dunya, what will happen to us?" Maria asked on their way home, as they climbed the Taganka hill.

"Trust in God, Masha." Dunya stopped to catch her breath.

As soon as they got home, Maria was about to start making dinner, but Dunya said, "Let's have tea first, Masha. I need a break."

"Good idea, dinner can wait. And maybe I can read to you?"

"Yes, how about Pushkin?"

"Very well, we can read *The Belkin Tales*." Maria rushed upstairs and brought back the tome she'd read many times before. But before she even had a chance to open the book, Dunya shook her head,

"He let those people burn? Oh, evil as evil might be." Dunya was referring to Dubrovsky, whose moral character she found questionable. The nanny had heard the story countless times, but to Dunya, it never got old. "I don't know why Pushkin would write about a man like that."

"But he was fighting an evil guy who had sued his father."

"But Dubrovsky stole money. Why was he stealing?"

"He was only stealing from the rich, Dunya."

"So he knows better than the Lord himself? He thinks he should decide who should be rich and who should be poor?"

"But Dubrovsky is so brave, Dunya. Masha should have run away with him," Maria said wistfully. "I wish I had a man like that, who would whisk me away, risking everything."

"That's a bad idea. You want a practical man. A stable partner. No, she's a smart girl. She did the right thing by marrying the rich guy."

"Dunya, this is just in the book." Maria sighed, bile rising in her throat, as she thought of her own broken engagement to Count Nikolai and her tryst with Andrei. "Men like Dubrovsky don't exist in real life, anyway."

"But that young bride, she took an oath in a church. Now, read the passage to me again. How she rejects Dubrovsky, I sure like to hear how she sends him on his way." Dunya pointed at the book, and that's when Maria had an idea.

"Dunya, what if I teach you how to read?"

"What? Me? I'm too old." The nanny shook her head, pushing the book away.

"Please!" Maria gave her elderly nanny an encouraging smile. "Why didn't we think of this sooner?"

"How in the world?" Dunya crossed herself, and Maria suddenly knew what to say.

"Wouldn't you want to read the Bible?"

"The Bible?" Dunya pushed her chair back. "I'll have to think about it."

* * *

IT TOOK MARIA SEVERAL WEEKS, but finally she convinced Dunya to learn how to read. The two of them started dedicating one hour each night to studying. Maria found her old ABCs book and sat patiently with her nanny, teaching Dunya the alphabet. After two months, Dunya was able to read and write her own name, moving the pen carefully on the page, and then they progressed to other words, then on to sentences.

"Dunya, this is fantastic!" Maria cheered, watching Dunya confidently read a whole paragraph.

"I never thought I'd be able to do this. Never in my life. An old woman like me." Dunya wiped a tear from her wrinkled cheek.

"Now we can write letters to each other." Maria proposed.

"Letters?" Dunya chuckled. "We're right next to each other all day."

"Maybe little notes?" Maria smiled. "That way you get to practice writing."

Reluctantly, Dunya agreed, and each morning the two of them exchanged notes, that they then read out loud together.

* * *

IN LATE OCTOBER 1917, Maria woke up to a loud noise. It was still dark outside.

Bam.

Another loud bang.

Maria jolted upright. The walls of the house shook.

"Dunya!" Maria threw on her housecoat and rushed downstairs, skipping steps.

"What's happening?" Dunya emerged from her bedroom, looking around in confusion, crossing herself. No matter how many times Maria had suggested she take up one of the other bedrooms upstairs, Dunya refused, preferring to stay in her bedroom by the kitchen.

"Is it an earthquake?"

"I don't know," Dunya said.

"I'll go out and check," Maria said and rushed upstairs to get dressed. She came back downstairs not more than two minutes later to find Dunya blocking the entrance, the front door bolted.

"No. I won't let you leave." She stood guard, hands on her hips. "It's too dangerous."

"But I need to know what's happening, Dunya, please."

"It must be the hoodlums." Dunya knitted her brow. Since the summer, she had started referring to the revolutionaries as 'the hoodlums'. This term included not just those against the tsar, but anyone whom the nanny considered to be suspicious.

Another bang.

"I'll just take a peek outside. Quickly." Maria moved to the door, but Dunya showed surprising agility, blocking her.

"Stay inside." She shook her head. "I won't let you go anywhere."

"It sounds like something is happening right down the street, on the Kotelnicheskaya embankment," Maria mumbled to herself, walking away from the door in resignation.

The loud banging continued through the day, stopping very late in the evening, only to start again in the morning.

The day after, the same thing repeated.

Maria could not concentrate on anything for more than a few minutes. When Dunya suggested they read together, Maria refused. It wasn't until the fourth day, when the loud noises subsided, that Dunya let her leave the house. The street in front of the Suvorov mansion was completely empty, as if all the residents of the city had disappeared.

With a sinking feeling, Maria climbed up the hill to the Taganka square. At the entrance to the Bolvanovka church, she saw an old woman, dressed in all black, hair covered by a thick scarf, standing at the gate. The woman's face was criss-crossed by wrinkles, her eyes cold.

"Matushka, good day to you." Maria stopped to greet her.

"Good day?" The woman crossed herself. "Haven't you heard? They've been firing cannons on the Kremlin."

"Cannons? Is that what it was?"

"Yes, cannons. For three days. Now, go, you shouldn't be out." The old woman narrowed her eyes. "Unless you're looking for trouble."

Without waiting for Maria to respond, the woman stepped back and slammed the gate shut.

"Thank you," Maria mumbled and turned back home. She was half-way down the block, when she felt something soft brush against her leg. Looking down, she saw a rat scurrying away.

"No!" Maria shuddered in disgust. She reached for her shin, rubbing the place where the rat had touched it. "No!" she yelped again.

A young man dressed in raggedy clothes approached out of nowhere, smirking.

"Just a rat, nothing to be afraid of. These aren't the rats you should worry about," he announced insolently and spat.

Maria froze in stunned silence.

"Did you hear what I said, lady?" The man put a fist up as if to punch the sky. It was the gesture she'd seen Ivan do. "It's a great day! We won! The Kremlin is under control of the proletariat, lady. Remember this day! November 3rd, 1917. Yes!!! We got those damned cadets out of the Kremlin and now the Revolutionary Workers Party is in charge of Moscow." The man pumped his fist again.

"In charge of Moscow?"

"Where 'ave you been, lady? Lenin. The revolution of the proletariat." The man shook his head indignantly and walked off.

Maria stared after him in confusion. She'd heard of the Revolutionary Workers Party but had never taken it seriously. Since the abdication of the tsar earlier that year, several parties fought for power. She remembered Ivan, their chance meeting, Ivan's promise to go to St. Petersburg, his zeal for the revolution.

How did they manage? This can't possibly be true. And I gave him money. Did I contribute to this?

But she shook off the uncomfortable thought and continued home. She was almost at the gate, when she had an uneasy feeling of being followed. She threw a panicked look down the street and ran into the house through the back entrance. Maria rushed to bolt the front door and check the windows. She yanked the curtains shut and took a deep breath.

CHAPTER 19

"Dunya, what do you think it means, the revolution?" Maria asked her nanny later that day.

They were huddling together in the kitchen, the curtains drawn, as if blocking the light would give them additional safety.

"The hoodlums will stop at nothing, I just feel it," Dunya said and shivered, wrapping a shawl around her shoulders.

"I'll go get the firewood," Maria said.

They'd been heating the rooms they used since October, the fall unusually cold that year. The firewood Potap had left before leaving had given Maria the impression of an endless supply, and she marched confidently to the shed, to find the supply half-depleted already. Maria grabbed two neatly chopped logs instead of four, as usual.

"Misfortunes never come singly," Maria said, plopping the wood in the middle of the hall. "We're halfway through the firewood supply, Dunya."

"How I miss Potap," Dunya exclaimed, throwing her

hands up in frustration. By then, the two of them had already established and accepted that Potap wasn't coming back.

"You know what? Why don't we stop heating my bedroom during the day?" Maria suggested. "I'll move downstairs, and we'll only need to heat the kitchen and your room. That way the firewood will last us all winter."

"And where will you sleep?" Dunya raised her eyebrows.

"In Fekla's old room?" Maria shrugged.

"Fekla." Dunya crossed herself. Since the cook's disappearance, they hadn't spoken of her, but still referred to the tiny bedroom on the other side of the kitchen by the cook's name.

"I'll help you air it out." Dunya sighed, and so it was done.

Maria moved downstairs, settling in the cozy bedroom on the other side of the kitchen.

The upstairs rooms stood empty, with ice forming on the windows. When Maria went up there, she put on her warmest coat and boots, and even so, it was freezing. She walked through the empty rooms in a daze – her childhood a faint memory.

But despite these efforts, the remaining firewood lasted only through the end of January. Maria had seen men with axes walking around the city, chopping down trees and fences for their own heating needs. Some even cut into houses that looked deserted. They reminded her of lumberjacks from the fairy tales she'd read as a child, but, when she shared the observation with Dunya, the nanny frowned. "These hoodlums… look how we live now. No food, no heat. How are we supposed to survive like this? No order at all with these people."

"But didn't Potap have an axe somewhere?" Without waiting for an answer, Maria ran to Potap's toolshed and produced his axe. She dragged it behind her into the house.

"This is man's work, Masha. Forget it." Dunya shook her head.

"I'll figure it out. Men aren't the only ones who can chop things." Maria grunted, trying to pick up the axe, which was surprisingly heavy.

"Listen, stop this nonsense right now. I don't want you dropping this thing on your foot. Or, God forbid, chopping it off!"

"But how do we heat the house? We are going to freeze to death in here."

"We won't freeze to death. We got all these chairs." Dunya pointed to the living room. "What do we need all of these chairs for?"

"But Papa…I don't know. What do I tell him if he comes and asks what happened to the furniture?"

Dunya put her hands on her hips. "You tell your Papa that he shouldn't have left you in Moscow all alone! That's what you will tell him, I reckon."

"But Dunya, he didn't know it would be like this." Maria jumped to her father's defense.

"He had four years to figure it out." Dunya shook her head. "Leaving a child alone like this."

"I'm not a child. And remember, I was engaged." Maria threw a surprised look at Dunya, who had never criticized her employer before. "Papa thought… Oh, never mind. Let's chop up the chairs."

"Why don't we use the saw?"

"Oh, yes!" Maria went back to Potap's shed and got the tool. Together, they sawed the chairs and heated the house for another week.

* * *

A WEEK LATER, after examining her hands that had gotten rough and calloused from the sawing, Maria found a street boy, who brought her firewood in exchange for meals. The logs looked like they had been torn out of a fence, but Maria didn't care. As long as they burned and heated the downstairs rooms, it was enough.

Over the long winter months, Maria grew even closer to Dunya. They'd been spending nearly every waking hour together, and Maria felt like there was no one dearer to her in the whole world than her nanny.

"We have made it, Dunya," Maria exclaimed. It was Easter Sunday, May 5th, 1918.

"I never thought we'd survive this winter." Dunya nodded. "But we sure did. God's miracle."

Fasting during Lent that year differed little from how they normally ate, their diet consisting of mostly cabbage and potatoes, ever since they'd stopped buying meat at the bazaar months prior. They hadn't had eggs since the previous summer, and butter was so scarce they had cut it out of their diet long before Lent.

But to celebrate Easter, Maria and Dunya bought eggs at the market, trading a silver serving spoon, and painted them dark brown, boiling the eggs in onion skins. Dunya's friend, Akulina, brought over a Paskha, a special Easter cake she'd made in exchange for several eggs.

"The godless hoodlums can't stop true believers," Dunya said, examining their Easter spread in satisfaction. "Akulina told me the other day they were trying to stop the Easter procession on the Red Square. Oh no they don't."

"Dunya, don't worry, we are still able to celebrate. That's what matters." Maria smiled. She'd been in a great mood ever since the Saturday night service at their church.

"Christ has Risen," Dunya said, crossing herself.

"Truly, He has Risen."

They had just finished the meal, and Maria rose to clear the dishes when she noticed a figure walking down the path. Though she hadn't seen the woman in months, she recognized the cook right away.

"It's Fekla," Maria exclaimed.

"Let me see." Dunya squinted. "It's Fekla, alright. What's she doing over here? How dare she come back?"

"Look, she's carrying something," Maria said, pointing to the two large bags Fekla was carrying. "And she's wearing a winter coat and boots."

The cook walked up to the front door, fixed her scarf, stood still for a minute, let out a deep breath and knocked.

"Do we open the door?" Maria and Dunya exchanged glances.

"I suppose so," Maria said. "Maybe she's here to wish us a Happy Easter?"

"Alright then, let me deal with her." Dunya walked out of the kitchen and opened the door. She stood back, letting Fekla inside.

"Christ has Risen," Dunya greeted the cook, but Fekla didn't respond. She sniffled, put down her bags and cleared her throat. Then, her voice quivering, said,

"Look here, Avdotiya Timofeyevna, I came here because I'm trying to help you." Fekla pointed to her bags. "I'm going to move in here, help you out. Wouldn't you rather live with the people you know?"

"What? Are you out of your mind? Get out of here right now!" Dunya yelled.

Fekla raised her head up, crossing her arms. You're living all alone here. Haven't you heard? They're redistributing property."

"I've heard no such thing! Who is?" Dunya narrowed her eyes.

"The people in charge, that's who." Fekla sneered. "I'm

going to settle upstairs." She picked up her bags and was about to make a move to the steps, when she noticed Maria. "Countess," her voice trailed off. "I thought you'd run away."

"Hello, Fekla," Maria said, keeping her voice steady.

"Listen here, Miss. I work at the factory now. I get a ration." Fekla bit her lip. "And I'll be taking your room." She climbed the steps, dragging the bags behind her.

"No you won't!" Dunya rushed after Fekla, breathing heavily. Maria followed.

But Fekla was quicker. Pushing them out of the way, she ran to the bedroom and slammed her bags on the floor. They looked out of place in the neat space. The beautiful wooden furniture and the paintings on the walls only further accentuated the raggedy sacks.

"You get out of here right now," Dunya hissed.

"You have no idea, do you?" Fekla sniggered, pushing Dunya out of the way, and walking back downstairs. "Over here, over here, Vasya, Timka!" Fekla yelled out into the yard, and Maria, who'd followed Fekla down the steps, noticed a small man, also dressed in a winter coat and boots, walking down the path. He was dragging a huge bag, and behind him, three small children walked together, holding hands. They were all wrapped in gray scarves and dressed in dark brown rags.

"What's this?" Dunya yelled.

"My family. The future of the country. They deserve to live in this house," Fekla announced, triumphant. "I reckon the kids can take the other rooms upstairs, one each."

"You better get these lice-infested vermin out of here, fast." Dunya's voice was shrill. She'd made her way downstairs, and, wiping beads of sweat off her forehead, now stood guard at the bottom of the steps, blocking the way.

"I think you better shut up or I will report you to the revolutionary committee," Fekla replied. "We've got all the rights. As the proletariat, it's our turn to live here now. You're lucky we aren't throwing you out of the house and are letting you stay."

Dunya was about to react, but Maria rushed to the nanny.

"Dunya, please, calm down." She pulled the nanny into the kitchen. "Please, have a seat. Don't argue with her. We'll work something out. This is just temporary, I'm sure."

"This is awful. Just awful." Dunya plopped down and let out a sigh.

"But at least we know her. Fekla is right. If they're really doing this, who cares about the upstairs, right?"

"It's bad, bad, Masha. And I saw my mother in my dream the other night. She always comes to me in my dreams when something bad is about to happen," Dunya added after a pause.

"There you go with your dreams again, Dunya. It's Easter Sunday, remember? Come on, Dunya, nothing bad can happen on a day like this."

CHAPTER 20

$\mathcal{D}$unya had taken Fekla's return much harder than Maria, but after a week, they settled into an uneasy routine.

"See, this isn't so bad," Maria told Dunya one day, when they were in the kitchen alone together. They now took turns using the kitchen with Fekla during the day, but in the evenings, the space was all theirs.

"Now, what would you like to read tonight?"

Dunya scratched her head, about to respond, when they heard voices coming from the outside "Who's this?" Dunya walked up to the window.

Fekla walked down the path, followed by a group of men. There were five of them, all wearing shabby, worn clothes.

"I told you, this woman was trouble!" Dunya yelped, shuffling out of the kitchen. Maria followed her nanny to the front door.

"Right over here." Fekla entered and led the men inside. "Come right through."

Their smell hit Maria right away. The men stank.

"Listen," Fekla told the men, ignoring Maria. "Ya'll can get settled right here." The former cook pointed to the living room.

Turning to Maria, Fekla declared, "This lady right here, she don't mind. She knows she gotta be helping the prole," she stumbled, "the proletariat. Building our bright future." Fekla paused for effect. "Honest, working men."

"And I suppose you're letting them stay at the Suvorov mansion out of the goodness of your heart?" Dunya, hands on her hips, sauntered to Fekla.

"No, they're paying me a week's salary each." Fekla shrugged. "Nothing wrong with this. I'm just helping them out."

One of the group stood out. His hair caked in dirt, his rags were especially repulsive. He scratched himself, quickly moving his hands, starting with his head, then his neck, then reaching into his armpits and, finally, his crotch. And then starting the routine all over again. He belched as he followed Fekla into the living room, and that threw Maria into action.

"That is *it*," she said to Dunya and rushed to the front door.

"Masha, where're you going?" Dunya asked.

"Dunya, I'm going to complain to the revolutionary committee," Maria whispered, putting on her coat.

"The revolutionary committee?" Dunya gasped, trying to block the door. "You're out of your mind. You can't go talking to these people."

"But how do we go on living like this? We are going to get infested with lice and flees and who knows what!?"

"But what's your committee going to do?"

"I'll just go check. I promise, I'll be very careful. And I won't attract any attention. No one will ever know who I am."

Dunya tried to protest, but Maria would not stop. She

could tolerate Fekla and Fekla's family, but having the strange men staying in her home was too much.

Maria headed straight for the revolutionary committee local headquarters that, she knew, had been established in the basement of a small house at Taganka Square, right behind the Bolvanovka church. Akulina and the church ladies had complained about the proximity, and, over the last few months, Maria had seen people going in and out of the building. Maria had never considered doing so herself. Until now.

Propelled by the indignity, she ran uphill and, a few minutes later, opened the door to the basement and walked down the dimly lit stairwell. Rubbing her eyes, she waited for them to adjust to the darkness. At the bottom of the steps was another door, and she pushed it open, finding herself at the end of a very long corridor, nearly bumping into two people arguing in front of a closed door with the sign 'Head'.

The stuffy, musky smell overwhelmed her and she felt faint. She leaned on the wall for stability. Maria swallowed hard, nausea rising in her.

This was a bad idea, she decided and nearly turned around to leave, but someone tugged at her sleeve.

"Hey there, what are you looking for?" A young man wearing a leather jacket was standing next to her.

"Nothing," Maria answered, her voice thin.

"Comrade, why did you come here?" His voice was insistent.

"I…I have come to get help," Maria squeezed out after hesitating for a brief moment. "There are these people, and they have moved into my house. Something should be done. They are just occupying every space, and they have no right. No–"

"Your house?" The leather jacket raised his eyebrows. In the faint light of the corridor, Maria could just make out his light blue eyes. He had ruffled hair, as if he'd just ran his hand through it.

"Yes, my–"

"And where is this house located, comrade?"

Maria felt her hands grow sweaty. "It's in this district," she responded vaguely, taking a step back.

"How interesting. Have you heard that private property has been abolished, comrade?"

"Umm."

"Not sure where you've been for the last six months, but no one owns their apartments anymore. And certainly not whole houses!" The young man sneered. His blonde eyebrows grew closer together and made him look like a frazzled bird.

"Well, it's not really a house. I misspoke. Thank you for your help." Maria tried to move to the exit, but the young man gripped her arm and held it tightly.

"Please, let me go," she pleaded.

"We'll go there together and see what's been happening," he announced loudly. The pair arguing in front of the door suddenly stopped and Maria felt two pairs of eyes on her. No one moved to help.

"Thank you for your assistance," Maria said, trying to maneuver out of the man's grip, but to no avail.

"Go," the man ordered and pushed her down the corridor, to the steps.

Maria nearly stumbled, but immediately felt his fist on her back. She climbed the steps, out of the basement. The man followed her out, and, in the daylight, Maria noticed he was very young. He could not have been older than twenty. Maria thought how strange it was that the two of them were probably almost the same age, but she was fully at his mercy.

"Comrade, you better stop resisting, or I will get you arrested," the man barked. "We've got to confiscate private property and log it into our records. There are proletarian families waiting for resettlement. We need apartments. So if you are saying you've got a whole house and don't know what to do with it, and you got people settling here illegally, we must address it right this minute."

"I will come back, I promise." Marie felt tears well up in her eyes.

"Stepan!" Someone called from the basement. The young man loosened his grip on Maria.

A wave of relief rushed over her, as she saw Ivan Engelghart climbing up the steps. He was wearing a leather cap, a matching black leather jacket, which looked brand new, and shiny leather boots. On his belt hung a revolver, Ivan's right hand firmly resting on it. With his normally greasy hair covered by the cap and the shiny new jacket, he looked like a person of authority.

Maria was about to say something, but he raised his eyebrows at her in a barely perceptible indication to stop her from speaking, so she closed her mouth.

"What is it you are up to? Harassing young women?" Ivan barked at the young man.

"Ivan Afanasievich! I would never!" Stepan's cheeks reddened, as he let go of Maria completely.

"What are you doing with this young comrade?" Engelghart pressed.

"This is no comrade, Ivan Afanasievich. She's an enemy capitalist and just told me she's got a whole house she still owns." Stepan was almost out of breath, as he scrambled to impress his superior. "She tried to run away."

"I see, I see! A capitalist enemy, you say?" Engelghart turned to Maria and looked at her curiously, as if seeing her for the first time. He then turned back to Stepan. "I don't see a capitalist. Don't you have anything more important to attend to? When our brothers in arms are dying at the front, you're running after a skirt? You are shameless, really!" Engelghart sneered and suddenly slapped Stepan so hard that the young man stumbled back.

Maria gasped.

"Now, you go back to the office and get back to work," Engelghart barked. He then turned to Maria and said, in a completely different voice: "Please, comrade, excuse the disturbance. If you still have an issue, come back tomorrow. You may go."

Engelghart turned and followed Stepan into the basement, slamming the door behind them.

Maria was left standing on the street.

She felt as if she had just woken up from a nightmare. What had happened to her in the last hour was so improbable, the strange men invading her home, her near escape, Engelghart's sudden appearance. Maria felt nauseous and sat under a tree to catch her breath. After a few minutes, she decided it was best to go back home, and moved slowly, with frequent stops.

Entering her home, Maria overheard an argument.

"You go! It's weird, this thing. I'd much rather just have an outhouse, like back in the village," one of the men said.

"Oh, that's for sure. This fancy stuff is too fragile," the second man hooted. "Not sure it'll handle what I've got."

Rushing into her nanny's bedroom, Maria closed the door tightly behind her and broke down crying.

"What happened?" Dunya embraced her. "Please don't cry."

"I almost got arrested. It was just by chance I saw someone I knew. And he let me go," Maria said through the tears, pressing a handkerchief to her face.

"My little girl. What's happening to us?" The nanny rocked her. "At least you're safe now. Safe right here, next to me. You sleep right here, in my room tonight. You just stay here with me."

They pushed another mattress into the nanny's bedroom, and that night, Maria dosed off into a broken, troubled sleep, with Dunya sleeping right next to her.

Loud banging awoke them in the middle of the night.

"Open the door!" a man's voice commanded outside. Maria tried to get up, but Dunya hushed her.

A few moments later, they heard Fekla's sleepy voice respond, "Please, please come in."

Footsteps followed.

"What do we have here?" someone asked, and Maria recognized Engelghart's voice. "Who are the occupants of this property? Where are your papers?"

"Papers? I ain't got no papers," Fekla replied. "I've worked here for ten years as a cook."

"If you have no papers, you must vacate the premises right this minute," Engelghart barked.

"But I got my babies upstairs, they're sleeping, please your excellency." Fekla's voice took on a pleading, desperate tone.

"Who are you calling 'excellency'?" Engelghart screamed. "Don't you know how to properly address a revolutionary? You've got ten minutes to pack up and vacate the premises." After a pause, he added, "And who are these people?"

"It's just some honest folk, factory workers." Fekla said meekly.

"Factory workers?" Engelghart sneered. "Comrades, this looks like a brothel to me. Operating right here, in the Taganka district."

"Oh, these are just some good citizens. They are sleeping here, just for one night," Fekla rushed to explain.

"I see drunk bums who, instead of supporting the revolution and fighting for their country, are boozing and causing trouble." Engelghart kicked a bottle that rattled across the floor. A loud snore followed, as if confirming the statement.

"Comrade Boyko, wake them up right now," Ivan ordered, and immediately there was slapping and kicking. "Get up, you pig, get up, you disgusting pig, and you too."

There was the noise of bodies being moved, shuffling, struggling and grunting, and, less than ten minutes later, the mansion grew quiet.

"Now, that's better. And if I see you here again, you'll go straight to jail," Ivan said.

"But Mr. Comrade, there are more people inside," Maria heard Fekla say, the cook's voice smarmy.

"Are there now?"

"Yes, yes, there is the real enemy hiding out next to the kitchen!"

"The real enemy? You don't say?" Engelghart guffawed.

"Yes! If you must know, it's Countess Maria Suvorova, the daughter of the nobles. An actual countess! And she is living in the cook's room, next to the kitchen right now, right at this very moment. You must have her vacate also! And arrest her, put her in jail. She has been abusing us, poor pro… protarians for years and must be punished. I'll show you right now."

Maria felt a knot form in her stomach, as she heard the door being opened, and guessed, Fekla was showing Ivan the cook's old room.

"Dunya, they're looking for me," she whispered.

The elderly nanny pressed her hand over Maria's, and shook her head, saying nothing.

"And where is this woman now?" Engelghart shouted. "How dare you lie to me?"

"But she was here," the cook started to say.

"You shut your mouth right now," Engelghart shouted. "You expect me to believe an enemy countess is living in a cook's room? I've never heard of such a thing. I doubt you've ever met a real enemy countess. You want to know what I think? I think you're trying to disrupt the revolutionary committee from doing its job and from clearing the premises of illegal occupants such as yourself. I think you're trying to derail the revolution by distracting us from our work!"

"Me? No, no, I am just trying to help, Comrade sir," Fekla squealed. "Just trying to help."

"Do I look like I need your help?" Engelghart inquired in a sinister tone.

"I, I, no, no, I will get going now."

"Comrade Boyko, you follow her and her brood, and make sure they don't come back," Engelghart ordered. "I will stay here and take a look around. Everyone else, outside!" Maria heard Engelghart's confident steps echoing in the hallway.

"Maria, you may come out now," he called. "I know you're here."

Maria and Dunya exchanged glances.

"What do I do?" she mouthed to the nanny.

"Hide, Masha," Dunya whispered, as she pointed to the trunk.

Maria sighed. "He knows I'm here." She got up and straightened up her dress, grateful she'd started sleeping in regular clothes ever since Fekla had moved into the house. Ignoring the shocked look on Dunya's face, Maria stepped out into the hallway.

"Ivan Afanasievich, hello." Maria stared at Engelghart, wide-eyed.

"Maria, you've been incredibly careless," he said, pressing a finger to his lips, warning her to lower her voice. Outside, they could hear the bickering of Ivan's men with the intruders. "I'm surprised you're still here." He shook his head.

"But where would I go? I don't want to leave my house. This is where I belong. This is my city, my home."

"I've come here to warn you. The revolutionary committee is about to requisition your property. You've got twenty-four hours to leave."

"What?" Maria gasped.

"They won't let you stay. I've seen the papers. You've helped me and saved my life, and it's only fair I return the favor."

"But I'm staying in this little space." Maria pointed to the cook's room.

"They've already reallocated the place to other families. Probably ten or eleven of them, one for each room. Because of who you are, you'll risk everything. The best thing for you is to leave."

"But I'll lie. I'll pretend, I'll figure something out," Maria pleaded. "I grew up here."

"You heard your cook just now. Someone will give you away," Engelghart noted ruefully. "That's what always happens." Ivan adjusted his jacket, and Maria noted the revolver hanging casually in the holster on his belt.

"But where can I go?" Maria yelped, but quickly caught herself and put her hand against her mouth. "And what about Dunya?"

"Dunya is a proletarian and a citizen of the new country, not an enemy element," Engelghart responded. "So she gets to stay. I will issue a form, granting her the rights to her room."

"I am not staying here without Maria," Dunya said bravely, and Maria realized her nanny had been standing right behind her the whole time. "I'm no proletarian."

"Then both of you will need to leave within twenty-four hours." Ivan raised his eyebrows.

"Ivan Afanasievich, please. You know this is impossible. We have nowhere to go."

"Maria." He looked at her, and she read sadness and regret in his eyes that did not match his tone. "I shouldn't be doing this." He leaned in and Maria could smell his sour breath.

"Go to Irina Kutuzova's mansion," Ivan said.

She remembered their first toast at Irina's, the champagne, the glitter of the evening, and blinked at the memory that was so out of place.

"What?" Maria swallowed hard.

"There is a room under the stairs. It's hidden. I've stayed there myself when Irina helped hide me from the *okhranka*. It's all set up. Everything you need is there. Do not tell anyone your real name. You're to forget who you are. If anyone recognizes you, they've made a mistake. You hear me?"

"Yes." Maria nodded.

"And never, ever, tell anyone I've helped you." Ivan gave her a cold stare. "It's good to see you, comrade." He smirked and disappeared into the night.

* * *

MARIA SPENT the following morning bickering with Dunya, as the nanny tried to stop her from leaving.

"Masha, who was this man? Why was he telling you where to go? I'm coming with you!" Dunya hovered over her, as Maria went through her clothes, trying to pick the essentials and pack them into a large suitcase, which, she decided, was what she could carry with her to Irina's house.

"Dunya, I've met him before. Remember? I think I've told you. At the salon, it was ages ago."

"I did not know you've met people like that. Hoodlums!"

"Ivan isn't a hoodlum. He's a good person."

"He's kicking you out of your home!" Dunya crossed herself. "Oh, the world is ending, the world is ending, save us, Lord Jesus."

"Dunya, please, don't worry. I know where to go. I'll be fine. And Ivan is trying to help me."

"Oh, my little girl." Dunya hugged Maria tightly.

"I'm not going far. And I'm sure this is just temporary."

"He said he's giving me some paper. How will I live here without you? What am I going to do?" Dunya clasped her head. "Take me with you, Masha, please."

"Dunya, I'll just go for a few nights and then I'll come back, okay? I'll come back and let you know how I'm doing. And we can write letters to each other." Maria smiled. Be strong, Dunya, we'll both be alright. It's good we've spent all that time practicing writing, isn't it?"

"If I'd known it was for this, I would have never learned." Dunya shook her head stubbornly. "I don't want to lose you."

PART III

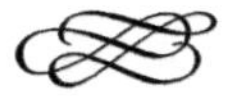

CHAPTER 21

On the afternoon of May 13th, 1918, Maria departed her childhood home. Dunya tried to stop her, telling her leaving on the 13th was bad luck and to wait until the following day. But Maria insisted on going, remembering Ivan's warning and not wanting to put off the inevitable.

She fought her own tears, trying to stay calm for Dunya, but the knowledge she was leaving her home forever made Maria's heart ache. She told herself it was bound to happen, was, if anything, overdue, and it was just a matter of time.

Had I married Count Nikolai, I would have left four years ago, Maria thought ruefully, dragging her suitcase outside, but this did little to console her.

Maria gave her nanny a tight squeeze.

"I'll write when I'm settled, Dunya. And I'll come see you as soon as I can."

Dunya crossed herself. "Go now. Just go. I can't take this." The nanny turned around and shuffled back inside.

Remembering Ivan's warning, Maria left through the back door of the house. She turned to look at the yellow exterior of the Suvorov mansion, the building she loved so much, and felt as if her whole person was being ripped apart. She wore a light travel coat and her most comfortable shoes.

Right before her departure, Maria and Dunya opened the hiding place. Maria had taken out several pieces of jewelry, including her mother's garnet bracelet and the diamond earrings she'd worn to her first ball, and sewn them into lining of the jacket. She took two thousand rubles in cash and left the rest of the money. There was no more silverware left: the two of them had traded all of it for food.

Her father hadn't sent funds in months, and Maria pushed away the troubling thought of how she would survive once she'd sold the jewelry and spent the money.

Having never gone to Irina's mansion on foot, Maria quickly realized she'd miscalculated the distance. As she walked along the Moscow river embankment, carrying the suitcase, beads of sweat formed on her forehead. She had to make frequent stops and change hands, the handle rubbing uncomfortably. The valise that had seemed so manageable when she first left her home, got heavier and heavier.

Maybe Dunya was right and I shouldn't have left today.

Maria's resolve faded and she'd almost turned back, but then she'd turned on to Lenivka Street. The Museum of Fine Arts stood in front of her. She'd been there once with her mother, shortly after the museum's opening gala on May 31st, 1912, and had always thought fondly of the place.

The landmark was not far from the red mansion, and Maria forced herself to continue. Soon, she saw the familiar outlines of Irina's home with the lion guarding the tower. Approaching the mansion, Maria realized she didn't ask Ivan what had happened to Irina, and now wondered whether the woman was still living there.

Pausing at the front door, Maria suddenly considered her move to the red mansion to be brazen and careless.

What if Ivan has set me up? She gulped at the thought, but then remembered Fekla and the squatters. The events of the night before in her own home. She took a deep breath and knocked gently. There was no answer. She knocked again, and the door gave way.

Maria pushed it open and entered. As soon as she walked in, it was clear to her Irina Kutuzova was long gone. The glamorous socialite would have never let her home go into such a state of disrepair. The living room, once the centerpiece of the mansion, had been turned upside down. Maria peeked into the space. The walls were still covered with the red wallpaper Irina had ordered from Italy. But gone were the Venetian vases. The grand piano had been pushed into a corner, its strings sticking out. One of its sides looked like it had been chopped off with a cleaver. Next to the piano stood a bed, covered hastily with a blanket. Maria gulped at the realization the living room had been requisitioned as a bedroom.

Stacks of books had been thrown casually in a corner. Dust had settled on the once-thick velvet curtains that now were peppered with large, mole-eaten holes.

Maria heard voices coming from the kitchen and rushed down the corridor. She was half-way down the hallway, when she heard the front door open and slam shut behind her.

Her heart was in her throat, and Maria just barely had time to hide behind the stairs when she heard footsteps approach.

She froze in place and could barely breathe. But the footsteps receded, and a moment later one of the doors upstairs slammed shut.

This spurred her into action.

HER MOVEMENTS CAREFUL, calculated, she brushed her hand along the wall and found the secret compartment with the lever Ivan had mentioned. Her fingers trembling, she pushed, and it gave way.

A door opened, leading her to a tiny space that, she suspected, must have once been a closet. It was narrow and windowless, housing a bed, a nightstand with a lamp directly behind it, and a washbasin attached to the wall.

Ivan was right. The room had all the essentials but barely so.

Once Maria dragged the suitcase inside, it completely blocked her passage, fully occupying the narrow space next to the bed. She pulled it onto the bed to open it, but the next moment she was hit with a smell, so offensive and unpleasant, she nearly gagged.

It was the smell of fish on the verge of rotting. It made it impossible for Maria to stay in the tiny space, and, pinching her nose, she carefully opened the door and peeked out.

In the corridor, the smell was strong but not as disagreeable. Maria noticed an open vent in her room, right above the bed. She rushed to close it, sighing with relief and considered leaving the door to the room open to let it air out, but decided it was too dangerous. She sat back on the bed and surveyed the room. It felt stifling.

I can't last here more than a few hours, Maria decided. *This is no way to live. Be as it may, I'm going to see what's going on in this place. And if anyone asks, I'll just pretend I've been living here all along.*

Anxious to act, Maria went out to explore the mansion. Her first stop was the kitchen, which, she'd learned during Fekla's short stay at her home, was shared among all residents.

Maria had never been to Irina's kitchen before. It looked much like the one at the Suvorov mansion, only it had been partitioned. The stove and the sink were separated from what must have been turned into a sleeping space by a makeshift curtain. A middle-aged man, red-faced and scrawny, stood by the stove. He was dressed in pants with suspenders and an undershirt. The man was wielding a large spoon, stirring something in a large pot boiling over on the stove. Two fish tails stuck out of the pot. Maria guessed them to be the source of the terrible smell that had made it into her room.

"It was your idea. Your idea, Klava, please," the man muttered. "Now, you do it."

"No, no, I cannot." With that, the woman covered her mouth and ran out of the kitchen, heaving.

A large herring was splayed out on the kitchen table. The woman ran back into the kitchen a moment later and approached the fish. She picked up the knife, but no more than thirty seconds later ran out of the kitchen again, covering her mouth.

The man started speaking, half-turning to Maria, as if also addressing an invisible audience.

"I got her this fish. She said she wanted fish soup. So, I bought her herring." He dropped the ladle and scratched his head. "How was I to know she ain't able to keep her food down? I even boiled the water, got the pot ready." The man's red face turned an even darker shade of scarlet.

Klava had run back into the kitchen, picked up a knife and approached the herring. "Gavrila, Gavrila," she squealed, as if repeating a prayer.

"See, ain't so hard, is it?" Gavrila nodded in approval. "Fish soup, like you wanted, we haven't had it in months."

Klava, pressing a hand to her mouth, threw the third herring into the pot and then, wiping her hands, turned to Maria. By some unwritten code, Maria realized, a woman would need to acknowledge her presence first, rather than a man.

"I'm Klava." The woman smiled. She had a button nose,

arched eyebrows and blue eyes, and looked about Maria's age.

"And this here is my husband, Gavrila." She pointed to the man. "We're the Sidorovs."

"Ma…" Maria started to stay, when she remembered Ivan's warning. "Martha," she introduced herself.

"And your family name?"

"Goncharova," Maria said, quickly adapting the name of her street, Goncharnaya, to a last name.

"Martha, eh." The man sneered. "I don't think I've seen you here before." There was menace in his voice. "Have I?" He turned to Klava, who fell silent.

"I just moved in." Maria swallowed hard.

"A, I see. Which room did you get? Are you by yourself?"

"I am. I got the closet." Maria attempted a smile. She decided there was no sense lying to the couple.

"Makes sense." The man nodded, seemingly satisfied with the explanation. "We're upstairs, in the large room. Got the partition by the window." He turned to Klava. "On the account of the baby." There was pride in his voice.

"Nice to meet you," Maria said.

"We come from Voronezh, trying out life in Moscow. Tough out here, but more money than back home," Gavrila said. "I got a job at the factory."

Maria was just about to react, but at that moment she heard the door to the kitchen open and confident footsteps followed.

"Gavrila, what are you making today? Up to your old tricks, I see?" a man's voice said and Maria froze in place.

Slowly, so as not to dispel the dream, she turned around to see Andrei standing in the middle of the kitchen.

Four years had passed since their last meeting. Andrei's eyes, deep, dark-gray, stared right at her. The look of instant recognition in them.

"Andrei?" Maria mouthed. She took an imperceptible step in his direction, but then stopped, remembering Ivan's warning.

"You two know each other? Small world, ha! You at the theater also?" Gavrila pointed at Maria. She pulled back.

"We may have met before." Andrei shrugged.

Maria felt her face flush a deep shade of red. Her heart pounding, she squeezed her hands, remembering their kiss.

"Please remind me who you are again. They say actors never remember the audience, and it's true. I can hardly keep track! It must be all the lines I have to memorize," Andrei noted casually.

She wasn't sure, but Maria could have sworn he winked at her as he spoke.

"Martha Goncharova," she said coldly, extending her hand. "I moved in today."

"I'm Andrei Zurov." Andrei took her hand, and she felt a current run through her body at his touch. "I suppose we'll be neighbors then."

Andrei's eyes pierced right through her, and Maria gulped.

Oblivious to this development, Gavrila noted, "Must be nice to have so many fans. And nice-looking ladies, too!" He clicked his tongue, gawking at Maria. "Eh, Andrei, if I were in your place, I wouldn't waste time. Life is short!"

"Thank you, Gavrila. I'll take that into consideration," Andrei said.

Maria mumbled an excuse and rushed out of the kitchen. Gavrila's leering, Andrei's indifference. All of it was too much. As she left, she heard Klava chastising her husband.

Bypassing her tiny room, Maria went to the garden. She remembered Irina Kutuzova had once employed the best gardener in Moscow. Trained in England, the gardener was known as 'Sir William'. According to Irina, he had adapted the English garden tradition to Russian taste. Flowers were planted so they would bloom in succession all summer long, the colors beautifully coordinated.

It was still too early in the season for the full splendor of the garden, but the lily of the valley had just bloomed, the delicate white flowers mixing with the greenery.

Maria sat on a bench, deep in thought. She noticed the lilac buds, the bush about to blossom. A thrush had landed on the ground and stared at her expectantly, opening its beak.

"Hey there, little guy," Maria said. "I wish I had food to give you."

The shock of her meeting with Andrei was slowly sinking in. Andrei would now be her neighbor.

In a different life. She remembered Andrei's words. *Was this it?*

Maria sat on the bench, deep in contemplation. The sun was about to set, and it grew colder. She shivered and rose to go inside, considering whether to go to the kitchen or back to the tiny closet that was now her bedroom. She opened the door and nearly bumped into Andrei.

"Is this really you?" he asked, looking at her in wonder. "Masha. Are you real?"

"Yes," Maria said, stepping back out to the garden. Andrei followed her outside. There was no sense lying to Andrei and pretending she was Martha Goncharova.

It was like she'd never left Andrei's side. The years, the separation melting away in an instant.

"Masha." Andrei smiled at her. He said her name so softly, her heart leaped. "What happened to you? I never thought I'd see you again. I thought that you'd be living in Constantinople. Or in France by now. Married to that husband of yours."

"What husband?" Maria shook her head.

"Is there more than one?"

Maria read incredulity in his eyes. "Not quite."

"But you were engaged."

"It didn't work out." Maria shrugged. "I don't really know what happened. He went to war, and his family… well, they just stopped talking to me one day. After that, I never heard from him again."

"I'm sorry."

"It's for the best," Maria said. "I'm sure."

"So, you never left Moscow? It was like you disappeared off the face of the earth. But you've been right here?" Andrei stared at her in disbelief.

"I was here." Maria bit her lip.

"Masha." He reached for her hand. "I've thought of you often. I've wondered, thought maybe one day, if I made it to France, I'd find you there. I had dreams. Strange, wild dreams, you and I were together. The last time we saw each other. Do you remember?"

"I do." Maria nodded.

"Remember how we used to talk? I missed that the most," Andrei said, his voice full of conviction. "And you're here now. What made you come here?"

Maria was about to tell Andrei how she'd run into Ivan Engelghart, but stopped herself just in time, remembering her promise not to reveal Ivan's role in her move.

"I got kicked out of my house." She shrugged. "And so, I decided to come here. Lucky that I found a spare room here. It's the only place I knew."

"I'm so sorry, Masha. So, your home got resettled, like Irina's?"

"Yes. It was just so sudden." Maria's voice quivered. "I didn't know the revolutionaries were doing that sort of thing."

"Yes, they are starting with the larger houses first. Big apartments, too. Private property doesn't exist anymore and there is a housing crisis in Moscow," Andrei said simply.

"This is how I got to live here, actually. Irina asked me to keep an eye on her place before leaving for Paris, and when it got resettled I got to stay."

"When did she leave?"

"Well, the first time, she left right after you'd warned us about the *okhranka*." A sad smile crossed Andrei's face. "But then she came back briefly last year. She was going to join the revolution, you see."

"Irina?" Maria raised her eyebrows. "I guess it makes sense, she'd supported the revolution before."

"Exactly. So, she met with Ivan. Remember him?" Andrei asked.

"Of course, I do. I ran into him once, on the street. A few years back," Maria said, again reminding herself not to mention her recent meeting to Andrei.

"Small world." Andrei hummed. "Well, he never told me. He's a big time Bolshevik boss now, rising through the ranks fast. We see each other often, Ivan and I. But anyway, Irina came back to Moscow and went to see him. She wanted to help the revolution. I don't know exactly what they spoke about, but when she realized she wouldn't be able to keep living in her house and keep her servants, she returned to France. It might have been the food shortages in Moscow, too. You know Irina, she loves to live in luxury."

"So, she won't be coming back?" Maria's mouth gaped open.

"I very much doubt it, Masha. But I'm glad you're still here. I just thought, well, I thought most aristocrats would have left by now."

"Not me." Maria shook her head. "There's nothing for me in France. So, are you still at the theater?" How many times had she been to the Eliseyevsky market, right near the theater, wondering about Andrei? How many times had she stopped herself from going there, from seeking him out?

"Yes. I am the Communist Party representative there, too. In charge of making sure we reach the masses. That's our mission now. Theater is for everyone." Andrei smiled proudly. "It was Ivan's idea to assign me to that job."

A light breeze sent a shiver through her body.

"You must be cold." Andrei took off his jacket and put it around her. "Here. Would you like to sit down?"

"Sure." She nodded.

That night, they sat on the bench for hours, talking about everything. At first, they reminisced about the salon, but then told each other stories of how they passed the years of their separation, as if they'd made a pact to see each other again. As if their chance meeting had somehow been preordained.

It was past midnight, when they went inside. Maria's heart fluttered in anticipation, as she walked down the hallway with Andrei. She wondered if he'd kiss her again, yearned for it. But remembering it as the moment that had marked their four-year-long separation, she was also afraid of it.

"Masha," Andrei said as they stood in front of her door. "I don't want to lose you again." He looked into her eyes and she held his gaze, a flame burning inside of her.

"I don't want to lose you, either."

He reached for her and kissed her softly. She felt as if she were melting into him, a sense of completeness and belonging.

That night, Maria dreamed of the man in uniform. He was the same man she'd seen in her dream after the divination. She asked him to turn, and he agreed. She saw it was Andrei. "It was always you," she said in her dream. "It was you!"

"Yes, Masha, it was always me," said the dream Andrei.

She was certain of it now: he was the one.

* * *

MARIA WOKE up the following morning, unsure of whether her evening with Andrei had been real. She sat up on the bed and took in the shabby, narrow bed, the tiny closet that was now her bedroom. She checked the time. It was two in the afternoon and she nearly jumped off the bed.

How did I sleep so late?

She splashed water on her face, checking herself in the mirror, and sat down to brush her hair. A soft knock on the door followed. She rose to open it. *Andrei.*

"Masha, is it okay if I come in? I've got you something," he said, a shy smile on his face.

"Yes, of course." Maria let him in.

"Ouch," he exclaimed and hopped on his foot. "I just stumped my toe."

"Yes, the room is a bit small," Maria said. "Why don't you have a seat." She pointed to the bed. "I don't know how Ivan…" she started, then stopped herself.

"Masha, it's okay, I know Ivan told you about the room," Andrei said, sitting down.

"You do? But he asked me not to tell anyone." Maria averted her eyes.

"I just saw him. And look." Andrei's eyes sparkled as he handed her a small piece of paper.

"What is it?"

"A residency permit for one Martha Goncharova." He scanned her face for a reaction. "Isn't that your new name?"

"Yes," Maria's mouth gaped open. When she blurted out an alias to Klava and Gavrila, she never expected it to become permanent, let alone have it be documented. But seeing it written on the card made it real.

"You just have to take a photo and then you'll glue it here." Andrei pointed to the permit.

"I'll help you."

"But Andrei, how did you get this?"

"I have my ways." He winked at her. "Ivan helped me, and a little luck. Listen, I've got an idea. Let's go to the theater. I was thinking about this all night and I think this plan might just work."

"Alright." Maria stared at Andrei in awe and fascination. He was like an angel sent to help her. "Won't you tell me what it is?"

"I will." He nodded. "When we're on our way there."

An hour later, the two of them were walking down Volkhonka Street to the Moscow Art Theater. Andrei held her hand, and Maria reveled in the new sensation of being together. Of having Andrei at her side. She felt carefree and protected, as if all the travails of living in Moscow were easy to conquer. The feeling was so unlike going to the market with Dunya, when danger lurked at every corner, and dishonest sellers were out to get them. Even the passersby didn't look so grim that day.

"I love to walk," Andrei shared. "Even when the weather isn't as nice as today. Much prefer walking to taking the tram." He gave her hand a gentle squeeze. "And with you right here, I feel like I'm dreaming, Masha."

"Me, too." Since seeing him again, she'd been having the sensation of a dream, of something incredible that had finally happened to her. A fairy tale unfolding in front of her very eyes.

"I'm taking you to meet someone. His name is Trifon," Andrei said.

"Who is he?"

"He is the head manager at the Moscow Art Theater," Andrei said. "He runs everything, the staff, the building, the lights. Without him, we would not exist!" There were notes of admiration in Andrei's voice. "I don't know how he does it."

"I thought Stanislavsky ran the theater. He is so gallant," Marie noted, remembering the talented director and their meeting, how Stanislavsky kissed her hand and murmured, 'Enchanté, mademoiselle.'

"Stanislavsky runs the productions, of course. But the day-to-day, that's Trifon Kirillovich."

"I see."

"If it weren't for him, we wouldn't have gotten the rations."

"The rations? What rations?"

"We get rations at the theater, of course. Or we'd have nothing to eat."

"I don't get any," Maria noted ruefully.

"We'll see to that," Andrei said cryptically. "Otherwise, most of our performances are free, the patrons can't pay, and people like Irina, well, they have fled the country." Andrei furrowed his brow. "No one pays for performances anymore. The revolutionary party is trying to educate the soldiers and is giving away free tickets. Even to the people who can't read. So, everyone gets exposed to culture. Isn't that great, Masha?"

"It is. But you know, it might be good if they taught people to read as well. Dunya," Maria paused, "She and I, well…" She trailed off.

"Who is Dunya?"

"My nanny."

"You don't need a nanny now, do you?" Andrei chuckled.

"She's the closest person I've got in this world. After my mother died, and then, when my father left, it was just Dunya and me."

"I see." Andrei nodded in understanding.

"So, Dunya learned how to read, Andrei. Just last year.

And she's in her seventies, or maybe even older. I don't know for sure."

"How did she learn?"

"I taught her," Maria said.

"You did? But that's incredible, Masha."

"I mean, Dunya is really amazing. I'm so glad she learned to read and write, and now we can write to each other." Catching a curious look from Andrei, Maria added, "Since I shouldn't go back to my house. That's what Ivan told me."

"Oh, yes. Well, Masha, listen, this guy you're going to meet, Trifon Kirillovich. Let me tell you about him, so you know what to expect."

CHAPTER 23

"Trifon never takes a day off, ever," Andrei said. "He grew up very poor, comes from a circus family, and he lost his mother very young. She was a famous acrobat but lost her balance and fell to her death during one of her acts."

Maria gasped. "How awful."

"Their circus went everywhere, from Siberia to Sochi. He tells us he still remembers the terrible winters and the terrible feeling of waking up in a freezing tent, his fingers blue from the cold and his teeth chattering. So, he left when he was twelve years old. He stayed behind in Moscow after the circus had packed up and left."

"So how did he manage in Moscow?" Maria gasped. "All alone?"

"He says he settled in Khitrovka," Andrei noted casually.

"Khitrovka? But that's where all the thieves are." Maria reacted. "At least, that's what I've been told. My house, well, the estate." She blushed. "We lived not far from it."

"Trifon jokes about it, believe it or not. He always tells us how he ended up at the Moscow Art Theater by chance, because at first, he went there to steal on a tip from one of the Khitrovka thieves."

Maria shook her head. "That can't possibly be true, Andrei."

"Maybe not, but it's a good story. Somehow he got noticed by Stanislavsky, and the director made him an errand boy, and then, this part I believe, Trifon was so resourceful, so helpful, he quickly rose through the ranks to become theater manager. He knows everything about everyone at the theater, Masha," Andrei said emphatically. "And with Stanislavsky, if he wants something, it has to be done right away. If a decoration has to be redone, without Trifon, it would be impossible. But he gets everything done, whatever Stanislavsky's whim is."

"Wow, you have such amazing people working with you," Maria said. "Too bad I can't be an actress. I really wish I could get to know them, too."

"Masha, you'll see." Andrei turned to her. "You just might get a chance to meet them."

They walked into the vestibule of the theater, which was quiet during the afternoon hours, and Andrei led her to the management offices. Maria couldn't help but think back to the time she'd met Andrei in his dressing room and blushed, following him down the corridor. Andrei knocked on one of the doors, and, after hearing a curt 'come in,' they entered. It was a large room with wooden panels on the walls.

A man, whose appearance matched exactly Andrei's description, sat behind a large oak desk. Seeing them enter, the man rose to greet them, and Maria noticed he was short and stocky. His head was completely bald, and his long mustache had been freshly waxed and curled upwards.

"Andrei, good to see you. Is everything alright with the rations?" Trifon asked.

"Yes, Trifon Kirillovich. I wanted you to meet a friend. This is Martha Goncharova."

It took Maria a moment too long to react to the new name, and she felt the theater manager's astute eyes on her, his eyebrows slightly raised in expectation.

"Pleased to meet you, young lady." Trifon kissed her hand. Maria felt as if he could see right through her and her heart beat fast. *Can he tell that's not my name?* she wondered.

"I see you're not an aspiring actress then," he noted and chuckled in satisfaction. "Or you'd be introduced to the great man instead. Am I right?"

Having caught her bearings, Maria managed a smile.

"Now, how may I be of service?"

"Trifon Kirillovich, I remember you mentioned you were going to hire a typist," Andrei noted.

"That's right."

"Have you posted the ad already?"

"Not yet, not yet."

"I was thinking, maybe Martha could do the job."

"Ha." Trifon scratched his head. "This young lady? Let's see. Let's see." He turned to Maria. "How is your grammar?"

"My grammar?" Maria croaked. "It's good."

"Good? Or perfect? We need it to be perfect."

"It's excellent. I've always been complimented on how well I write, and my grammar and spelling are excellent." Maria had been taught to never speak of herself highly. This was considered a huge faux pas in fine society, but something told her those rules of civility no longer applied.

"Good, good, I expected as much. And have you ever used a typewriter, young lady?"

"Umm… I am sorry, I can't say that I have." Maria bit her lip. She couldn't lie to this man. "But I've seen one. My father had one."

"We write a lot of letters here, and do it by hand, as if we were in the nineteenth century. Not everyone reads short-hand, you see. Stanislavsky agrees with me. We need to modernize and become more efficient."

"Of course." Maria nodded. She assumed this was a hypo-thetical discussion, because, surely, she didn't qualify for the position, having just admitted to barely knowing how to type.

"You can start immediately," Trifon announced.

"As a typist? Me?" Maria asked and looked at Andrei in wonder. He gave her a quick nod.

"Yes. You'll be working right here." Trifon pointed at a small table in the corner of the office, and Maria noticed a typewriter that sat there. It looked just like her father's.

"Thank you for trusting me," Maria said, her voice quivering.

"It's a relief to have someone based on a recommenda-tion. And someone who isn't an aspiring actress." Trifon rolled his eyes. "I swear, it's as if every young woman in Moscow wants to act. Or is already an actress just waiting to be discovered by the great Stanislavsky."

"Thank you, Trifon Kirillovich," said Andrei. "Thank you!" He turned to Maria. "Mash… Martha, let's go."

"Don't forget to register her, so you can get the rations processed," Trifon added, as they walked out of his office.

Andrei led her to another room, where Maria received a work card which established her under the identity of Martha Goncharova, as an employee of the Moscow Art Theater. The card would provide her with a modest salary and monthly food rations. Maria was a now a fully-fledged resident of Moscow and the new Soviet state.

"Andrei, thank you," she said, as they left the office.

"You're welcome. I'm so glad this plan worked. Let's talk at the end of the day. I've got rehearsal. I'll drop you back off at Trifon's office."

"Andrei, wait." She lowered her voice. "Listen, you don't think anyone will recognize me, do you?"

"You mean from before?" Andrei scratched his head.

"Yes, I met Stanislavsky that one time. Remember?"

They exchanged a look, both of them remembering Maria's visit backstage.

"He won't remember you. He meets thousands of people." Andrei gave her a confident smile.

"I just don't want you to get into trouble because of me."

Andrei turned to her and took her hand.

"Masha, I'd take a bullet for you," he said, and, despite herself, Maria thought of Dubrovsky.

She returned to Trifon's office, where her good mood evaporated, as soon as the theater manager pointed at the typewriter and announced:

"I'll give you a week. I've seen young ladies who can type without looking at the keyboard. I need you to be able to do the same by next Monday."

Maria's knees buckled as she stared at the machine, hesitant to approach it.

"It won't bite," Trifon said. "It's good you're joining us when the season is about to end. You'll have time to practice over the summer," he added and left the room.

Hands trembling, Maria walked up to the typewriter and stood, contemplating her actions. She brushed her finger on the case and sat down. She examined the keyboard, taking in the layout. Maria gently placed her hands on the keys and pressed them. It was just like playing the piano, but she needed to press harder to make an imprint of a letter.

A click. Another click.

She put in a piece of paper and started to type her name as she sounded it out. "M." "A." "R." She found the three letters easily, and was about to add the 'I', when she gulped, remembering she was now Martha. She typed out the new name, her fingers feeling stiff. Her fingers moved, but her movements were jagged. She had to search for each key. Frustrated by the slowness, she gave up in the middle, then started all over again. She made a mistake and had to retype the word several times before succeeding.

When Trifon came back two hours later, Maria was still sitting at the typewriter, several sheets of papers with text typed and retyped next to it.

"Why don't you write out the keys on a piece of paper? And you can practice at home. Come back when you're ready," Trifon said. "That way you won't be using up all this paper. How does that sound?"

"Oh, yes, thank you. That's a great idea." Maria nodded at the suggestion. She was hungry and tired, but she carefully traced the layout of the keyboard on a sheet of paper, trying to keep the keys true to size. At the bottom of the sheet, she added the space bar, which was particularly troubling to her, because she kept hitting it and then had to move the cursor back.

"So, what did you think?" Andrei asked her on the way home.

"I'll make it work," Maria responded.

He took her hand in his, and they walked to the red mansion together, discussing the events of the day. They were half-way home, when it hit her. Whatever differences had separated them before, had been erased. Andrei's humble origins didn't matter any longer, nor did it matter she was the descendant of one of the finest aristocratic families in Russia. If anything, in the post-revolutionary Russia, her bloodline was seen as a flaw.

"Masha, are you listening to me?" Andrei asked.

"Yes," Maria said, "But Andrei, does this seem real to you?"

"What?" He stopped to look at her.

"Us," Maria said, her voice a near whisper.

"Yes," Andrei said and kissed her gently on the cheek. "Very real."

* * *

FOR A FULL WEEK, Maria stayed up late, studying the cut-out, running her fingers along the paper, then closing her eyes to visualize the keyboard. The following Monday, when she accompanied Andrei to the theater again and Trifon asked her if she was ready, Maria said with resolve, "Yes, Trifon Kirillovich."

"Excellent, let's try it out, shall we? I've got a passage from *Pravda*. Here." He unfolded the paper. "This one, right here." He cleared his throat and started to dictate.

"Decree calling for full mobilization of the workers and peasants born in the years 1896 and 1897."

Maria typed, as thoughts swirled in her head. 1896 was the year she was born, and she suddenly wondered whether Andrei would be drafted. But then she calmed herself. *Andrei is older than me, he can't possibly be born in 1896, he must be a few years older, so he's fine.* She forced herself to continue typing. Her fingers moved confidently, and, though slow at first, not once did she hesitate and or make an error.

"Let's take a look," Trifon said after she was done. He peered at the paper, which Maria had taken out of the type-writer and then nodded in satisfaction. "Impeccable! Impeccable!" He smiled at her, handing the paper back to her. "I knew I'd made the right choice when I hired you. My intu-ition is always on the spot."

CHAPTER 24

"It's official, I passed the test today!" Maria shared the good news with Andrei later that day as they were walking home. It was late afternoon, but still light out, the summer day long.

"Congratulations!" He squeezed her hand.

"Andrei, how old are you?" Maria asked suddenly, just as they were about to cross the street.

"Twenty-five. A quarter of a century, Masha. I won't ask you. I know better than to ask a woman her age." He chuckled.

"I'm asking, because I read about the draft today. They're calling for everyone born in 1896 and 1897 to go to the front." Maria bit her lip.

"You don't want me to go?" He fixed his gaze on her.

"No. Please don't joke like this. Of course not."

"I guess I'm too old, I was born in 1893." He curled his lips in a smile. "But it wouldn't be so bad if I got drafted, Masha."

"What?" Her blood ran cold at the thought of Andrei fighting. "No."

"Why not? I wouldn't mind supporting the Red Army. I believe in the cause. It's the right thing to do."

"But you can do other things, like you're doing now," Maria said, her voice trailing off, as she considered Andrei's words.

"Don't worry, Masha, I'm not going anywhere. And why don't the two of us celebrate your new job?"

"Andrei, I'd love to, but I've got to send news to Dunya. She's waiting to hear how I'm doing."

"You're lucky you have someone like that," Andrei said, a flicker of sadness in his eyes.

"Yes, I don't know what I would have done without her. I'm not supposed to go back. Ivan told me to stay away."

"He's right. It's too soon."

"But I have the papers now," Maria protested.

"You've lived your whole life on the same street, papers or not, someone is bound to recognize you, Masha. Why don't I go there instead? And I can check on the place," Andrei offered.

"That would be great, Andrei, thank you."

Andrei touched her face, then kissed her. A deep, passionate kiss right in the middle of the street.

"Not right here," Maria mumbled, pulling away. Kissing a man in public was not done. "Andrei, not like this," she said, and those words made her turn a deep shade of crimson. "We aren't even engaged."

Andrei paused, blushed, and smiled at her, then he squeezed her hand and gave her another kiss. A soldier, who was passing by, whistled at them, and Andrei smiled at the man, eager to share his happiness.

"I know what I'm doing. Don't worry, Masha, we're living in a new society. The bourgeois prejudices are in the past."

"But what does that mean?" Maria stared at Andrei, wide-eyed.

"It means in the new society; a man and a woman don't need to be bound by the formalities of marriage to express love for each other."

"So, people don't get married anymore?"

"Not in church." Andrei shrugged. "You can register your marriage, but it's not really a big deal. Religion doesn't matter. What matters is having feelings for each other and enjoying your time together."

"I see." Maria nodded, doing her best to process this piece of information. "It's just that I'd always thought I would get married."

"People get married now, too. But what's more important, do you enjoy being with me, Masha?"

"Yes." Maria nodded. "I do."

"Same here." Andrei kissed her on the cheek. "I really like being with you."

They walked together in silence, still holding hands.

"Aren't we lucky to live during this time?" Andrei said, as they approached the red mansion. "The Soviet world is full of possibilities for the young people like us. We can build a relationship, and no one will judge us. All that matters is our feelings for each other." Andrei kissed her again.

"You know, the other day I thought of something. Remember, four years ago," she paused, "when we said goodbye to each other."

"Yes."

"Well, I thought of how my background doesn't even matter anymore. And we lost all that time, Andrei."

"We didn't, darling." He kissed her. "Being back with you makes me appreciate you so much more."

As soon as they got home, Maria wrote a note to Dunya and gave Andrei directions to her childhood home. She saw him off, despite badly wanting to go with him, to see her nanny and hug her. Maria tried to picture his encounter with

Dunya. Would Dunya suspect something about the nature of their relationship? Would she know this was the very Andrei that Maria had met before?

To calm her nerves, Maria went to the kitchen. There, she found Klava, who was making soup.

"No fish this time." The neighbor smiled and wiped beads of sweat on her forehead. "But I think Gavrila will like this one. He got pearl barley," she spoke in a hushed tone. "Extra ration, real tasty."

"That's great." Maria nodded in approval. She hadn't eaten pearl barley in months and immediately salivated at the mention.

"And good for the baby." Klava rubbed her belly, and Maria noticed a tiny bump. "I'm due in November," Klava added. "I think it's a boy."

"Really? How do you know?"

"My belly is pointy, so it's a boy."

"I didn't know that."

"Well, when it is your turn, I'll help you out. Figure things out."

"Oh, I'm not, well…" Maria averted her eyes.

"Just a matter of time. You and that actor, aren't you an item?"

"I don't know." Maria sighed. "I'm not really sure where things are going. He just told me he doesn't think getting married is important."

The sudden confession made Maria blush.

"That's alright, my Gavrila used to say the same thing." Klava giggled. "That's how all men think. They'll try and see if you'll give it away for free, of course they will." Klava stirred the soup. "Alright, boiling now," she muttered, then looked back up at Maria.

"Really?" Maria stared in awe at Klava and the important information the neighbor shared. A whole world of possibilities opened up to Maria, whose only source of information about men for the last six years had been the unmarried Dunya.

"Of course. Men just want to run around. And that actor, he's easy on the eyes." Klava winked. "You gotta be careful with a guy like that."

"I think I'm being careful." Maria raised her hands up in protest.

"Don't take no offense, Martha. What I mean is, the guy needs to chase you. Men, they like that a lot. Gets them all excited. And then he'll have no choice but to marry you to get what he wants. Hasn't your mama taught you nothin'?"

"My mother died," Maria said. "It's been six years."

"I'm real sorry. Listen, I'll help you. My mom, she done raise five girls, me and my sisters. I know all there's to know about being a woman." Klava opened her eyes wide. "Us girls, we gotta stick together."

"Thank you." Maria's eyes lit up.

"Listen, Martha. My Gavrila, he didn't want to get married at first. And I didn't have any older brothers to beat him in case things went wrong. But now, he thinks he's the luckiest bastard alive, married to me." Klava giggled. "And got a job at the factory to support the baby. Even quit drinkin'." She leaned in, whispering confidentially.

"So, you two are properly married?" Maria asked. What Klava was sharing was nothing like Andrei's words about the new, modern society where mutual enjoyment mattered more than the formalities of marriage.

"Of course we're married." Klava stuck out her hand with a gold band on her right ring finger. "That used to be his grandmother's," she said proudly.

"But isn't marriage abolished now?" Maria swallowed hard.

Was Andrei lying to me?

"Abolished? What's that mean?"

"Like, people don't get married anymore," Maria said, then, noticing the confused look on Klava's face, added, "I heard Lenin got rid of marriage, that's all."

"Look," Klava came up close to her, "Martha, I wouldn't normally say this, but on the account of you being an orphan and all, men will say whatever to get under a skirt. So maybe Lenin canceled marriage 'cause he wants to run around. But I'm not letting any man in there without a marriage certificate." Klava pointed at her waist. "What am I, a common whore?" Klava put her hands on her hips. "And just think," she tapped her head, eyes narrowed, "if you're not married, your man can just walk away at any moment. And what am I supposed to be doing with his baby?"

"That makes sense. I didn't think of that." Maria frowned.

"Like I said, if you ever need help in that department," Klava winked at her, the expression on her face calmer now, "just come find me."

* * *

MARIA CONSIDERED BRINGING up the issue of marriage with Andrei again, but then decided it wasn't the right time. She tried to picture Andrei chasing women, tricking them into intimacy, just like Klava said all men did, but something didn't click into place.

If he was like that, he would have seduced me four years ago, Maria decided. *Andrei is different.*

By the time Andrei got back from visiting Dunya, Maria had put the conversation with Klava out of her mind.

"So, how did it go?" she asked.

"Avdotiya Timofeyevna is a lovely woman, Masha," Andrei said, handing her a carefully folded, sealed note from

Dunya, and Maria recognized her nanny's curly, childlike handwriting.

"Did you tell her about the theater?"

"Yes, of course. I told her you got settled, and got a job, and I told her you've mastered typing in a week."

"Thank you! And she understood why I couldn't come and see her myself, right?" Maria asked.

"Yes. She told me to tell you not to worry, and that she is doing just fine."

"Was there anyone else living there?"

"Not yet. She was by herself, Masha."

"And she was fine?"

"Yes."

* * *

ANDREI AND MARIA settled into a happy routine. They were both busy at the theater. Andrei, with the end of theater season, and Maria with her new job as a typist. Trifon Kirillovich was a demanding boss. Maria spent her days glued to the typewriter, typing letters, documents, and manuscripts.

And after Andrei learned Lenin would come to the last performance of the season, he joined the troupe in extra rehearsals. Though the play had been running all season, they rehearsed 'The Village of Stepanchikovo' with a newfound zeal, preparing for the visit of the leader of the revolution, who was now also the leader of Communist Russia.

On the last night of the season, after the curtain closed, the troupe stayed behind to celebrate. All staff were invited to join the party to mark the successful end of the Moscow Art Theater's twentieth season. Stanislavsky gave a speech, congratulating the troupe on its success. Other toasts followed. Despite the food shortages, Trifon Kirillovich had arranged for a banquet with champagne and caviar. Maria was hesitant to go at first, but Andrei was right, and she quickly realized Stanislavsky had no recollection of meeting her before.

When Andrei introduced her to Stanislavsky as Martha Goncharova, the theater director gave her a polite smile and welcomed her on board.

The party lasted long into the night, and it wasn't until the early hours of the morning that Maria and Andrei returned home. The warm June air, the light breeze, made the night magical.

"Masha," Andrei whispered into her ear. "I love you."

"I love you, too."

They held hands as they walked quietly into the mansion. It was silent, all of its residents asleep. Andrei squeezed her hand, and, without a word, she understood his question. She followed him upstairs to his room, a bedroom in the farthest corner of the mansion.

"Masha." He kissed her, and she leaned into his touch.

With trembling hands, she reached for him, unbuttoning his shirt. She then, surprised at her own bravery, undid his belt. Her hand paused, but he guided it lower, and she allowed him, feeling him, but then stopped, remembered Klava and the warning she'd been given. Maria froze in place.

"What is it, Masha?" Andrei kissed her neck. His voice was low, almost a growl. She could feel his desire, his want for her, and her own passion responding in her.

"I, I don't..." she croaked, afraid to displease him, the desire for him, the want to melt into him, fighting with the voice in her head, warning her against taking the step forward. "I'm scared," Maria said, at last in a thin voice. "Really scared."

"What are you scared of?" Andrei pulled away. It felt as if

she'd stepped into an abyss, as if a rift had appeared between them, never to be repaired.

"I've never done this before." Maria gulped.

"I know. I'll be gentle." Andrei looked at her, his eyes dark, almost black. For a moment, in the dim light, she thought he looked like a demon from the painting by Vrubel.

"Andrei, I, I can't." Maria shook her head. "I can't. Not like this. I'm not modern." She blinked away tears. "I'm sorry."

"Masha. Didn't you hear what I said?" Andrei looked sad, and the expression on his face unsettled her.

"About marriage being abolished?"

"No." He shook his head. "I love you, Masha." Andrei took her hands into his. "I love you. And if you don't want to be together yet, I will wait. I don't want you to be scared. I want you to *want* us to be together."

She scanned his face, then leaned into him, hugging him, holding him close.

"Andrei, Andrei, but I want to be with you. I love you, too. But I care about marriage. It's how I was brought up."

"Masha, I have thought about it."

"You have?"

"Yes. But church weddings aren't allowed." He gave her a sad look. "And we can't get married in the registry because you're living under a fake name."

"I am." Maria nodded. "I forgot. But you told me marriage was abolished. And we should just enjoy each other." She stared at Andrei in confusion.

"I did." He kissed her. "It was only so you'd let me kiss you on the street."

"What?" She shook her head in mock shock, her fear and doubts disappearing. "You were trying to trick me?"

"No." He pulled her close. "Are you still afraid of me?"

"Yes," she squealed.

"I'm afraid of you, too. Afraid of how wild with desire you

drive me. I've wanted you for so long," he whispered. "Since the first day I saw you, I've waited for this moment. I know we can't get married, but I wanted you to have a ring."

Andrei produced a small box. Maria opened it and gasped. It was a narrow golden band encrusted with emeralds.

"Do you like it?"

"Yes." Maria nodded. Andrei slipped the band on her right ring finger. It fit perfectly. "I love it," she said, admiring the ring.

"Masha," she heard his voice.

Their love for each other was a primordial force, something out of this world, something uncontrollable that bound them. A tie between them that had always existed, now finally set free.

They made love through the night, exhausted, but unable to let each other go. Each time, they reached for each other, as if for the last time. They fell asleep in the early hours of the morning, when the sun rose on the horizon and woke up in the afternoon.

Maria felt a sense of completeness she'd never imagined existed in the world. This was the reason for all the serenades. The inspiration for all those poems she'd read.

Maria knew at once. This was love.

She lay next to Andrei, embracing him, unable to speak. He kissed her gently then.

"I love you," he said, reaching for her again and again. His desire for her awakening the force within her she didn't know she possessed.

CHAPTER 25

Their relationship, which began so suddenly, fully consumed them both. They called each other 'kitten' and 'darling,' held hands in public and spent as much time together as possible. Their desire for each other was strong, overpowering. It drove them into each other's arm each night. In the mornings, Maria woke up in a state of altered reality, and first checked for Andrei, leaned into him, pressed herself against him, reveling in the closeness and unity.

After their first night together, she'd moved into Andrei's room, and used her own tiny space only as storage.

They talked about everything and quickly established that, despite their differences in class, despite having been born into completely different circumstances, they shared the same principles of morality and ethics. They believed in humanity, believed in the ultimate good in people, believed in the triumph of good over evil, and were optimistic about their future together. Meanwhile, their love for each other made them generous and kind to the world around them.

"Masha, how lucky we are," Andrei loved to say to her, "we're here, together, we found each other."

"Yes, Andrei."

"And the Soviet state, the transformation. Communism will arrive soon, and, in a few years, we'll live in a utopia," Andrei added.

"Well, I don't know about that." Maria brushed her hand on his cheek. "Maybe in ten?" She looked at him expectantly. "And Andrei, do you think I'll still be Martha then?"

"Darling, don't worry." Andrei kissed her. "You'll get your name back in no time."

But Maria couldn't help the feeling of living a lie.

Countess Maria Suvorova had ceased to exist, disappeared without a trace. And a new woman, Martha Goncharova, had taken over. Under the new identity, Maria had a great job, received a modest salary and food rations, and, more important, had a room registered in Irina's mansion. Each time, returning after a long day at work, Maria still paused in awe at how her life had turned out.

As a young girl, she could never have imagined the twist that would have put her in the red mansion with the beautiful lion, with this handsome, incredible man who was her husband. Here, Maria stopped herself, because Andrei wasn't exactly her husband.

He was her beloved. Yes, that was the word.

Almost a husband, if only they could get married officially. Maria would then check her gold band with the emeralds as a reassurance of their relationship.

Andrei visited Dunya every week and brought news of the nanny's well-being to Maria. Maria sent food and once even sent Dunya a Napoleon pastry, which Trifon Kirillovich had procured through his many channels. After that visit, Andrei reported that Dunya was in tears, thanking him and

Maria profusely, and nearly refused to eat the pastry, wanting to save it for Maria.

"That sounds just like her," Maria said. "I miss Dunya so much. Isn't there a way for me to go? I'm sure it's all different people living there now. Don't you think it will be alright?"

"Masha, but what if someone recognizes you?"

"I'll just tell them they made a mistake. I've got my ID right here. I'm Martha Goncharova!" Maria took out her papers. "Right?"

"What if it's taken away? Then I'll be in trouble. And Ivan." Andrei furrowed his brow.

And so, Maria didn't go back.

* * *

"Masha, the Moscow Art Theater will go on tour. They asked for volunteers," Andrei told her one evening in February 1919. "We'll go to Kharkov, then to Crimea, in the summer. We'll perform there to get more people to appreciate the new Soviet state."

"That sounds lovely, Andrei. How long will the tour last?"

"Just a few weeks. I'd like to volunteer. And they're letting actors bring families with them. Would you like to come along?"

"Yes, of course, I would love to!" Maria clapped. "It can be an adventure."

"Oh, is that right?" Andrei picked her up and carried her to the bed. "Is that what you want? An adventure?"

"Yes." She giggled in excitement as he pressed his body against hers.

"And when we're on tour, we'll make love in all the new cities, Masha," Andrei whispered into her ear.

That spring, preparations for the tour had taken over the Moscow Art Theater. Those who were traveling rehearsed separately, often on top of regular rehearsals and perfor-mances of the 1918-1919 season, and Andrei was often at the theater until late into the night.

Stanislavsky had shared several times that the tour was expected to establish the Moscow Art Theater as the leading art institution in the new Soviet nation, and, though the famous director would stay behind in Moscow and not join the tour, he had empowered Kachalov, a renowned actor, to lead the troupe and to have full authority on his behalf.

"So, Martha, I hear you'll be joining the tour?" Trifon Kirillovich rubbed his hands together. "Good idea, good idea." He nodded in approval. Maria had just finished typing up a long manuscript and placed it aside, about to review the papers.

By then, Maria had gotten to know her boss well. He'd been trusting her with confidential documentation, financial statements, everything that ensured the running of the theater. Maria was now more than a typist. She had become his secretary.

"I've given it some thought, and I've decided to come along as well," the theater manager said after a pause. "Might be nice to take a break, to leave Moscow for the summer. I always say, it's good to travel. I used to travel quite a bit when I was young." He chuckled. "It wasn't by choice, mind you."

Maria nodded. Trifon Kirillovich had told her the story of his youth, which she'd heard from Andrei before. "What an amazing life you've had. How you've succeeded against all odds."

"Ha, I don't know about that. But like I said, it'll be good to travel out of the city. And the troupe can use a bit of help with the provisions, the organization. And for me, a change of scenery. Those actors," he shook his head, "can't trust them with getting themselves fed, can you?"

"Yes." Maria smiled in agreement. She and Trifon had long established that actors, often lost in their own world, could use the assistance of organized people like the two of them.

"Now, Martha, we'll need to get your travel documents ready. Do you have a passport?" Trifon asked.

Maria, who until that moment had been lost in a pleasant reverie of funny theater anecdotes, froze in place.

"I don't have a passport," she mumbled, her mind running wild. It could be going too far by using the fake ID for another document. *A passport. What if I get caught?*

"We're all going to the registry office next week to submit the papers, and they'll get them ready by the end of April," Trifon Kirillovich noted. "And remind Andrei, please. I've told the actors, but they always forget."

"Of course, Trifon Kirillovich." Maria did her best to stay calm, but her heart beat fast. She bit her lip and turned to the typewriter in an effort to conceal her doubt.

"You know, we're going to need passports to travel," Maria said that evening, when Andrei got back. It was late and she'd come home before him, too tired to wait at the theater until after he finished rehearsal.

"Oh, yes, Trifon Kirillovich told us. I completely forgot." Andrei had just taken off his jacket and was unbuttoning his shirt. Maria noticed one of the buttons had come loose and noted to herself to sew it on later.

"So, with my ID, how do I get a passport?" Maria stared at Andrei, wide-eyed. "As Martha Goncharova?"

"Yes, Masha." Andrei came close. "Come on, don't worry so much." He put his arms around her.

"But I just didn't think this farce would last that long. Do I live my whole life as Martha?"

"No, Masha, but it's best for your safety. Your last name,

it's too risky. You don't want anyone to suspect your origins, do you?"

"But I can't keep living a lie, can I?" Maria frowned.

"Kitten, please." Andrei reached for her. He kissed the top of her head. "You're my Masha, and I know exactly who you are. That's what matters."

"Yes," she murmured. When in Andrei's arms, she felt safe and her troubles melted away, as if on their own. "I love you."

"I love you, too. So much. You can't even imagine, Masha."

* * *

MARIA SUBMITTED the papers with the rest of the troupe and, by the end of April, she received a brand new passport under her assumed identity. Flipping the document in her hands, Maria had an idea.

"I'd like to visit Dunya," she said to Andrei. "Now that I have two IDs, no one would ever suspect I'm not actually who I say I am."

"Masha, you're really taking a big risk," Andrei started to say, but Maria shook her head.

"I'm about to travel all across the country as Martha Goncharova and you're telling me I can't go see Dunya, who lives right here, in Moscow?"

"I suppose it's okay now," Andrei said after a pause. "If you're careful."

"I'll be careful. Why don't we go see her together for Easter? It'll mean a great deal to Dunya. And the last time we saw each other was on Easter a year ago, Maria added, seeing Andrei's raised eyebrows.

"Masha, are you sure this is wise? The Soviets don't want people going to church."

"We won't, we'll just stop by for an Easter lunch, that's all. I'm so sure. I feel great about this." She held up the passport.

"And thanks to this, I'm definitely Martha. I can even dress up for the visit."

"Why don't you wear that navy-blue dress of yours? It's beautiful."

"The silk one? Alright." Maria smiled. She knew Andrei had meant the dress she'd sewn from her mother's, the one she'd worn to the salon the first time they met.

For the visit to see Dunya, Maria used several weeks' worth of food rations. Just like the year prior, she bought eggs, boiled them in onion skins, and consulted with Klava on the best recipe for a Paskha.

"Are you celebrating Easter?" Klava asked Maria.

"I'll just go visit my na…" Maria started to say, but immediately corrected herself. Martha Goncharova couldn't have had a nanny. She came from a simple family. "A relative. After my mother died, she took care of me," Maria added.

"Oh yes. Some people are like family. Better than family," Klava noted, rocking the baby on her hip. Much to Klava's shock and Gavrila's delight, she'd given birth to a little girl on the anniversary of the revolution. For that reason, Klava had named the baby Kira, which was one of the most fashionable names that year. It stood for Communist International Revolution. Gavrila immediately announced that 'boys were no good' and 'at least girls wouldn't be going to war,' and cooed over the baby whenever he was at home.

"But still, they say the Soviet state doesn't want people going to church." Klava lowered her voice. "So be careful if you go. They've even closed a few churches altogether." Klava crossed herself. "Gavrila doesn't know I still go." Her voice was down to a whisper.

"You go to church?" Maria opened her eyes wide.

"Of course. I prayed to the Virgin Mary for a baby. And it worked. If you want a baby, I'll help you out." Klava grinned. "Tell you where to go pray."

"Thank you." Maria nodded. "Maybe after this summer."

"Why after the summer? You know, the Virgin, she'll know if you don't really want something. She sees everything."

"We're supposed to be traveling this summer," Maria said. "With the theater troupe. So probably better if I get pregnant after."

"Oh, that's real nice." Klava nodded in approval, then, turning to the baby, cooed. "Isn't that nice, Kira? Yes?"

A baby, Maria thought. *A baby would be great.* It had to be a girl. She imagined Andrei cooing over their daughter, just how she'd seen Klava's husband do. And they would likely be given a larger room, since it would be the three of them.

And maybe – here Maria knew the dream was nearly impossible to achieve – but maybe they could all move back to her childhood home and raise the baby girl in Maria's old bedroom.

CHAPTER 26

$\mathscr{A}$ndrei and Maria set out to see Dunya on Easter Sunday morning. Maria assumed her nanny would have gone to the night service at the church, but decided it was best to go early, knowing Dunya always got up at the crack of dawn.

"I'm just so nervous, Andrei, I don't know why," Maria said, putting on her shoes, as they were about to leave. She checked herself in the mirror and stepped outside. Andrei walked out a moment later, and they were half-way down the mansion steps, when Maria gasped. "We forgot the basket."

"What basket?" Andrei reached for her hand. Normally, the gesture would reassure her, but not this time. Maria pulled her hand back.

"The one with the Paskha. It's bad luck to return. Something bad will happen. I just feel it." She felt a knot form in her stomach. Maria turned back, ran upstairs, and grabbed the basket with the eggs and the Paskha she'd prepared since the previous evening. She looked in the mirror again, following the superstition she'd been taught by Dunya, but the aching feeling was with her the entire way from the red mansion to her childhood home.

As they neared the Suvorov estate, Maria half-expected a patrol to appear, to stop them and request papers. To be arrested and led away. But none of that happened. They arrived at the familiar yellow mansion with no incident.

"See, everything is just fine." Andrei kissed the top of her head. "My little kitten."

"I love you," Maria whispered into his ear, as they walked into what used to be the Suvorov estate.

The first thing that hit her was the smell. Maria remembered her home smelling of freshly baked bread in the morning, when Fekla was still around, of a fire burning, and of pine mixed with oranges in the winter when they put up the Christmas tree. And at Easter, it smelled like vanilla and sugar, sweets, the smell of treats. Now, her childhood home smelled of fermented cabbage, stale sweat, and mold.

The second thing she noticed was how dark it was inside. The living room had been partitioned into separate rooms, and all of them had blocked access to the large windows, submerging the place into semi-darkness.

"I don't recognize my own house," Maria whispered to Andrei.

An older woman passed them, carrying a boiling teapot, which was spewing hot water. The woman, red-faced, scowled and, without saying a word, disappeared upstairs. Andrei was quiet. He had been here since the requisitioning and was not surprised. The place looked much like Irina's mansion, with many families living together and trying to make the best of it. The door to Dunya's room was closed, and Maria knocked softly.

"Come in," she heard the familiar voice and her heart leaped.

"Dunya!" Maria ran into the room. She expected her

nanny to be sitting at her table, drinking tea, but Dunya was in bed. The light was off, and Maria stopped in her tracks. "Did I wake you?"

"Masha, so glad you came," Dunya said, her voice faint. It was so unlike the voice Maria remembered, she balked. Dunya's face looked gaunt, much thinner than before. "I've been hoping to see you one last time," the nanny squeezed out.

"Dunya? What are you saying?"

"Before it's my time." A tear rolled down Dunya's cheek. "Oh, Masha." She shook her head.

"I'll wait outside," Andrei mumbled and left the two women alone.

"My little girl. I love you–"

"Dunya, what's going on? Why are you saying this? Are you sick? I'll call the doctor."

"It's too late.

Maria heard a wheezing noise. "Are you in pain? Show me, please." Maria was hysterical now. "Dunya, you can't do this. I just got here. You're not dying."

"Not yet. Not yet," her nanny said, her voice weak. "But I can't walk, Masha. My legs." She pointed and Maria saw them wrapped tightly with a blanket. Lifting it, Maria gasped. Dunya's legs were bloated, the skin red, blotchy, and cracked. They looked like they had doubled in size. Liquid seeped from them, trickling down Dunya's shins.

"Water! There's water!" Maria gasped. "Dunya? What's going on?"

"It just started this morning. It hurts so much," Dunya said. "I can't walk." She clasped her heart.

"I'll call the doctor," Maria yelled. "Dr. Petrovsky. I'll be back soon. Please stay put." Realizing the absurdity of the request, Maria hugged her nanny and bolted out of the room.

"Andrei, I've got to go get the doctor," she called to Andrei on her way out. "I'll be back, please stay with her."

Dr. Petrovsky lived nearby, in one of the newer apartment buildings near Taganka. Maria ran uphill, hoping she could find his building. She remembered it was gray, had five stories, and was not far from the church. As she passed the Bolvanovka church, Maria saw a crowd of churchgoers assembling for Easter Mass, dressed in festive clothes, all ignoring the order to stop celebrating the religious holiday. She briefly wondered who would prevail.

To her relief, once at Taganka Square, she quickly recognized the dark-gray building, which had just two entrances. The plaque for Dr. Petrovsky was on the first one. She rang the bell for Apartment 12, displayed on the plaque, and entered. Inside, the building was somber, quiet, imposing. The wrought-iron railings, the tall ceilings, everything had been constructed to impress. Maria ran up the steps to the third floor, deciding it would be faster than waiting for the elevator. She was about to knock, but the door to apartment 12 opened and a little girl stepped out. Another one followed.

Maria remembered Dr. Petrovsky as an older man, but not old enough to be a grandfather, and wondered whether the girls were his daughters.

The smell that hit her was surprisingly similar to the smell of her own transformed childhood home. The sour mix of unwashed bodies, sweat, and cooking. She nearly gagged. Right away, she understood the apartment, which had once housed Dr. Petrovsky's family and served as his office, had been requisitioned. The dark corridor had a set of doors on each side, all of them closed. Maria, unsure of what to do next, wavered at the entrance.

"Are you here to see the doc?" A small woman popped out

of one of the rooms, wiping her hands on a dirty apron. "He's over there, third door on the right."

"Thank you," Maria said, but the woman had already disappeared.

Counting the doors from the entrance, Maria walked down the corridor. Another plaque, a smaller, more elegant version of the one she saw outside of the building entrance, hung on the right. Maria figured it must have been once hanging at the entrance to the apartment. She knocked.

"Come in," she heard a woman's voice and entered.

The space was cluttered with furniture that looked to have been randomly thrown together. An enormous oak desk was squeezed in by the window, two chairs pushed against it. A bookshelf bursting with volumes, two or three to a row, was crammed against the wall. A cabinet stood on the other side, pressed against a bed. In the middle of the room, was a sewing machine, a burgundy Singer. A yellow dress laid on it.

"Hello, please, have a seat." The woman pointed to a chair. She had large, kind blue eyes, and thick, dark blonde hair loosely tied in bun. The woman held a needle pillow in her hands and a measuring tape hung around her neck.

"Hello," Maria croaked. She wondered whether the woman had mistaken her for a client, assuming she'd just walked into a seamstress' office. "I'm sorry." She took a step back to the door. "I'm here to see the doctor. I'll go now."

"Dr. Petrovsky will be back shortly. Have a seat, don't worry. I'm his wife, Ekaterina." The woman smiled such a disarming, genuine smile as if the two of them were good friends. But then Maria remembered Dunya and bit her lip.

"It's urgent. Do you know how long he'll be?"

"He went to see a client. We're closing the practice, you see." Ekaterina pouted. "It's impossible to go on."

"When?"

"Eventually. This fall. I assume you've seen Dr. Petrovsky before? He doesn't take on new clients. We've been spreading the word."

"Yes, but it's not for me. It's my nanny. Does he still do house visits?" Maria opened her eyes wide.

"Yes, yes, don't worry."

"We used to be patients of his." Maria averted her eyes. The realization that she'd have to share her real name to establish the connection was sudden. She drew a deep breath.

"What's the name, dear?" Ekaterina raised her eyebrows.

"The Suvorovs."

"Oh, my dear. Of course. Countess Suvorova, what a tragic story. You're the daughter? It was right after your first ball. Of course. Whatever happened to your father? And your mother was a lovely lady, lovely. I remember Dr. Petrovsky was shocked. A heart attack, and at such a young age."

"Yes, that's me. My name is Maria." Saying her real name for the first time in nearly a year made her blush.

"Life is full of surprises, isn't it? So, were you able to stay at your house?" Ekaterina gave her a look full of wonder. "I assume your house has been, ahem, vandalized as well?"

"I'm staying at a different place," Maria said, hoping to change the subject.

"Oh, my dear, I'm just asking so that I can confirm Dr. Petrovsky's appointments for the afternoon. Don't worry, I know these days we're all hiding from each other." Ekaterina looked at her kindly and Maria suddenly felt ashamed for doubting this woman.

"I'm sorry." She sighed. "I'm staying at Irina Kutuzova's mansion. It's a crazy story, really, but I've got a room there and I have papers. Though they're not quite—"

Ekaterina pressed a finger to her lips. "These walls are

remarkably thin. Sometimes I wonder whether they're there at all."

Maria fidgeted. The warning jerked her back to reality.

"I can wait outside," she noted.

"Oh, don't worry, Dr. Petrovsky should be back soon." Ekaterina took a seat at the sewing machine and pushed the pedal. The noise provided a low hum, and she spoke softly to Maria.

"I worry about our neighbors. You know, it's almost impossible to exist here. It's been a year, but I can't get used to it. How has it been for you?"

"It hasn't been too bad. And I have a job at the Moscow Art Theater. As a typist," Maria said with pride in her voice, but then the image of Dunya, weak, on the bed, stood in front of her eyes. "But your husband, will he be able to come with me right away? It's urgent. I, I would have come sooner," Maria said, more in an apology to Dunya, who couldn't hear her. "I just didn't know."

"My dear, of course, of course. Would you like a cup of tea while you wait?" Ekaterina stopped the machine and rose from her seat. "We've already had breakfast. Easter, though we aren't allowed to celebrate," she whispered.

"No, thank you." Maria got up. Moving felt good. She needed to act, to get help for Dunya. She was about to walk out of the room, but the door opened and Dr. Petrovsky appeared on the threshold. The kindly, slightly detached expression on his face was that of a man who had long ago accepted the state of imperfection in the world and took it in stride.

"Hello, darling," he said, giving his wife a kiss and handing her his jacket and fedora.

Maria wasn't sure whether he'd noticed her.

"Darling, this is Maria. You may remember the Suvorovs?" Ekaterina said in a hushed voice.

"The Suvorovs?" Dr. Petrovsky frowned, then rubbed his neck. "Oh, the countess?" His voice trailed off as he turned to Maria. "Oh, yes, I saw you once. It's been a few years. Nerves. And, if I remember correctly, your mother, the countess," he cleared his throat. "How may I be of help?"

"It's my nanny. She can't get up. And her legs," Maria's voice broke. "They are swollen."

"Has this been going on for a long time?" The doctor furrowed his brow.

"I, I don't know." The image of the cracked skin, the rashes she saw, the pained, helpless expression on Dunya's face, and the guilt, the overpowering guilt of not having been there for her nanny sooner, crushed Maria. "I just went to visit. It's my nanny, she stayed at the mansion, but I had to leave." Maria dug her nails into her palms to stop herself from crying. "So I went today, because of Easter and I found her like this."

"I see."

"Her legs look terrible, Doctor."

"Well, let's go and see the patient, shall we?" Dr. Petrovsky put on his jacket and fedora. "Darling," he turned to his wife, "I can fit it into my schedule, right?"

"Yes, darling." Ekaterina smiled and turned back to her sewing. Maria heard the humming of the Singer as they walked out of the room.

CHAPTER 27

"Thank you so much for coming to see Avdotiya Timofeyevna," Maria said, as they walked out of the building.

"Don't worry," the doctor said. "I'll examine her at once."

It was only then that Maria noticed Dr. Petrovsky was carrying a black case. Despite his reassuring tone, Maria felt a sense of foreboding. A premonition of something terrible about to happen. Dr. Petrovsky was a man of few words, and they walked the rest of the way to the Suvorov mansion in silence.

"It's right this way." Maria pointed to Dunya's room, but the doctor gave her a kind smile. "Is there a sink with running water?" he asked, and Maria was initially stumped by the question, but then led him to the kitchen.

She hadn't been there since leaving the mansion and was shocked to discover the space now cluttered with a multitude of pans and pots, all, she guessed, belonging to different families. A rope hung in the middle of the kitchen with drying laundry, which concealed almost entirely the kitchen table that stood at the opposite end. Maria noticed a gaunt-looking woman, who was sitting at the table, eating porridge. Steam rose from her bowl, and the woman gave them a hungry, wolfish stare, before turning back to her meal. The doctor nodded to the woman, and, ignoring the clutter, moved to the sink to wash his hands. He shook off the water and gave Maria an expectant look.

"Over here." Maria opened the door and led him back to Dunya's room. The doctor mumbled incoherently to Andrei, who'd opened the door, and walked straight to the nanny. Her eyes were closed, and she was moaning softly.

"Hello, Avdotiya Timofeyevna," Dr. Petrovsky said. Maria was surprised he remembered Dunya's name, since she'd only mentioned it once. "I'm Dr. Petrovsky." From that moment on, he was focused only on the patient.

"Doctor?" Dunya opened her eyes and blinked, staring at him. "I don't need a doctor."

"I heard you have swelling in your legs?" The doctor gave her a kind look. "I'd like to see what's happening and make you feel better."

"Oh, I can't walk, Doctor. I can't walk." Dunya shook her head. "I've never been to a doctor in all my life. I don't want to make a fuss. Masha, did you send for him? Oh, my little girl." Tears streamed down Dunya's face, the expression of gratitude and pain.

"Dunya, yes, please. Let him see your legs." Maria bit her lip. Then, seeing the hesitant look on Dunya's face, turned to Andrei. "I think maybe you should wait outside," she whispered to him and Andrei nodded and immediately left the room.

Maria turned back to find Dr. Petrovsky sitting on a chair next to Dunya. He examined her legs, then took out his stethoscope and measured Dunya's heart rate.

"Doctor, what is it? Can you help her?" Maria asked after he was done.

"Let's speak outside." Dr. Petrovsky's voice was kind, but she recognized the tone. It was the tone she'd heard before, the tone that was supposed to soothe her into accepting death. It was how people had spoken to her after her mother had died.

Something inside of Maria snapped.

"No." She shook her head, following the doctor out of the room. "No." Dr. Petrovsky and Andrei exchanged glances.

"It's her heart," Dr. Petrovsky said, once they were standing out of the room, the door firmly shut. "It's not working properly, and it's affecting her kidneys. This is causing water retention and what you see now is a symptom of an illness that's progressed very far. Unfortunately," Dr. Petrovsky cleared his throat, "at this stage, you'll need to think about palliative care."

"Palliative?" Maria swallowed hard. "What does that mean?"

"You want to make sure Avdotiya Timofeyevna doesn't suffer."

"You mean she will…" Maria shook her head, unable to say the word. "But can't you do anything? Can't you take her to the hospital?"

"In a case like this, it's best to stay in the comfort of her own home."

Maria suppressed a sob.

"Masha, I'm sorry," Andrei said.

"Why didn't you tell me she was sick?" Maria blinked away tears. "Why didn't you say anything?"

"I didn't know. She never told me." Andrei shook his head. "She was fine when I saw her."

"The onset of something like this could be gradual," Dr. Petrovsky said. "So likely even Avdotiya Timofeyevna didn't realize things were getting worse. But something like this is impossible to reverse. I will prescribe her diuretics, of course, for temporary relief, but her heart is too weak."

"Too weak? So, what can I do?"

"I can recommend a nurse. I understand you have a job at the Moscow Art Theater?" He said to Maria.

"How did you know?"

"Avdotiya Timofeyevna told me. She is immensely proud of you. Told me you've succeeded against all odds."

"Oh God." Maria couldn't speak. Tears were streaming down her face. Andrei pulled her close, and she leaned into him, grief rushing over her in waves.

"I will also prescribe morphine," Dr. Petrovsky said to Andrei. "Please make sure you only use it if only completely necessary. Every eight hours."

"Yes, of course." And then Andrei asked a question Maria did not dare to raise. "How long, doctor?"

"A few months," Dr. Petrovsky noted. "Could be as long as a year. The human body is a mystery, you see."

"Thank you, doctor. For the payment, we will arrange…," Andrei started to say, but the doctor raised his hand.

"With my wife, please. She deals with accounting matters."

* * *

A NEW ERA BEGAN. Maria no longer cared if she would be recognized. She went to her childhood home every day after work. All of her energy was focused on Dunya, on being by her side. Maria hired the nurse Dr. Petrovsky had recommended, and, though Dunya initially protested, she allowed the woman to attend to her and to administer morphine. Maria sat with her nanny and held her hand.

"Masha, life is a blessing. Don't forget," Dunya said to her. "And you came back. I'm blessed, truly blessed. God is great."

"Dunya, but I could have saved you. I've failed you."

"No, no, it's my time to go. It's my time. And I'll go in peace, knowing you love me."

"Please, don't say that. Please live. Just live."

"I love you, Masha. I love you more than anything in this world."

"I love you, too."

"And just think, you taught me, an old woman like that, to read and write." Dunya lifted her hands, knotted, red, shaky. "So, I could do fine things like writing. Read God's word myself." She looked up at Maria, her eyes clear.

"Dunya." Maria leaned into her.

"Life goes by fast." The nanny sighed. "So fast. And I remember the day I came to your family. I was so scared."

"I can't imagine," Maria said.

"Oh, yes, I was just thirteen years old. Young girl. Came here barefoot, never done knew no shoes growing up."

"No shoes?"

"No shoes, Masha. And now I don't need them shoes anyway. Can't walk." Dunya sighed. "That's life."

"Dunya, are you in pain?" Maria asked. "Let me move your pillows."

"Oh, don't you fuss." Still, she accepted Maria's help to fluff up her pillow and give her water.

"Never did I think I'd have a Suvorov take care of me. Never in my life."

"Please, after what we've been through together." Maria hugged her gently. "I love you."

"Before I forget, Masha," Dunya whispered into her ear. "Remember the hiding place?"

"Of course."

"Well, I've added to it. Make sure you take everything out before it's too late." Dunya's hands were hot. "Make sure the bad people don't get any of it."

"Of course, Dunya."

Maria snuck into the hiding place late at night, after making sure everyone at the house was asleep. Andrei was waiting for her outside. She lifted the floorboard and reached into the space. In addition to the jewelry she'd hidden away that day with Dunya and Potap, she discovered several gold coins in a velvet sash.

Dunya, Maria sighed. *How did she manage?*

Maria took the unexpected bounty with her and hid it in a wall compartment in Andrei's room. It was a place he had created, and Maria wondered if everyone in Moscow had stashes like theirs.

"Dunya, thank you," she told her nanny the next day.

"Did you find everything, Masha? You keep it for your dowry, you make sure you have money put away, you hear me?"

"I will, Dunya."

"That man of yours, is he a good man?" Dunya asked.

"I think so, Dunya."

"Well, then you have my blessing."

CHAPTER 28

"*A*ndrei, I won't be going on tour," Maria said a week before the troupe's departure.

She'd been mulling this decision over in her mind. The idea of leaving for a few weeks, of 'getting out of Moscow' as Trifon called it, was tempting. And everything was ready. It would be a wonderful adventure, a new experience, and she would be with Andrei, on their first big trip together. A promise of a new life. But Maria couldn't leave Dunya.

"I'll never forgive myself if anything happens to her while I'm gone," Maria whimpered.

"But it's only three weeks, Masha. The nurse is taking good care of her."

"No, darling, I don't think I can. I still need to keep an eye on that nurse. I have to stay here to make sure she takes care of Avdotiya Timofeyevna."

"Can't you ask her friend? That woman?" By then, Andrei knew about Dunya's best friend.

"You mean Akulina?"

"Yes."

"Akulina is too old, and she's got a newborn grandchild

she's taking care of. I'm the only one who can help Dunya," Maria said.

"You have a good heart, Masha," he said and kissed her forehead.

When Maria informed Trifon of this development, he took it in stride.

"I suppose this is the right choice. In this day and age," he opened his arms wide, "rather uncommon. I have come to rely on you, Martha, for quite a bit, and you will be missed on tour," he added. "But once we're back, I expect you to be ready."

"Of course, Trifon Kirillovich."

The next few days were a flurry of activity as Andrei got ready for the trip. Maria helped him pack. Since reuniting, they had only been apart for a few hours at a time, and the possibility of separating seemed impossible. Maria had gotten so used to Andrei's presence, she did not understand the full impact of his departure until the very day.

"Masha, we're going to have three whole boxcars booked just for the troupe," Andrei told her on the way to the train station.

They found the actors assembled in the middle of the train hall, waiting for the track announcement. Some brought their families, eager for a trip outside of the dusty Moscow, and children ran around, playing tag.

No one expected the train to leave on time. Wartime complications, various disruptions were inevitable, and no one was the least bit concerned when a delay of several hours was announced. The only person displeased was Trifon, who paced the station, a grim look on his face, his mustache pointing down to follow the shape of his downturned mouth.

"Hello, Martha, Andrei," he said, seeing them approach. "So, I suppose we'll be off. If the train ever shows up."

"It will, Trifon Kirillovich."

"Alright, Martha, don't get too comfortable now. We'll be back before you know it." A smile crossed the theater manager's face. "And you'll get your Andrei back." He shook his head. "Just kids, just kids," he mumbled to himself, walking off.

"I'll write to you every day, Andrei," Maria promised.

"Same here, kitten."

They embraced. His touch, so familiar.

"I'll miss you so much."

He took her face into his hands, and, looking into her eyes, said, "When I'm back, we'll have a wedding. I promise you."

"Okay." She smiled.

"Stay strong, darling. I know you've got to take care of Dunya."

At the mention of her nanny, Maria straightened up and checked her watch.

"Andrei, I'll need to leave soon. She's probably waiting for me to come. But I so want to be here when you board the train." Maria's voice cracked.

"Darling, don't worry. These trains, there's no way to know when we'll actually leave. You can't spend all day here waiting for us. Maybe just ten more minutes?"

"Alright, ten more minutes."

They found a spot on a bench and sat together, holding hands, in silence. Ten minutes turned into fifteen, then twenty. Maria left an hour later, after hearing the announcement of yet another delay, pushing the departure by three more hours.

* * *

THEATER SEASON HAD ENDED for the summer, and with Trifon away, Maria didn't have to go to work until the troupe's return. She spent her days at Dunya's side and went back to the red mansion in the late evenings. Sleeping alone in the bed she'd shared with Andrei unsettled her. Maria woke up in the middle of the night, searching for him, expecting to feel him next to her.

She ached for Andrei, for his smell, the feel of his touch on her. She found a shirt he'd left behind and slept in it until his smell disappeared.

Taking care of Dunya occupied all of her time. Dunya's health was uneven. One day she felt better and the swelling in her legs reduced. She tried getting up and managed to stand with Maria's help. But the next morning, Maria found Dunya in tears, crying in pain, and asked the nurse to administer a larger dose of morphine. This cycle repeated several times, and Maria was left feeling constantly on edge, expecting the inevitable.

Going back to her childhood home every day under an assumed identity, Maria wondered what she would do if a letter arrived for her from her father and was half-relieved when none came.

Her only solace were Andrei's letters. He wrote several times a week and updated Maria on their journey. His letters were full of funny details, and Maria reread each one several times, smiling to herself, picturing the troupe and their everyday activities.

In early July, she received another letter from Andrei, and, preparing to read it, settled on her bed.

Masha, my darling kitten. Please don't worry, the letter began, and Maria's heart sank.

There's been a slight change of plans, and

we won't be returning to Moscow soon as expected. You see, darling, Denikin, the White Army general, has made unexpected advances and has taken over Kharkov. The city welcomed the White Army, and all access out of the city back to Moscow has been blocked. We are finishing performances in Kharkov and are considering our options.

Please don't worry, darling Masha, we're safe, and there is absolutely no danger.

Andrei

Danger.

That was the first word Maria registered. Her heart beat faster, and she closed her eyes, forcing herself to breathe normally. *Danger.* And then the realization that Andrei was not coming back hit her. She reread the letter. *Considering other options. What other options?*

She jumped off the bed and paced the room. She needed answers, right away. Maria checked the time. It was after ten in the evening, and she was about to get dressed to go to the theater, but then remembered they were still on break. There was nothing else to do but wait.

But Maria couldn't resign herself to inaction, and so, the following morning, she went to the theater anyway. She found the Moscow Art Theater locked. She knocked, and a small, hunched-over man opened the door, peeking out at her.

"Hello, excuse me, is anyone around? I work here," she said.

"No, no, closed until August 1ˢᵗ. Come back for rehearsal

then," the man grunted and, before Maria could protest, slammed the door shut.

She received several more letters from Andrei, but none of them mentioned a return date. She wrote back, asking Andrei about the troupe's plans, but it was as if Andrei didn't get her letters at all. Her questions went unanswered.

Counting down the days to August 1st, Maria waited. And when the day came, Maria woke up early and got ready to go to the theater. She nearly ran all the way to Kamergerskiy Lane and knocked on the doors of the theater. The same little man opened the door, squinting at her from the darkness of the vestibule.

"What do you want?" he asked.

"It's August 1st," Maria responded. "The theater should be opening today, I work here. Please let me in."

"I didn't get any orders." The man tried slamming the door shut, like last time, but Maria pleaded, "Please, I work with Trifon Kirillovich. He might have sent me a letter."

"Trifon Kirillovich?" The man raised his bushy eyebrows, the look on his face turning from menacing to incredulous. He scratched his head and sighed. "Alright, alright, come in." Reluctantly, the man let her inside, following her down the vestibule to the office.

"I'll check the mail." Maria turned to him. "Trifon Kirillovich may have sent me a letter."

"Alright, alright," the man responded, his tone almost kindly.

Maria assumed it was because of the respect the theater manager commanded. In the office, Maria went through the stack of mail and found a letter from the theater manager addressed to her.

Dear Martha,

I am sorry to inform you, but our troupe has faced delays in Kharkov. Although I shouldn't assume, but as you may have already heard from Andrei Zurov, our troupe is unable to return to Moscow as planned. After much deliberation, and, having finished our performances in Kharkov, the Moscow Art Theater troupe under the leadership of Mr. Kachalov has taken the decision to travel to Crimea, where we will put on shows and stay through September to finish the tour. We will reassess the situation at the end of September and plan on returning to Moscow thereafter.

Please continue reporting to work.
Trifon Kirillovich Arbuzov

"Crimea? Andrei is in Crimea?" Maria mumbled, as she stared at the letter. Then, following the instructions from her boss, sat at the typewriter and got to work.

August was a terrible month for the theater. Moscow Art Theater turned into a sad place with half of the troupe on tour. Once the actors had learned the news about the troupe's delayed return to Moscow, they started spending most of their days gossiping over Kachalov's motivation and whether their theater would survive.

Stanislavsky wandered the hallways, frowning, complaining that he couldn't start the season, that there were no provisions, no rations, and no money to pay his staff. Maria, just like the rest of the staff, hadn't been paid since June.

At first they were told to wait for the start of the season, which was on September 1st, but then they quickly learned the theater had no money and barely any food rations left. With Trifon away, no one took care of the practicalities of theater life. To survive, the actors started selling off their belongings. Instead of rehearsals, they exchanged tips on which pawn shop was the most generous.

Their diet consisted almost exclusively of cabbage, potatoes and millet, and they shared recipes of how to prepare these three ingredients in creative ways.

The stagehands went on strike, then returned to work, but only part-time, and every performance was a struggle. The actors were in a disarray. The performances the theater had ready for the season needed the second part of the troupe, and Stanislavsky hastily moved to hire and train new actors. He was unhappy with the results, fired most of the new hires, then hired some of them back. Everything was in flux.

Each new day at the theater turned into a calamity, nothing seemed to be going right.

There wasn't much for Maria to do. She still came to work, each day hoping to receive good news of the troupe returning and the situation stabilizing, and each day brought a new disappointment.

There was no news from Andrei, and Maria assumed he had no way of reaching her. She'd stopped writing to him, because the troupe was moving through different towns, and she had no way of knowing for sure if her letters reached him. The idea of contacting Trifon to ask him about Andrei's whereabouts occurred to her, but Maria didn't want to mix her personal life with work. And so, she resisted the temptation.

At least Dunya was doing better, and Dr. Petrovsky hinted that Dunya's case was special. That she was a miracle to have survived so long. That it was thanks to Maria's care and presence that her nanny had managed to be doing so well. Maria even started to believe that her dear nanny's illness would somehow improve. That however poorly Dunya's heart was doing, it would keep on going.

But then, as the cold weather had set in, Dunya took a turn for the worst. In early November, just as the city was about to celebrate the second anniversary of the great Revolution, and red banners popped up all over the city, declaring victory of the proletariat, Maria found her in so much pain she was crying.

"What about the morphine?" Maria asked the nurse.

"I cannot. We need to check with the doctor. I've already given her the maximum prescribed," the nurse hissed. "If I give too much, she might not handle it."

The relationship with the nurse had gotten tense over the last few days, as Maria delayed paying her.

"Alright, I'll go check with the doctor," Maria said and rushed to see Dr. Petrovsky.

CHAPTER 29

$\mathcal{M}$aria found the doctor alone in his room, sitting by the window, eating soup, and Maria apologized for the disruption. Ekaterina walked in, carrying a steaming teakettle.

"These communal kitchens!" His wife shook her head in indignation. "Turned making tea into wartime negotiations. I now have my own allocated time when I have access to the stove." She set the kettle down on a trivet and turned to the doctor. "So if I want to make tea when my husband, who treats patients mind you, has his thirty minutes for lunch," Ekaterina crossed her arms, "I have to beg and plead with those women."

"Darling, please, don't worry," Dr. Petrovsky said, but Ekaterina interrupted him.

"It's just unnecessary. I'd like to meet the person who decided stuffing eight families into one apartment was a good idea. Did that person ever consider the practicalities of daily life?"

"Maria is here."

"Oh. Sorry! Is everything alright?" Ekaterina asked, now seeing the distressed expression on Maria's face.

"I think Avdotiya Timofeyevna might need a larger morphine dose," Maria said.

"We were at fifty, weren't we?" Dr. Petrovsky put his spoon down.

"Yes." By then, Maria had become very familiar with the dose levels and other medical jargon. "It's been at fifty for the last month or so."

"Alright, I'll stop by later today." Dr. Petrovsky promised. "I've got a few more patients to see." He turned to his wife. "I can go over to the Suvorovs at the end of the day, right, darling?"

"Yes, darling, but please finish eating your soup while it's still hot." Ekaterina hovered over her husband. "You've got to eat. It's chicken soup, with bones," she said proudly.

"Yes, darling," Dr. Petrovsky muttered, moving his spoon faster now.

The mundane expression of care between the couple made Maria yearn for Andrei, for their closeness, the year they had spent together. Maria had just re-read Alexander Kuprin's love story, *Olesya*, and recalled a passage, which stood out to her. 'Separation is like the wind to a fire. It extinguishes a small love, but it fans a big one to make it stronger.' After reading it, Maria decided her love for Andrei was a big one. It got stronger, deeper, her feelings for him growing as their separation continued.

"We're going to leave next month. Once the ice thickens, we'll cross over into Finland from St. Petersburg." Ekaterina's voice pulled Maria out of her reverie. "Are you thinking of leaving, Maria?" Ekaterina turned to her. "To join your father in France? That's where we'll be going."

"I can't leave Avdotiya Timofeyevna." Maria shook her head.

"Oh, yes, of course." Ekaterina exchanged an almost imperceptible glance with her husband. "And your job? How is that going? The Moscow Art Theater used to be such a wonderful place, but I heard they've run into some trouble this season." Ekaterina gave her a pointed stare. "But I suppose everything under the Bolsheviks is bound to collapse."

"A part of the troupe went on tour this summer and didn't come back. I'm engaged to one of the actors who's away. I was actually supposed to go with them," Maria said.

"My dear, that's terrible you are apart. Dr. Petrovsky and I are never apart, are we, darling?" Ekaterina gave her a look full of such compassion, something inside of Maria snapped and her lower lip quivered.

"I better go now. I'll see you at later today," Maria said to the doctor and left.

When Maria returned to the Suvorov mansion, she found Dunya sitting up, propped up on the pillows. Her eyes sparkled, as she said, "Masha, you know what I'd like?"

"What is it, Dunya?" Maria smiled. "Anything you want."

"That Napoleon cake. Do they still make those?"

"Of course, Dunya, of course they do." Maria nodded. "They started selling them again. I passed by the Eliseyevsky market just the other day and saw them."

"I would sure love me a slice of that Napoleon pastry." Dunya wriggled on the pillows and Maria rushed to help her.

"I'll go get it for you right now, Dunya, how about that?" Since getting sick, Dunya had not had an appetite, and Maria's heart leaped at the request.

"Tomorrow, get it for me tomorrow. There is no rush. Just stay with me, Masha, stay right here next to me." Dunya's hand reached for hers in a familiar gesture.

"Alright, Dunya, of course."

Maria hadn't been to the Eliseyevsky in a long time, and,

sitting next to Dunya, imagined herself going up Tverskaya Street, and walking into the grand entrance of the Eliseyevsky market after work. She could almost smell the vanilla and sugar of the market and salivated at the memory. It would be a nice excuse to stop by the bakery section and say hello to François.

"Yes, yes," Dunya mumbled, dosing off. "Don't fuss, Masha, don't fuss."

Maria sat next to her nanny, deep in thought for a while, and left, feeling unusually at peace after the visit.

Maybe Dr. Petrovsky was wrong, Maria thought on her way home. *Dunya might get better. This must be that miracle case. One in a million. And the human body is a mystery.*

Maria smiled to herself.

* * *

INHALING THE SCENT OF PASTRIES, Maria hurried along the aisles of the Eliseyevsky market. The few precious coins in her purse would be enough to pay for the treat and to cover the nurse's backpay. So little in exchange for her mother's ring at the pawnshop two hours prior.

The secret compartment in Andrei's room, once stuffed with treasure, now sat half-empty. Of her mother's jewelry, only a few items remained, and Maria had set aside Dunya's gold coins, sure the nanny would ask for them once she got better.

The Eliseyevsky, having lost some of its luster, still boasted a good collection of cold cuts, baked goods, and cheeses, though no longer imported from France. Its prime location, right down the street from the Kremlin, made it an important fixture in the country's life. The Soviet government had made sure to keep the store open and running to signal the stability and splendor to come, once they prevailed in their fight against the supporters of the tsar and the White Army.

François was pleased to see her, and gave her the largest slice of Napoleon available, nearly double the usual. Having thanked the clerk profusely, Maria walked out of the store into the drizzly November day. Freezing rain fell, turning into slush.

Normally, Maria hated November. The month had no redeeming qualities, as far as she was concerned. The weather wasn't fall anymore but not quite winter, with the fluffy snow it promised. Just the days getting shorter and shorter and the two seasons fighting for primacy.

Each year, the month was a reminder of the loss Maria had suffered. Her mother's untimely death. But now, as she made her way through the city back to see Dunya, clutching the generous portion of the Napoleon, Maria decided she may have been wrong. She was about to present Dunya with a wonderful treat.

"Dunya!" Maria rushed into her nanny's room. "Guess what." She stopped at the door. The air in the room was unusually thick. And then she saw it.

A sheet had been pulled over the nanny's face. Dunya's hand hung lifelessly down on the side.

"No! No! No!" Maria screamed. "No! Dunya, I brought you cake, like you asked. Dunya!"

"She passed this morning." The nurse walked in. "I've been waiting for you in the kitchen."

"This morning? When?" Maria glared at the nurse. "Why didn't you tell me? Why didn't you stop her from dying? I could have called the doctor!"

"Stop her? The nurse shook her head. "It was her time. She was ready."

"No! She asked me to bring her a pastry! She wanted to

live! She wanted to be here with me." Tears streamed down Maria's face and she heaved. "She didn't want to die."

"You come see her face now." The nurse pulled Maria to the bed. The woman's kindly, round face suddenly looked sinister, and Maria fought the urge to run away. Only then did Maria notice the mirror had been covered with a cloth. The room had been prepared for death.

"I can't, I can't." Maria shook her head. "She can't be dead."

"Look at her. You're gonna feel better once you do. I never done see no one look so peaceful when dead," the nurse noted, pulling back the sheet with a practiced gesture.

Maria gasped. The nurse was right. The look on Dunya's face was peaceful. Eerie, otherworldly, but peaceful.

"She's done living, see? You go make those arrangements now," the nurse said. "And you owe me for the month."

"Yes." Maria reached for the money she'd prepared. She would have to pawn something else to pay for the funeral.

Maria put down the slice of Napoleon and felt like gagging, the dessert now associated in her mind with losing Dunya. With grief.

* * *

Dunya's funeral, organized at the Bolvanovka church, was well attended. All the church ladies, her friends and their families, came together, informed by Akulina, who was the first person Maria told of Dunya's death.

Maria couldn't help but compare the service for Dunya to her mother's funeral, when the Moscow elites had gathered, in part, for a social occasion. The empty expressions of condolences, the cold faces of those who had attended the funeral only because of her family's social status. Others, who came to gawk, to gossip over the cause of her mother's sudden death, in her prime and right after the opening ball of the season.

Her dear nanny's funeral was different. All who came knew Dunya well, loved her, and came to pray for her soul and to celebrate her life. They embraced Maria, shared in her grief, comforted her, and made her loss feel almost manageable.

"You were like a daughter to her," they all said, and their words were sincere.

Akulina had put herself in charge of the wake. Through intense negotiations and bargaining, Akulina managed to secure the agreement of all residents in the Suvorov mansion to hold the wake there. She was like a general, leading an army, taking control of the communal kitchen, temporarily got rid of the drying laundry, borrowed pots and pans, and cooked all day long to prepare the meal.

"A saint, a saint, they don't make them like Dunya anymore," Akulina mumbled, as she roasted a chicken, which, Maria later learned, someone had donated for the cause.

Amidst the hungry days in Moscow, the constant struggle for survival, this level of generosity was unmatched, a testament to Dunya's uniqueness.

CHAPTER 30

It wasn't until after the wake was over and Maria was washing the dishes, so she could return the kitchen to the communal residents of her old mansion, that she felt the magnitude of her loss. Tears rolled down her face, dropping into the sink where grimy water had pooled.

Maria had the sudden urge to smash the plates she'd so carefully washed and set to the side. She turned the water off and wiped her face, took a deep breath, and bit her lip to stop herself from screaming.

Dunya's death left a void in her life, but it also was a complete rift with the past. The last thread connecting Maria to her childhood home was gone. There was no turning back. The room where Dunya had lived and died, Maria was told, had already been reallocated, and a new family would soon move in. She didn't argue, having learned the rules.

Maria was left in a limbo. She couldn't move forward until Andrei returned to Moscow. Though she hadn't heard from Andrei since the summer, she hadn't lost hope.

A few weeks later, Maria was walking through the theater vestibule, when she overheard two actresses speaking. She didn't know them well but remembered one of them was named Polina. The two women had been recently hired by Stanislavsky, and Maria decided to introduce herself.

"Europe, Poland, Germany, they're going to Berlin," Polina said.

"Did you say they're going to Berlin?" Maria tried to give her face a calm expression, to not reveal the sense of panic and doom rising inside of her. "I'm Martha, by the way. I'm a typist here."

"Nice to meet you. Polina Smirnova." The actress was beautiful, very tall, with almond-shaped eyes, a thin nose and full lips. "Yes, Kachalov wants to go. He thinks they'll do well there." Polina shrugged. She turned to the other woman, a somber-looking brunette. "Isn't that right?"

"That's correct. But I believe they are going to Paris," the brunette responded, her voice full of authority. She didn't introduce herself, as if expecting Maria to already know her name.

"To Paris?" Maria gasped.

"Yes." The brunette rolled her eyes. "To perform at Cabaret Buffe." She pronounced the last two words with a terrible French accent but did so with some pride.

"What's Cabaret Buffe?" Maria asked, opening her eyes wide.

"It's a theater, in Paris. It's famous." The brunette sighed. "I wish we'd been with the troupe last year, so we could have gone with them. They're probably having the time of their lives. I wouldn't want to come back to Moscow either if I were them. Right, girls?"

"Right!" Polina giggled. "Eating cabbage seven times a week. Though it's doing wonders for my figure." She twirled, showing off her tiny waist.

"Very true." Maria brushed her hands down her dress and noticed it hung loosely.

"You should wear a belt," Polina suggested. "That way, you'll look dainty, not gaunt."

"Or I could take it in," Maria said, oblivious to the jab.

"Polina, what are you saying, she doesn't look gaunt." The brunette jumped to Maria's defense.

"Well, it doesn't matter, does it?" Polina shrugged. "She doesn't have to be on stage, like us."

"If you do take the dress in, just be careful not to take it in too much. We might start eating well someday." The brunette shrugged.

"Don't hold your breath!" Polina said, and the two women broke out laughing.

Maria walked away from them; her spirits shattered.

* * *

ONCE AT HOME, Maria examined herself in the mirror for the first time in months. What she saw shocked her. Since Andrei's departure and Dunya's illness, she'd stopped taking care of herself. Now, checking her reflection, Maria realized how she looked to the two actresses. Her face was pale, her eyes dull, with dark circles under them. Her hair, once a rich shade of light brown, had lost its luster and had turned a mousy color. The daily ritual of brushing her hair nearly forgotten. It hung like a rat's tail down her back instead of the thick braid she'd once had. But worse of all was her figure.

Polina was right. Maria did look gaunt. She could see her collarbones sticking out, and, when she lifted up her dress, her legs were thin and bony. *How did I not notice this before?* Maria twisted her ring. It, too, was loose on her finger, though it had fit her perfectly once.

A part of her was glad Andrei didn't see her looking like

this. *But Europe? Did Andrei travel to Europe?* Maria thought. She heard a knock on the door and jumped.

"Martha, there's a man downstairs, he wants to see you," Klava said in a hushed voice, opening her eyes wide. "He said to get dressed." Maria noticed little Kira hiding behind her mother, and smiled at the little girl, but something in Klava's expression made her pause.

"What man? Is it someone from the theater?"

"No, I think he's like an army man. A gun and all," Klava whispered. "Listen, if you need help, you just let me know, okay? You don't worry about nothing, okay?"

"Yes, thank you." Maria took a deep breath, trying her best to stay calm. She threw a coat on and followed Klava downstairs.

A man stood by the front door, hands in his pockets. Something in his expression, the cold, assessing stare, the eyes of a man who was used to being right, reminded her of Stepan, the young man who had tried to arrest her before Ivan rescued her.

"Citizen Goncharova?" The man spat out her name. "Come with me." He produced an ID. She couldn't see his name, but clearly noticed the words CheKa printed in red. The Soviet Secret Police. Her heart sank.

"Yes."

Maria followed the man out of the red mansion, barely feeling her body. This was the end. She knew it. She'd heard of the All-Russian Extraordinary Commission, the CheKa, the Soviet Secret Police, which had replaced the *okhranka* in tracking its citizens. Before leaving, Trifon had mentioned it, always with reverence mixed with fear. Maria knew the CheKa investigated crimes against the new Soviet state.

They must have found out about my alias, Maria thought.

She'd been living with false documents, hiding her true

identity for almost two years, and her lie was about to blow up in her face.

"Where are you taking her? Where is she going?" Klava yelled after them. Her daughter started crying. Gavrila appeared and pulled Klava back, mumbling to the CheKa man, "Don't mind her, don't mind her."

A black car was idling in front of the steps. Maria got into the back seat, and the man got in next to her. He ordered the driver to go. Once the car was on the move, Maria, clutching the coat around herself for warmth, stared at the city. Her fingers felt numb as she ran them through her hair. She thought of Andrei, and tears welled up in her eyes at the thought she'd never see him again.

The ride was over before Maria could fully contemplate the futility of her existence. The car turned onto Lubyanka Square and pulled up to a large brick building, which had once housed the All-Russia Insurance Society headquarters. A large clock adorned its front.

"Get out of the car and follow me," the man ordered.

Maria considered running away, but noticed two soldiers, rifles in their hands, standing guard at the door, and obeyed the man, following him inside. She climbed the massive steps to the entrance, then continued another set of steps up to the vestibule.

The hallway, despite the late hour, was full of people. All men, most of them in uniform, hurried up and down the corridor. Maria followed her guide in silence. No one looked at her. It was as if she were invisible and the men with their expressionless faces and blank stares saw right through her. Mid-way down the long corridor, the man stopped in front of a white door. A plaque read: Fight Against the Counter-revolution Department.

The man leading her knocked. Maria bit her lip. She heard muffled voices coming from behind the door, then the sound of footsteps approaching, and the door opened. Maria gasped. Ivan Engelghart stood on the threshold. His eyes shone brightly with the same zeal she'd seen when he delivered his speeches at Irina's.

"Citizen Goncharova, come in," he told Maria and, with an almost imperceptible nod, dismissed the man who had brought her there.

She entered a large room that looked as if it had once housed an insurance agent. The space conveyed wealth and prosperity, as if to assure its visitors of stability in life. A map of Russia hung on the wall. There were two bookcases full of gold-rimmed volumes. Maria crossed the thick carpet to the large desk covered with a red velvet cloth.

Ivan pointed to a black leather couch that stood in front of it. "Have a seat right here."

Maria sat down and noticed a green lamp on the desk, much like her father's, a telephone, and a cast-iron inkwell next to it.

"Hello, Maria Olegovna," Engelghart said, as he walked behind his desk and took a seat across from her.

"Ivan Afanasiev–"

He raised his finger to his lips. "Maria Olegovna, I am in a bind. Please, allow me. You see, I value old friendships. This is why you're here tonight. If you remember our last meeting," he raised his eyebrows, "I told you to never come back to your house. To disappear. And I even gave you a suggestion where to stay. I also told you not to mention my involvement to anyone. Is that correct?"

"Yes," Maria said.

Engelghart sighed and put his hands behind his head, leaning back in his chair.

She wondered whether Ivan had been eating well. Like her, he looked thinner, and there were dark, almost purple circles under his eyes. The man did not look well. Maria remembered his terrible cough when she saw him on Tver-skaya and suddenly felt incredibly sorry for him.

This feeling of pity, of a desire to help this man, was so incongruous to her situation that she nearly gasped, wondering what force inside of her was driving her emotions.

"I've been put in a difficult situation, Maria Olegovna. My department, as you may have noticed, deals with the counter-revolution. We are a young country, and we're fighting for survival. We have many enemies. Countless, one might say. So, my job is extremely important." He paused for effect, and Maria nodded. "Now, who are these enemies?" He raised his eyebrows. "The White Army, of course. And who is leading the White Army? The aristocrats. People like you. Supporters of the tsar. Those who want the old times to come back." He sighed. "Maria Olegovna, I blame myself for this situation. I really do. I should have forced you to leave the country back in 1918, but I hesitated. Back then, I didn't realize the magnitude of our fight. I thought we would be done with the capitalist hydra by now. But war is still raging on, Maria Olegovna."

Maria listened to Ivan's speech in stunned silence.

"I was informed you've been seen with a certain Dr. Petrovsky, bringing him to the place of your former residence. The informants implied you were planning counter-revolutionary activities."

"What?" Maria gasped. "Ivan Afanasievich, it was Avdotiya Timofeyevna. Do you remember her? You let her stay. My nanny, she was dying." Maria nearly shrieked and grabbed the edge of the seat to stop herself from screaming. "Dr. Petrovsky was treating her."

"Maria Olegovna. I am well aware of the situation. This is why I allowed it to continue as long as it did."

"You allowed?" Maria's throat suddenly felt parched. "You knew?"

"Yes," Engelghart uttered. "How did you think Andrei got you the documents? Your ID? And your passport?"

"What? Everything? Oh, I've been so naïve." Maria buried her face in her hands.

"The situation cannot continue. The best thing for you is to leave the country."

"But I can't." Maria shook her head. "You likely know why."

She turned beet red from the realization this man may have been privy to her most intimate moments. Knew about her involvement with Andrei, of their affair. Her love story was now property of the Bolsheviks.

"Andrei Zurov is not coming back to Moscow anytime soon, Maria Olegovna."

Maria swallowed hard. "How can you be so sure?"

"I'm telling you, leaving would be the best thing for you given your situation. You always have a choice. But this might make a difference. Your father, Maria Olegovna, has been trying to find you." Ivan produced a stack of letters. "These have been intercepted in the last year."

"All of these are from my father? You've read his letters to me?" Maria stared at Engelghart in horror.

Maria hadn't heard from her father in over a year. After being forced out of the mansion, she initially felt ashamed, and was sure her father would blame her for what had happened. Her father had expected her to guard it, had put her in charge, and she'd left it with almost no resistance. She couldn't explain in a letter that she was hardly to blame. That she was forced to leave, that she would have been homeless, but for the kindness of a Soviet bureaucrat she'd helped in the past. And then there was another problem.

Even if she wanted to write to her father, she could not.

Maria Suvorova no longer existed. The link between Martha Goncharova and her true name could not be established. And if she wrote to Count Suvorov as Martha Goncharova, Maria would compromise her cover.

"I'm just doing my job, Maria Olegovna," Ivan said.

"I see." She paused. "And from Andrei?" Maria bit her lip. "Do you have any letters from him?"

Ivan shook his head ruefully.

"Farewell, Maria Olegovna."

"Goodbye, Ivan Afanasievich." She rose to leave.

Engelghart rubbed his eyes, and, with a sigh, picked up the receiver.

CHAPTER 31

When Maria returned to the red mansion a mere two hours after leaving, Klava followed her upstairs, repeating,

"I prayed for you, oh, Lord Jesus, I prayed. I prayed to the Virgin Mary to protect you from harm and to deliver you back. I prayed."

"Klava," Maria turned to her neighbor, tears of relief and gratitude in her eyes, "thank you. I don't know how to thank you."

"What did they do to you? What did they want? Was it the CheKa? Gavrila done tell me it was the secret police."

"Yes." Maria nodded, unlocking the door to Andrei's room, where she was now staying. "They asked me some questions, that's all."

"Some questions? Where did you go? Was it the building on Lubyanka? He said no one comes back from there."

"Really?" Maria gulped, walking in.

"Will you tell me everything?" Klava asked, following her inside. "Was it because of him? That actor?" Ever since learning Andrei had not written to her in months, Klava announced he was likely 'runnin around' like all men,' and encouraged Maria to forget the actor.

"Kind of." Maria nodded, taking a seat on the bed.

"You see, men, they're all trouble." Klava crossed her arms. "Gotta watch out."

"I guess so."

"You, Martha, you shouldn't have let him leave on his own. You gotta grab them by you know what." Klava gave her a disappointed look. "You see, he gotta be chasin' after you, not leaving you behind. He should've stayed."

"It was only supposed to be just for three weeks," Maria protested.

"Yes, and three weeks is a long time. Were there other women on that train?" Klava paused. "Yes, there were. You practically threw him away."

"No! I did no such thing."

"Well, it's too late now anyway."

"Don't you think he misses me?"

"Maybe. But a man can't be alone for long. That's impossible, Martha."

"Impossible?"

"Yes, impossible. And now because of him, you're going over there, answering questions. That man of yours, does he even know what you've been through here? Where is he when you need him?"

"I heard they can't come back..." Maria started to say, but Klava put the nail in the coffin.

"If a man wants somethin', he gets it. That much I know," Klava said categorically. "So, what're you gonna do now? What did the CheKa want?"

"I gotta think about something, Klava." Maria rose.

"You just think about yourself, Martha. Stay safe," Klava advised. "I'll see you in the morning. Gotta check on Kira."

Maria stayed up most of the night, reading her father's

letters. There were ten of them, written in his neat cursive, pages and pages of them. The first two had arrived right after Maria had left the mansion, and were full of questions about the house, requesting to share the latest accounting.

But by the fall of 1918, her father had stopped asking those questions. Instead, he urged Maria to leave Moscow and to travel to France. In each letter, her father shared stories of immigrants, families Maria knew, who had successfully arrived in France. Count Suvorov expressed regret at having left Maria in 1914.

The last few letters were short. Her father asked her to write back, or for whoever was reading and receiving his letters, to respond to him, to let him know what had happened to his daughter.

Having flipped to the last page, Maria ran her fingers over his writing.

I am nothing like how Papa remembers, she thought ruefully and her thoughts turned to Andrei. *Ivan wouldn't lie to me. He knows Andrei isn't coming back.*

Then Maria immediately remembered Klava's sobering assessment, the reference to 'the men that were runnin' around.' The six months of separation, the majority of which Maria had spent with Dunya until her death, had turned Andrei in her mind into a mythical figure. A part-phantom, part-man. She vaguely recalled being with Andrei, remembered the feeling of joy and belonging, but now doubted whether those feelings had been mutual. Whether she hadn't mistaken her own love for something else. Whether she'd read Andrei's feelings correctly.

He hasn't written to me in five months. He's probably with someone else.

Maria pictured Andrei with other women, beautiful actresses, giggling, sitting on his lap with glasses of champagne in their hands. She imagined Andrei caressing the giggling actresses and felt bile rising in her throat.

But then there was the ring. The gift from Andrei, the reminder of their vows to each other. The promise. Maria twisted the narrow band she wore every day, ran her finger against the tiny emeralds. Then she reached into the hiding spot. Out of the jewelry she'd inherited from her mother, there was the sapphire ring, large, imposing, a ring her mother had told her a woman could only wear after turning forty. There was the garnet bracelet. And the diamond earrings. The ones Maria wore to her very first ball. She flipped them, staring at them against the light. Their under-stated elegance, a reminder of the glamor of her past. A life she could have had. Maria wrapped the jewelry up and put it back in the hiding spot.

Maria fell asleep late and woke up after being startled awake by a strange dream. She had dreamed of Dunya and Potap, of the day they had hidden the jewelry under the floorboards. And the vision was so vivid, Maria felt as if she'd just relived those moments together. In the last part of the dream, she saw Dunya's face, staring at her, telling her to 'sew the jewelry in'.

Maria bolted upright and flicked on the lamp.

Of course! What am I even doing? I have to leave immediately.

The thought pierced her mind. The decision to leave Moscow for Paris wasn't her own. But when she reached it, Maria felt such an immense sense of relief, as if pieces of a puzzle she'd been trying to solve for months had suddenly fit together.

She got up, laid out her clothes and started sewing. She had a thick winter coat, which she would take with her, and she ripped the lining and sewed the jewelry into it, concealing several pieces at the bottom. Dunya's gold coins Maria sewed into the lining of the travel dress.

As soon as the sun rose, Maria left the house and went straight to the Petrovsky residence.

Please still be there, please still be there, she repeated all the way to Taganka. She hadn't seen them since Dunya's death. Maria quickened her pace. It was completely irrational. She had only decided to leave Russia several hours prior, but now she felt she couldn't stay any longer.

As she climbed the familiar steps to the Petrovskys' apartment, Maria had a sinking feeling she wouldn't see them. She remembered the urgency with which Ekaterina insisted they would be leaving, and then Ivan's words about the doctor. And so, when she knocked on the door and was greeted by a scowling woman, who informed her "the doc and his missus ran off', Maria wasn't surprised.

I'll go on my own, Maria decided. *I'll figure it out.*

The Petrovskys had mentioned traveling first to St. Petersburg, then waiting there until the 'ice got thick enough', and crossing by foot over the narrowest spot in the Gulf of Finland. There was, according to Ekaterina, a path known to the locals, and local guides who accompanied those trying to leave across the ice. Maria remembered the crossing at Sestroretsk, and a fairy tale image popped into her mind. The three horses of a troika pulling a carriage across the ice to Finland and then, the magical journey would continue and she would be in France, safely reunited with her father in Paris.

* * *

IT TOOK Maria two days to get ready. She finished sewing the rest of the jewelry and coins into her travel coat and dress, packed her clothes, and got a train ticket for Petrograd, which was what St. Petersburg was now called. She didn't tell anyone at the theater she was leaving but stopped by to check whether any of the rations or salary payments arrived. She was in luck and was able to collect two months' worth of payments for September and October. This would be enough to get her to Petrograd and to pay for the travel across to Finland.

Then Maria went to say goodbye to her childhood home. She knew she wouldn't be able to enter, not after the warning from Ivan, but she wanted to see it one last time. Maria walked on the snowy streets of Moscow and approached the yellow mansion from the Taganka hill side. It was a sunny winter day, and the yellow of the mansion gave it a festive appearance. The beautiful white accents matched the color of fresh snow that had fallen overnight.

Smoke rose from the chimney and Maria could picture her younger self returning home after a winter walk, running down the street, Dunya following her, yelling for her to slow down. How she would ignore Dunya's warnings and run down the hill, sliding at the very end, and be greeted by Potap, carrying firewood inside. Her mother would be waiting for her at the door and hug her tightly, as Maria shook off the snow and showed her mother a treasure – a beautiful, iced-over branch she'd found. The ice would start melting, dripping off the branch, but Maria held onto it until the very end.

"Look how pretty it is, Maman," she would say, and her mother would nod and kiss her on the cheek, then take her inside to warm up.

All in the past, Maria thought, standing at the top of the hill and looking at what used to be the Suvorov residence one last time.

She returned to the red mansion. There was one more thing she had to do before leaving.

"Klava?" She knocked on her neighbor's door. It was the

middle of the day, and Maria hoped to catch Klava on her own, when Gavrila was at the factory.

"Martha, so, you made up your mind?" Klava opened the door, brushing hair off her face. "Kira's sleeping." She pointed to a cot in the corner. Klava's room was submerged in semi-darkness, the toddler snoring fitfully. Though the room was cluttered, it felt cozy, rather than stuffy.

"I'd like to speak to you," Maria said, keeping her voice low.

"Sure, are you alright?" Klava scanned her face. "Come in." The two women sat down on the couch that doubled as a marital bed at night.

"Klava, I'm leaving," Maria said. "I'm going to France."

"To France?" Klava gasped. "Is that where that man of yours is now? Are you going to chase him down?"

"Maybe. I don't know for sure."

"But why are you going, then?"

"There is something I need to tell you. My name is actually Maria Suvorova. I'd like you to know my real name before I leave. So if anything happens, or if you hear anything, you know it was me."

"Suvorova? Like those counts?" Klava's mouth hung open.

"Yes," Maria said, then corrected herself. "Yes, the Suvorovs are my family. That's why I changed my name."

"Maria Suvorova." Klava stared at her in amazement. "You mean to tell me you're a countess? An actual princess? But that can't be."

"Yes." Maria smiled. "Well, not a princess. Just a countess."

"But you seem like a normal person. You're kind, you're real. You feel things." Klava shook her head in disbelief. "Them counts aren't like us."

"Well, I am."

"A countess. You mean, all this time, I've been friends with a countess?"

"Yes. We're friends, aren't we?"

"Yes, we are."

"Klava, I wanted to leave you something. It's for you, but also for Kira."

Maria took out a small velvet pouch she'd been keeping in her pocket. "Go ahead, open it." She urged, but Klava was hesitant.

"What's all this?"

"You'll see." Emotions overwhelmed Maria. She'd pictured this moment differently, imagining a quick and easy goodbye. She watched as Klava pulled the strings of the pouch apart and, with two fingers, took out the earrings Maria had worn to her first ball. The tiny diamonds sparkled in her hand.

Speechless, Klava flipped them in her hands.

"A gift. So, you remember me. I don't have anyone else left in Moscow," Maria said. "And you have been so kind to me. A true friend."

"Are you leaving forever?" Klava shook her head. A tear rolled down her cheek, and she wiped it. "Oh, Martha… Maria. I don't know what to say. Be safe out there. May God take care of you." Suddenly, she stopped speaking. "And I got nothing to give you. When are you going? Tell me, please?"

"Tonight," Maria said, biting her lip so as not to cry.

"Okay, okay. You'll be in your room until then?"

"Yes," Maria said. "I have to finish packing."

Klava came by two hours later, right before Maria was to leave, with two loaves of bread and an icon painted on wood. It was an image of the Virgin Mary, holding baby Jesus, her face beautifully done. Baby Jesus was pictured gently brushing his mother's cheek, his left leg unclothed.

"I got this just for you. To protect you," Klava said, pushing the icon into Maria's hand. "Keep it safe, pray to the Virgin Mary. And since your name is Maria, you should have told me earlier. I would have gotten this for you sooner. She's your patron saint, the Mother of Jesus. The Saint Virgin. Remember, Maria."

"I will. Thank you." The two women embraced.

"Alright, you be safe out there."

Maria gave Klava one last hug and stepped out into the night.

PART IV

*L*ater, when Maria thought of her journey to Paris, of the several months she'd spent on the road, she recalled it as nothing short of miraculous. The first part by train, that took her from Moscow to Petrograd, which Maria still struggled to call by its new name and kept referring to St. Petersburg. She then crossed into Finland, though not on a fairy tale troika, but in a car, driving on ice as terror paralyzed her body, imagining how it would sink into the Gulf of Finland and take its passengers with it, two men fleeing Russia just like she was, and their local guide, all going under water and dying in the freezing waters.

But none of it happened. She safely arrived in Finland, then, accompanied by the two men, got train tickets to go to Sweden.

Maria prayed to the icon each night. It was as if Klava's words had shrouded her in a blanket of safety and protection, She'd traded the gold coins for food, to pay for transport and shelter, and managed to stay safe.

In April 1920, Maria arrived in Paris unharmed and healthy.

Her funds had been nearly depleted, but she still had the bracelet and the sapphire ring that belonged to her mother sewn into her coat. She still wore the emerald ring Andrei had given her. She hadn't gained any weight but hadn't lost any more either.

As the train pulled into the Gare de l'Est, Maria took in the outskirts of Paris, the tall buildings and the broad boulevards of the city, staring out of the window in amazement. She slipped on her fur coat, took her suitcase, and alighted.

As soon as she stepped off the train, she realized her fur coat, so warm and thick, which had been so necessary in Petrograd and Finland, was completely out of place in Paris. Maria took it off, feeling the warm Parisian sun on her skin and stood with her suitcase next to her on the platform.

She had previously sent a telegram to her father informing him of her arrival. The stack of letters she'd received from Ivan contained all of Count Suvorov's contact information in Paris, where he had moved from Nice.

Her imagination did not extend as far as the actual reunion with her father after more than six years of separation.

The constant need to survive, to avoid a danger that could lurk in the most unexpected place, had driven Maria to a state of being constantly on guard. She looked around uncertainly and adjusted her hat. Then, she flipped her thin braid and noticed a boy.

He ran up to her and, frowning slightly, asked in an accented Russian, "Sister Maria?"

He said it in such a way that at first Maria shook her head, thinking the boy had mistaken her for a nun. But then something compelled her to ask him in French, "Are you baby Konstantin?"

"Konstantin Olegovich Suvorov." The boy extended his hand to her. "You're my sister, Maria Olegovna. Nice to make your acquaintance. We have been waiting for your arrival." He pointed to the end of the platform, and Maria saw a couple moving towards her. She could just make out their faces, but their expressions looked remarkably similar, just as she remembered, as if years of co-existence had now merged them into one.

"Maria!" she heard. "Oh, you've made it!" It was Antoinette. The former governess had gotten plumper. Her eyes shone brightly, like those of a cat that had just finished a nice meal.

"Yes. Hello, Antoinette," Maria said. "I've just met Konstantin."

"How lovely. We've been waiting for your arrival! Konstantin has been rehearsing his speech to greet you." Antoinette clapped. "But you probably want to say hello to your father."

"Maria." Count Suvorov approached, clearing his throat. "Now, where's your luggage?" He raised his eyebrows at the valise Maria had taken down from the train.

"This is it, Papa," she said.

"Sister Maria doesn't have any more luggage," Konstantin stated solemnly.

"That's it? I see." Count Suvorov hummed and rubbed his forehead. "Well, I suppose what's important is being safe."

"Oui, chéri. It is wonderful you were able to get your daughter back!" Antoinette gave him an adoring look. Turning to Maria, she said, "Your figure, it's absolutely lovely. You must tell me your secret."

"I'm not sure I know what it is." Maria shrugged. How could she explain to Antoinette the months, even years of deprivation, of eating watery cabbage soup, of pawning jewelry just so she could have something to eat the next day?

Even if she did, would Antoinette believe her and not think her gory and dramatic?

"You must have one." Antoinette giggled.

They walked through the train station, and Maria couldn't quite shake off an eerie feeling of her very existence being unreal. The reunion with her father, his new family, was all so mundane. As if none of her travails, none of the dangers of her escape from Moscow were real. The bustle of Paris, the expressions on the faces of the passersby, were starkly different from those of the scowling faces she'd seen in Moscow.

And then, there was the long-forgotten feeling of everything being arranged by her father. He was in charge. As they got into the car waiting for them by the train station, and her father instructed the driver, Maria fumbled for her purse to check if she had enough change to pay the fare, and then stopped, realizing she was, for the first time in years, under her father's care.

Count Suvorov, having settled in France before the war and the Revolution, was one of the more successful Russian aristocrats in Paris. He'd invested in real estate and bought a large apartment near the Alexander Nevsky Russian Orthodox Church. The Suvorovs occupied a five-bedroom apartment in the eighth arrondissement, on Avenue Hoche, with a view of the Arc de Triomphe, in one of the most prestigious parts of Paris.

The apartment was on the second floor of a cream-color building, which boasted a grand entrance, wrought-iron railings and bas-relief lions above the entrance.

"You know, where I stayed in Moscow, the mansion also had a lion," she told her father. They had just gotten out of the taxi and were standing at the entrance with her suitcase.

"Oh? Where did you stay, Maria?" Her father opened the front door of the building. "I couldn't find you, you know." The vestibule was even more impressive, with marble floors, large windows, and the sun streaming in.

"Yes. I got your letters later on. They had been collected by the CheKa."

"CheKa? What is that?"

"It's kind of like the *okhranka,* but the Soviet kind," Maria said, following her father up the stairwell. "Papa, I was staying at Irina Kutuzova's mansion. In one of the rooms."

"Wow, small world. Irina Kutuzova is in Paris, you know," Maria's father noted. "She is thriving, from what I hear."

"Irina?" Antoinette, overhearing the conversation, asked. She put an emphasis on the last syllable. "Yes, everyone knows her in Paris. She's a great socialite."

"It would be great to see her," Maria said.

"You know her? Oh, Irina is lovely." Antoinette gushed, leading Maria into the apartment. "Now, I think the first thing we must do is cut your hair," Antoinette noted casually as soon as they were inside.

"My hair?" Maria felt her braid.

"Yes, my dear, you need to fix it right away. And then we'll go to the ball. It's later this month."

"A ball? There are balls in Paris?" Maria stared at Antoinette in disbelief. Having been to just one in her whole life, Maria couldn't imagine anything further from reality.

"Oh, yes, there is the Russian ball. Well, several, I've been to them all." Antoinette opened her eyes wide. "I've met all the aristocratic families."

"Chérie, please." Count Suvorov touched his wife's hand in a warning gesture.

"But it's true, darling. And I think it'll be a good way to let everyone know of Maria's arrival in Paris," Antoinette said, turning to Maria. "And you know who's here? The Yelagins."

"I see." Maria nodded, unsure of how to react.

She had long ago forgotten about her failed engagement to Nikolai, but now the image of his long face, his mother, her insincere smiles, the broken promises, the endless lunches, and then the sudden break in the engagement. It all made her head spin.

"Oh, yes. Count Nikolai is a war hero," Antoinette continued, an eager smile on her face.

Konstantin had been absorbed in playing with a toy car, but his ears perked at the mention of a war hero. Maria wondered what was going through her little brother's mind and what kind of boy he was. What he had learned about Russia and its aristocrats while living in Paris.

"Yes, of course, he went to war," Maria said, keeping her voice flat.

"Yes. And Nikolai Yelagin is very active in the church," Antoinette started to say, but Count Suvorov interrupted her.

"Chérie, please, let's not bother with this now. Let's make sure Maria is settled in first."

"I'm just trying to help, so Marie is up to date." Antoinette pouted. "But yes, of course, darling. Let me show Maria to her room." She shrugged and shook off her disappointment.

"My darling, you know I've already made plans to invite the Yelagins over." Maria's father noted, smiling indulgently at his wife. "We will all spend time together, like in the old days."

Their conversation, the casual mentions of the noble families, the gossip that Antoinette so eagerly shared, all that Maria experienced in her first hours in Paris were so unlike the prior six years of her life, that she felt as if she'd just been dropped into a strange dream. A vivid one, where figures from her past had taken on new roles, had reappeared, having taken on unexpected functions.

The Russian aristocracy, long since forgotten by her, destroyed by the Soviets, had, in fact, been thriving in France. If anything, it had been made stronger by the Revolution. And not only that, had been making plans for a triumphant return to Russia.

Maria learned of this phantasmagorical undertaking from her father when he quizzed her on the Soviet state.

"And what of the people? Did they all accept Lenin?" Count Suvorov asked later that day, as they were about to sit down for dinner.

"I guess so, Papa." Maria shrugged. "It's hard to explain. Things were gradual, you see."

"But what about the churches, religion? How could it be? Russia is a deeply religious country. I heard the Bolsheviks were trying to stop people from going to church."

"Yes, Papa." Maria thought of Klava, of the strange mix of belief in God and her obedience of the Soviet state. "But people still go to church and pray. Or do so in secret." Maria did her best to explain how life in Moscow had changed after the Revolution.

Antoinette, who'd been listening to their conversation, sitting next to Count Suvorov with a quiet, focused expression on her face, followed their exchange with difficulty. Though she spoke Russian, it wasn't great, but Antoinette considered communicating in Russian a matter of pride.

Every Sunday, Antoinette attended service at the Russian Church on Rue Daru and knew the words of all Orthodox prayers in Russian by heart. Having converted into Orthodox Christianity before getting married to Maria's father, Antoinette became a zealous member of the community, as often happens with new converts.

"How terrible for the Russian people, this Soviet cauchemar," Antoinette said in Russian, passing the salad to her husband. She used the French word for nightmare, cauchemar, one of the many words the Russian language borrowed from French, and a proud smile crossed her face when she did so.

"Indeed." Maria nodded.

"Maria, I've asked my seamstress to come by," Antoinette said.

At the mention of a seamstress, Maria remembered the Singer sewing machine in the middle of the Petrovskys' room. She hadn't seen or heard from the couple along her journey and wondered if she would find them in Paris.

"Thank you, Antoinette." Maria gave a polite smile.

CHAPTER 33

By the time Maria arrived in Paris in 1920, Count Suvorov's marriage to Antoinette had been generally accepted by the Russian community. The aristocracy forgave him the indiscretion and, as many had hinted, he wasn't the first Russian noble to marry a woman of a lower social standing.

Another reason for the acceptance, Maria later learned, was the great melting pot of the Russian immigrant community in France, which quickly grew to nearly half a million, following the Russian Revolution. Many, unlike Count Suvorov, had lost everything and arrived in France destitute. The luckier ones got jobs in factories, opened small businesses focused entirely on serving other Russians, or became taxi drivers. All scrambling to preserve their dignity.

Many others, unable or unwilling to work, led murky lives on the fringes of society, became professional beggars, and many more drank to drown their sorrow.

The idea of seeing Irina, of reconnecting, of their shared past that included Andrei, was promising. Once in Paris, Maria had initially planned on looking for Andrei right away. She pictured going to Cabaret Buffe, the name she had retained well from her conversation with the two actresses, and finding Andrei there with the rest of the Moscow Art Theater troupe. But after months on the road, Maria was exhausted.

The lack of an explanation for Andrei's disappearance gnawed at her. She doubted herself, doubted their love. Doubted even her own decision to leave Moscow, though Ivan's warning had been unmistakable.

Did Ivan know something? Maria agonized, thinking back to the conversation in the Lubyanka office. *I should have pushed him. I should have demanded an answer.*

She clenched her fists in frustration. The not knowing, the gap in her understanding over why Andrei had stopped writing, made it difficult to focus on anything else, and Maria did her best to push these thoughts out of her mind.

* * *

Like Count Suvorov, Corporal Yelagin was one of the more successful immigrants. After reconnecting in France, the two men forgave each other the broken engagement between their children, which they had written off as a misunderstanding and due to the general disorder during the war. Maria felt she would never learn the real reason for the broken engagement, whether it was because of the birth of baby Konstantin, the sale of the estate, or her refusal to advance the wedding date.

When the Yelagins came over for lunch shortly after her arrival in Paris, nothing was mentioned directly, and no apologies were expressed.

Yelena Yelagina looked older, but the expression on her face was almost the same. It was that of eager condescension.

"Hello, my dear," she embraced Maria. "How lovely of you

to arrive in France!" The woman opened her eyes wide. "But what an adventure? I hear you came from the North. But how is Moscow? I miss it, our beautiful city. You must tell us all about it."

"Mother." Maria heard a low voice, and Nikolai Yelagin stepped out from his mother's shadow.

Maria barely recognized the young officer she'd been engaged to for several months. He'd gained weight and she could see a paunch protruding over his belt. He had lost almost all of his hair, and constantly ran his hand through his remaining few hairs as if to ascertain they were still there.

"Maria, a pleasure," he said solemnly. "We have a lot of catching up to do." He was holding a black case, which reminded Maria of the one she'd seen Dr. Petrovsky carry.

"Hello, Nikolai," Maria said.

"Look at this lovely reunion!" Yelena cooed. "But is there anything more important in life than old friends?"

They proceeded into the living room, decorated in various shades of yellow. The bright April sun shone through the curtains, giving it an airy, happy appearance. Maria sat across from Yelena, twisting the narrow golden band on her ring finger.

"My dear, are congratulations in order?" Yelena asked, curling her lips into an eager smile.

"Congratulations?" Maria followed Yelena's gaze. "Oh, this." She reddened. "No, it's nothing," Maria said. The words cut like a knife.

"But of course, it's very unfortunate, war, the upheaval. But as I tell Nikolai, one mustn't forget to live." Yelena nodded. "Right?"

"Mother." Nikolai's eyes bulged.

"Nikolai, why don't you show your project?" Yelena urged, seemingly oblivious to her son's discomfort.

"Yes, Mother." Nikolai turned to Maria. "I've started a

movement," he said gravely. "To restore order in Russia. It is taking most of my time at the moment."

"How will you restore order?"

"With the other Russian aristocrats here, in France. There are many of us are here, you see. In exile, for now. But it's just a matter of being organized. If we're to defeat the Bolsheviks and reclaim our land that belongs to us by birthright, we need to be united." Nikolai opened the black case and took out a stack of papers. "Take a look." He handed them to Maria.

She went through them. The papers were all the same. On top there was a last name, and then a drawing of a family crest. Underneath, she saw family trees, dates of births and deaths, and then, in a careful, slanted handwriting she recognized as Nikolai's, names of the estates in Russia.

"Nikolai, dear, tell Maria about the other part of your project." Yelena looked at her son with undisguised pride.

"Oh, yes, well, the other part is, of course," Nikolai scratched his head, "by itself, the list isn't very useful." He paused and fixed his gaze on Maria. "This is why I've also put together a map of Russia, but it's at home. And on that map, I've marked all the estates of these aristocratic families. I've collected all the information, piece by piece. So when we come back, everyone will be able to get their estates back." He rubbed his head. "I've collected most of the names and addresses. The Russian land, it belongs to us." He scanned Maria's face for a reaction. "God is on our side and we'll overpower the Godless Soviets. We'll triumph and soon. Of that, I am certain."

Maria nodded politely, still holding the papers in her hands.

"This looks like a lot of work," she said, handing the papers back to Nikolai, and he put them away, neatly sliding them into his case.

They were called to the table, and, as they rose to move to the dining room, Maria remembered Sergei. The young man she'd met at the Yelagins.

"And whatever happened to your cousin? I remember he was eager to join the military," her voice trailed off, as she thought of the eager young man, his clever eyes.

"Yes. He got his wish. Ran off to join the military. Sergei has been fighting with the Denikin army," Nikolai said.

"We've gotten a few letters," Yelena said. "A brave young man, a hero. Salt of the earth."

CHAPTER 34

"It's a place where all the artists and poets come together," Antoinette noted, her eyes sparkling, keeping her voice low so Konstantin, who'd been lurking nearby, wouldn't overhear. "Zey stay up all night drinking and partying, and zen zey sleep in the morning."

Maria was getting ready to go to Café de Flore on Boulevard St-Germain des Prés to see Irina Kutuzova. According to Antoinette, in the late afternoons, the socialite could be found there.

"She's so cultured. Please tell her I said hello." Antoinette blinked fast.

"I will, of course. Thank you, Antoinette." Maria checked herself over in the mirror once more.

She was wearing an outfit Antoinette's seamstress had made for her, a flowing skirt, narrow at the hips, and a short-sleeve loose top. The outfit was complete with a hat. Antoinette had also equipped her with a crocheted lace reticule decorated with the rosette pattern.

Barely recognizing herself, Maria smiled at her reflection in satisfaction: she looked elegant, chic even. Like a true

Parisian, were it not for her hair. Maria had refused to cut it, despite Antoinette's insistence that 'all modern women' wore their hair short. But Maria couldn't yet part with her long hair that now reached below her waist. Instead, she tucked her thin braid into the hat.

Despite looking the part, Maria felt some trepidation as she approached the cafe. She noticed it from across the boulevard, the elegant letters on the sign beckoning her inside. It was a late afternoon hour, which, Antoinette had told her, was when Café de Flore was at its busiest.

Round tables were set outside, right by the front door, each one full. Maria's determination faltered as she noticed the café-goers were all men. They were engaged in animated conversation and paid her little mind. Glasses of wine and coffee cups, half-empty or completely empty, were spread on the tables. A lone waiter with a look of quiet resignation stood at the door.

"Mademoiselle." He raised his eyebrows at Maria.

"I'm uh," Maria's face turned red, "I'm meeting someone."

The waiter nodded and slightly lifted his left eyebrow, as if to indicate Maria's meeting was none of his business and went back to silently observing the street. She walked in and took in the place. Noticing her reflection in the mirrors that hung on the wall, the expression of alarm on her face almost comical. The cafe was just as busy inside, the red booths at the perimeter of the cafe all full.

Her eyes fell on Irina and Maria sighed in relief. Irina was easy to spot: the only woman, sitting in the corner, a place that offered full observation of the room. Irina's blonde curls were like a gravity point, the center of the café.

Irina was chatting with two companions, young men, but, as her gaze met Maria's, she gave her a wave and smiled broadly. She must have told the young men to leave, because both pushed their chairs back and disappeared in a flash.

"Maria! I don't believe it!" Irina leaned over the table to greet her. "But I must be dreaming." Irina wore a flowing green dress, long, with a pattern of leaves sewn in small beads. On her head, she had a matching headband. "When did you arrive?"

"Only a few weeks ago," Maria said.

"My dear, but how in the world did you survive? I've heard you'd gotten stuck in dreary Moscow! Have a seat, please."

"I guess you could say that." A shy smile crossed Maria's face. Irina sat back down and pointed to a chair next to her, for Maria to sit down.

"What would you like to drink? How about champagne to celebrate finding each other?" Irina offered.

"Thank you. I stayed at your mansion, you know," Maria said after Irina had placed an order.

"Really?" Irina flipped her hair back.

"They've expropriated mine, and yours had already been reallocated. So I stayed in the tiny closet under the steps, Ivan's room. He was the one who helped me." As Maria told the story, she realized how fantastical it sounded, but Irina listened intently.

"I've heard, of course, but now, Ivan Engelghart. Hasn't he become a big-time revolutionary?

"Yes." Maria lowered her voice. "He works for the CheKa. The Soviet secret police."

"Oh, dear. Well, I'm still glad I've helped him and the movement." Irina sat up straight. "You know, I came back briefly after the revolution," Irina said. "But ran out of there after seeing what had become of Russia."

"I heard." Maria nodded. "And do you remember Andrei Zurov?" Maria asked. Her heart beat fast, as she said the name of her lover for the first time in months.

"Of course. The handsome actor. He was supposed to be keeping an eye on my place," Irina chuckled.

"Yes." Maria averted her gaze.

"Wait, do you mean to say?" A knowing smile appeared on Irina's face. "Now, my dear, that is an *interesting* development. I had a feeling about the two of you. Tell me, am I right?"

"I, I," Maria stuttered. She had not planned on revealing her connection to Andrei and had been sure she could keep it a secret, but, seeing Irina's understanding face, Maria hesitated. Since speaking with Klava about Andrei nearly six months prior, Maria hadn't mentioned her love story to anyone. The temptation was palpable.

"My dear, don't be shy. You can tell me everything. And I cannot blame you, he is a handsome young man. Delicious!" Irina's eyes glistened.

"Well, Andrei..." Maria started to say, but a wave of sadness rushed over her and she could not speak.

"So it's true then!" Irina clapped. "I knew it. You were together then? But you must have made a spectacular couple. Both of you are so tall, lean, and your faces oh! It's like you were made for each other." Irina stared at a distance. But then, noticing the expression on Maria's face, shook her head. "My dear, don't take it so seriously. It's just a romance, an affair. It comes and goes."

"Yes, I suppose so," Maria mumbled. "Andrei helped me. I worked at the Moscow Art Theater, as a typist. And thanks to him and Ivan, I got my papers, fake documents, so I could stay in Moscow. And then, Andrei and I were together."

"Oh, my dear, what a story."

"I had an alias," Maria continued.

"Really?"

"Yes, Martha Goncharova."

"Wow. So, tell me, Andrei and you, you must have been

the couple of the year at the theater! The one thing I truly miss is the Moscow Art Theater. Their productions…" Irina's voice trailed off. "Absolutely glorious." Irina snapped her fingers and the aloof waiter appeared at their table at once, topping up their glasses of champagne. As Maria took another sip, she was transported to Irina's salon, her first meeting with Andrei, the toast to friendship. It was as if her life had come full circle, only now Andrei wasn't there.

"So they aren't in Paris? I heard," Maria blinked fast, "they went to Europe on tour. The summer of 1918."

"Really?" Irina shrugged. "Not to Paris." She shook her head. "If they were in Paris, I would have been the first to know."

"What about a place called Cabaret Buffe?" Maria repeated the name she'd ingrained in her memory. "That's what I heard."

"No, no, the troupe, I'm still in touch with a few of them. They have moved to Poland and will be in Berlin this summer."

"Berlin?" Maria gasped. "I thought I would find him in Paris."

"Andrei? My dear. Did you come to Paris because of Andrei?" Irina stared at Maria with genuine concern. "Tell me this isn't so."

"I, Irina, not quite, but…" Maria averted her eyes. "It's hard to explain. But Andrei went on tour, and I stayed behind, and then everything was happening at once, and life in Moscow was just impossible. I had no one to turn to."

"My dear." Irina put her hands over Maria's. "So you haven't heard? Andrei left the troupe, almost right away. He joined the Red Army."

"The Red Army?" Maria balled her hands into fists. "But that's impossible. He was with the theater troupe; he wrote me letters…" She stammered.

"I know he left them and pretty early on. You know about his beliefs. And he and Ivan, they're very close." Irina sighed. "So, I'm not surprised. If anything, it would have been strange if he'd stayed with the theater once the White Army blocked passage to Moscow."

"You're right. Andrei was the theater's Communist Party representative." Maria furrowed her brow, trying to piece together the bits of information from her conversations with Andrei.

"I would imagine so. Andrei was one of Ivan's first followers. I know Andrei believed his mission was to serve the Soviet state, just like Ivan did. Now, those men, who knows what really goes through their minds?" Irina shrugged.

"So this is why," Maria mumbled. Pieces of a puzzle were moving together, shifting to form a picture that suddenly made sense. Andrei's sudden disappearance, the letters stopping suddenly, the hint dropped by Ivan. "Of course," Maria nodded. "I should have figured. Ivan knew Andrei had left the theater and was fighting with the Red Army, but he couldn't tell me."

"Listen, it's all in the past. There are better things in life than worrying about former lovers." Irina gave her a look full of compassion. "I'm certain now I must take you under my wing."

Maria blushed. "Irina, thank you, but you don't have to–"

"My dear, no, please, you must listen to me. I should have done it sooner, and you, having lost your mother so young, and your father marrying that woman. How trite."

"Antoinette is very kind to me."

"Of course she's being kind! After your father abandoned you in Moscow during the war? And that disaster of an engagement. My Lord," Irina fanned herself, "you're a fighter, Maria. And I'm sure Antoinette must realize she's also responsible for some of the terrible things you've gone through."

"Irina, thank you, but it's not like that. I'm fine." Maria raised her hands in protest. "And the broken engagement, Papa is friends with the Yelagins still."

"No, no. Don't get me started on that lot. Listen, please, please stick with me. We can accomplish so much together. And besides, it will be fun to have a girlfriend by my side." A sly smile crossed Irina's face. "It's hard to find an equal, you see."

"Very well." Maria blushed, looking at Irina in admiration. "Thank you."

"Don't thank me. I think destiny brought us together." Irina batted her eyelashes, and Maria suddenly saw that Irina, whom she'd always considered much wiser and more worldly, was a young woman in her prime. Now that Maria was twenty-four, and Irina, who must have been in her early thirties, their difference in age wasn't as intimidating.

"You know, I think you were younger than I am now when we met in Moscow for the first time," Maria said.

"Oh, yes, when was it? 1912?"

"Yes, 1912."

"Now, a woman never reveals her age." Irina took a sip of her champagne and winked. "So I won't confirm or deny your statement."

"Alright."

"But you know what I think?" Irina tilted her head. "I think we're going to find you a new lover."

"Irina! I'm not ready, I can't. I just arrived." Maria's face turned a deep shade of crimson.

"Trust me, my dear. You know what they say, like cures like. We've got to find you a new man." Irina straightened up and took a look around the cafe, as if a possible candidate were lurking nearby, waiting for her to spot him. "So much better than worrying about some actor running away to join the army. It might be a good plot for a play." Irina waved her arm. "Paris is full of great possibilities. I've been dating two young men." She lowered her voice. "Did you see? They both fawn over me, fighting over my time. Both handsome, smart. This city is a wonder."

"Two?" Maria's mouth gaped open. "And they know about each other?

"Yes."

"And what of your husband?" Maria blinked fast.

The world Irina was sharing with her was nothing like she'd been brought up to expect. Even the love affair with Andrei, their liaison, the fact that their union had not been formally registered, now appeared tame in comparison.

"Well, Count Kutuzov and I have an understanding," Irina noted vaguely. "We don't pry into each other's business. And there are other practicalities to be considered." Irina rubbed her fingers, indicating a financial transaction. "Our finances are tied, you see. For now."

CHAPTER 35

After that day, Maria met Irina several times a week. They saw each other at the Café de Flore, where Maria, too, became a regular.

Despite resisting at first, Maria decided to cut her hair, once Irina pointed out to her how nicely it would suit Maria's high cheek bones. And so, Maria adopted a style most young fashionable women in Paris sported, hair cut to the shoulders, laid in careful waves. Irina took her dress shopping, and, though Irina insisted Maria stay away from Antoinette, with the efforts of the two women, Maria now boasted a rich wardrobe, complete with several pieces for all occasions, from church to a ball.

Irina maintained a second residence, separate from the one she shared with her husband, and that gave Maria an idea.

"I was thinking, what if I got my own apartment?" Maria hesitantly mentioned to her friend one day, and Irina was more than supportive.

"Of course! I should have thought of it myself. You cannot continue to live with your father and his new family. It's simply ridiculous. You're a young woman. You must, after all, enjoy a certain ability to be discrete," Irina said, pushing her unfinished cup of coffee aside. Irina never finished the drink, complaining it made her jittery. "We must find you a cute place!"

"But I wasn't even thinking about that, I just want to be on my own." The idea of finding a new romantic interest was daunting. Maria still caught herself thinking about Andrei.

"I know I'm right, my dear. How do you expect to have a lover if you're to invite him over to your father's place?"

"But I can't quite use this as an argument with Papa."

"Trust me, I'm sure Antoinette is eager to be rid of you."

"Antoinette has been very generous."

"Darling, just ask your father about living separately and see what he says. I'm sure you won't need to explain your reasons. He's a smart man."

In the end, Maria mustered the courage to speak to her father and, as Irina had predicted, Count Suvorov was amenable to the idea of Maria moving to her own place. She had gotten to know Paris, and picked an apartment in the Marais neighborhood, a part of Paris she loved because of its meandering streets.

Irina, however, was appalled by the location and told Maria she might as well live on the streets. But the place was cheap, due to the Marais neighborhood's state of disrepair, and Count Suvorov agreed to purchase it for his daughter.

And so, a year after arriving in France, Maria had settled into her own place, which overlooked a courtyard and was right next to Place des Vosges. Each morning, Maria woke up with a feeling of deep gratitude and peace as she looked at the greenery outside. She furnished the apartment with light furniture and enjoyed the freedom of living on her own.

Now and then, she missed the company of Dunya and Klava, thinking back to her living arrangements in Moscow, but then remembered the communal kitchen, the noise, the neighbors taking turns using the stove.

Now, there was no one to greet her in the mornings. She was on her own.

"I will never visit you there," Irina had threatened initially, but after reluctantly coming to see Maria, admitted the apartment 'wasn't without a certain charm'.

With Irina's help, Maria had been on several dates, but something always stopped Maria from going beyond one or two dates. Each time she sat across from another young man, carrying on a polite conversation, she thought of Andrei. It was his face she pictured in front of her, his tall frame she yearned to see. She missed their conversations, their connection. She and Andrei understood each other, knew everything about each other.

Now, listening to another young man's story and his plans for the future, Maria found she had no interest in what he had to say.

Like a book with a plot she would immediately forget. Nothing and no one touched her heart – not since him.

And though Maria knew Andrei wasn't in Paris, she searched for him on the streets. She hoped he had somehow made it to Paris, had learned of her departure from Moscow and come to find her. The image of Andrei haunted her, especially in the early evening hours, and she found herself following a tall figure, accelerating her pace to catch up to a stranger, thinking the man Andrei, only to be disappointed.

On a cold November day, Maria and Irina visited the Café de Flore. Maria wrapped herself tightly in her coat.

"Dear girl, you are in France," Irina said. "There are so many lovely men here. Why do you want to limit yourself to the Russian immigrants?"

"But isn't it better to be with someone who can understand me?"

"Understand you? But you speak perfect French! I am sure the French can understand you."

"But culturally, we're different. The expectations," Maria started to say, and Irina interrupted her,

"In bed, my dear, I would recommend a Frenchman." That argument usually put an end to their conversation, but this time Irina pressed on. "This is simply ridiculous!" She raised her hands up in frustration. "Someone like you has to try very hard to become an old maid, but you, my dear, are going to succeed if you keep this up."

"It's fine. I'm perfectly happy on my own. I have a great apartment, great friends." Maria smiled at Irina. "And I've got a great job too."

Maria had just started working as a typist at a large law firm. She'd taken a course and qualified, having found that she still remembered how to type, and it was just a matter of learning and memorizing the layout of the French typewriters she needed to do before regaining the speed and accuracy with which she'd typed at the Moscow Art Theater. She thought back with gratitude to Trifon, and how he'd hired her on the spot to become a typist.

"Alright, alright," Irina said. "I suppose these things take time."

"Listen, I was just at church. It's Demetrius Saturday today," Maria said. She knew Irina did not go to church, but respected the Russian Orthodox tradition.

"Did you light a candle for your mother?" Irina gave Maria a look full of compassion.

"Yes. And for Avdotiya Timofeyevna." Maria sighed. She had told Irina the story of her nanny's passing. "November. Both of them passed in this horrible month."

"Yes, darling. I'm so sorry."

"And even in Paris, the weather is terrible in November,"

Maria said. As if on cue, she felt a rush of cold air, as the door of the cafe opened and a man walked in.

He was of average height but carried himself with confidence. His posture was that of someone who'd served in the military, shoulders pushed back, head held high. He had a broad, open face and very clever, slightly slanted eyes. Maria noticed him right away, and so did Irina.

"But take a look at this young man." Irina's opened her eyes wide, "Now, if you don't want to get to know him, I will."

"Irina, he looks young," Maria started to say, but then, to her surprise, saw he was heading their way.

"Hello," he said, taking off his cap. "I was told I'd find you here."

"Have me met?" Maria fixed her hair. The man was attractive.

"I believe so. Sergei Chegodaev."

"Sergei?" Maria paused, and then gasped, placing the name. "Of course. But the last time we met was ages ago."

"Yes, I was just a boy. Back in Moscow." Sergei smirked. He kissed her hand. Maria didn't pull her hand back and only after the kiss did she remember she wasn't wearing gloves.

"This is Irina Kutuzova." Maria introduced her friend.

"Pleased to meet you." Irina smiled, examining the young man with interest. "Would you like to join us?"

"Yes, very much so." Sergei smiled, a broad, open smile, while his eyes remained fixed on Maria. He lifted a chair back and sat across from her.

"And how do you two know each other?" Irina asked.

"We met through the Yelagins," Maria and Sergei said in unison and exchanged a look.

"I see." Irina raised her eyebrows and a sly smile appeared on her face.

"I'm their distant cousin. I stayed with them a while in Moscow," Sergei said.

"And Sergei, what brings you to Paris?" Irina asked.

"I'm like everybody else. En exile." Sergei bit his lip. "I was fighting with Denikin, the White Army general, then Vrangel, until the very end. Gave it everything, but we lost." He shook his head ruefully. "And so, I made it to Constantinople. Worked at a loading dock, tried to make ends meet. But then the Yelagins wrote to me, so I came here." His speech was simple, but Maria knew behind those words hid unimaginable suffering, hunger, war, destruction.

In Sergei's story, she recognized her own experience of fleeing Russia. The struggle for survival. The revolution that had ripped apart their country.

"So, you're a war hero!" Irina exclaimed emphatically.

"I'm no hero." Sergei shook his head. "I went to war without the slightest idea of what it would be like. I was only trying to do the right thing. And it sounded almost romantic. Beautiful." He sighed. "Well, it was nothing like that. I've learned that much."

"A true hero!" Irina repeated and glanced at her watch. "Now, would you look at the time? I must go. Bye, darling." She gave Maria a kiss on the cheek, got up, and, before Maria could ask her what appointment Irina had, left the cafe.

"That's a good friend you got here." Sergei winked at Maria and only then did she realize Irina had left them alone on purpose. Maria blushed, and noticed that Sergei was still looking at her, as if his clever eyes could see right through her. "Would you like to go for dinner?" He asked.

"Yes." Maria nodded.

Dinner turned into an evening out, and then, without giving it much thought, Maria decided to invite Sergei over to her apartment for a drink. She knew she was being reckless, but for once, she decided to follow Irina's advice. Being with Sergei was easy, their conversation flowed effortlessly, they had a lot in common, and he was, Maria knew, younger than her.

He can't possibly want anything serious, she decided. *Which is just what I need. It's exactly what Irina has been telling me to do.* They were standing outside of her building.

"Another time," Sergei responded, and Maria balked at the rejection, but he said, "I'd like to see you again. Tomorrow."

"Tomorrow? Alright."

"You know, the day I met you," Sergei said, "I fell in love with you. I remember thinking how lucky that cousin of mine was to be marrying you. And that he didn't deserve you."

"Oh." Maria opened her eyes wide. "I had no idea." She looked at Sergei again, as if seeing him for the first time.

"It's when you least expect it, or so they say." Sergei straightened up his shoulders. "I prayed to see you again. Prayed you were in Paris." He pierced Maria with his look. "I'll see you tomorrow. You're my redemption, Maria."

* * *

WHAT SHE THOUGHT WOULD BE a fling, a brief affair to help her forget Andrei, turned into a serious relationship quickly. Sergei courted Maria, doing all of the right things. He insisted it was fate that had brought them together, their union preordained, and Maria followed along.

Sergei knew what he wanted, and Maria was relieved to have a companion who didn't leave her room for doubt. Slowly, her memory of Andrei was pushed back, and Sergei occupied her thoughts more and more.

"What a brave young man!" Count Suvorov exclaimed after Maria brought Sergei over for lunch a month after their chance meeting. "A real war hero. How brave he is, how humble. Now, that's a real man, Maria. What a shame that he must live in exile."

"Maria, he is adorable." Antoinette practically purred, putting the emphasis on the last syllable. "I'm so happy for you."

"Thank you, Antoinette. But I'm not sure. Well, we're just getting to know each other."

"I'm certain things will work out for you this time." Antoinette glanced at Count Suvorov, as she always did when she spoke of matters of the heart.

Sergei proposed to Maria two months later, after asking Count Suvorov for her hand. When Maria shared the news with Irina, her friend giggled.

"Darling, you couldn't have a fling, even if you tried."

Maria blushed. "I guess I'm not made for light romance."

"I'm just happy you're over the actor."

"Oh, yes. Of course I am." Maria shrugged. "See, you were right. I just needed to find the right guy."

"Well, Sergei's an absolute catch, darling. I'm very happy for you. And the immigrant community is absolutely thrilled." Irina rolled her eyes. "They love it when aristocrats marry their own."

"Oh, yes, I've gotten so many invitations to their gatherings. I had no idea the Russian emigrés were so social."

"Be careful, darling, stay away from the gossip. Now, when's the wedding?"

"September 15th," Maria said and gasped, only then realizing the wedding had been set for exactly the day she was supposed to marry Count Nikolai nine years prior.

The strange coincidence made her pause, but she brushed it away. There was simply too much to do to prepare for the wedding.

CHAPTER 36

Maria spent the summer of 1923 in a frenzy of activity. The various social obligations, preparations, discussions of the guest list with Antoinette and her father, mailing and tracking invitations took an inordinate amount of time.

"Do we really need all this?" Sergei asked each time Maria shared with him bits of information about preparing for the wedding.

"I think so. We're the couple of the season." Maria would smile, averting her eyes. "Celebrities of sorts."

"I can't imagine." Sergei shook his head. "Don't these people have anything better to do?"

"I guess not." Maria kissed him on the cheek. "But I'm sure they'll forget about us as soon as we're married."

"Let's hope so." Sergei smirked and fixed his clever eyes on her.

Each time he did it, Maria felt as if he saw right through her, knew her deepest secrets, and wondered whether Sergei suspected she'd once loved another man.

Once we're married," he said, "we'll be done with all that socializing, won't we?"

"Yes, of course," Maria said, her voice faltering.

Sergei had been categorical in his intention to cut the Russian aristocracy from their lives, but Maria, while respecting his decision, wondered whether that would require her to cut ties with Irina, too.

"All those incredibly vapid people. All living in the past. Proud of their aristocratic roots. They're pathetic." Sergei pursed his lips.

* * *

IN LATE AUGUST, Maria met Irina to share the latest updates. With the wedding just a little over two weeks away, she assumed it would be the last time she met Irina as a single woman.

"Now, please don't become one of those boring women who never goes out once she gets married." Irina smiled at her friend.

"Of course not. But at least Sergei is happy to move into my place in the Marais." She took a sip of her coffee.

"I'm not sure it's such a good idea. Wouldn't you rather get a place together?"

"Sure, but not yet. He's only started courses at the Sorbonne."

"He's working hard, isn't he?" Having married an incredibly wealthy man, Irina had a rough understanding that one had to work for a living, but never got into the topic with too much detail.

"Yes, he's driving a cab. For now," Maria said. "Once he gets his degree, we'll be able to afford something else."

"And your father, he'll be helping?"

"Sergei refuses to accept a loan from my father." Maria

sighed. The subject of money had been a topic of much contention with her future husband.

"And how are the Yelagins handling it? Your engagement to their cousin?"

"They're fine with it. I think Nikolai is too busy with his project to care."

"At least something good came out of that failed engagement of yours. I'm very happy for you. You look great, by the way. Being in love agrees with you." Irina nodded at Maria in approval.

"It's been nice. Sergei wants to skip the church ceremony, have I told you?" Maria added after a pause.

"That's a bit unusual, isn't it?"

"I guess so. He says he doesn't like the church, that it's a corrupt institution."

"I see." Irina adjusted her bangs. "Listen, I just found out something. But promise me you won't do anything crazy."

"What is it?"

"The Moscow Art Theater is coming to Paris."

Irina's words were like an exploding bomb.

"What?" Maria's heart beat so fast, as if it was about to leap out of her chest. "When?"

"Next week." Irina gave her a pointed stare. "I got us tickets to the performance. And we can stop by to say hello to Stanislavsky."

"Do you think it's okay?" The tips of Maria's fingers felt like icicles. "Do you think..." She pictured Andrei, their reunion, and the image of her former lover was so vivid in her mind, it was as if nothing else in the world ever existed.

"Listen, I really don't think Andrei will be there." Irina's voice reached her, as if through a fog. "I doubt the theater would have taken him back regardless, but who knows whether he even came back from the Red Army."

"Andrei," Maria mumbled. The equilibrium, the sense of

peace she'd achieved since meeting Sergei, was all gone in a flash.

"We're just going to watch the play, Maria." Irina looked at her with concern.

"Of course. And I can also say hello to Trifon. My old boss."

* * *

THE FOLLOWING WEEK, Maria spent in nervous anticipation. She barely slept, forgot to eat, made mistakes at work, and once even left the house wearing a mismatched pair of shoes, noticing this error only half-way to the office.

A certainty she would see Andrei overtook her, and Maria dreamed of her reunion with him, imagined how he would tell her he'd thought of her every day in the four years they had been apart, how he would hold her hand, kiss her, and tell her she was the only one for him in the world. Then she told herself Andrei had died and gnawed at herself for her silly fantasies. Maria had lost so much weight that she had to wear the ring Andrei had given her on her thumb. Right before leaving her apartment to see Irina, she put the emerald ring on a chain to wear it as a necklace. She hadn't told anyone, not even Irina, the story of the ring, and claimed it had been her mother's, continuing to wear it even after getting engaged to Sergei.

The two friends had agreed to meet at Café de Flore before going to see the Moscow Art Theater debut in Paris. Irina took one look at Maria and groaned.

"Alright, I would rather not take you looking so stressed, but what the hell!" Irina rarely used strong language, and Maria flinched. "Let's go." Irina ordered and, without waiting for Maria to answer, headed outside.

They made their way to the theater, arriving several

hours ahead of the performance, as planned, to give them ample time to reconnect with the troupe. Even so, some of the Russian immigrants were already there, and the entrance in front of the theater glittered with theatergoers, dressed in their best, eager to see one of the best shows in the world.

"Thank you, Irina! I am so glad you told me the troupe was coming to Paris!" Maria exclaimed, as they walked into the vestibule.

"Seeing how you are right now, I should have kept my mouth shut," Irina hissed. "This is a fool's errand!"

Irina expertly made her way backstage, and, as Maria followed her friend down the long theater corridor, she couldn't shake off the feeling of déjà vu. It was almost as if they were back in Moscow, in the familiar halls of the Moscow Art Theater. They passed two women in the corridor, speaking Russian, and Maria stopped cold in her tracks.

In one of them, she recognized the young actress she'd met back in Moscow, the languid Polina with her almond-shaped eyes. Polina's hair had been dyed red, but it was definitely the young actress.

"Polina?" Maria called softly.

"Have we met?" The woman furrowed her brow, staring at Maria in confusion.

"Martha," Maria said. "I used to work at the Moscow Art Theater. In Moscow."

"I don't think I remember." Polina shrugged.

"I live here, in Paris now." Maria started to say, but Irina interrupted her.

"Polina? Listen, dear." Irina spoke with authority. The young actress straightened up. "We need your help. Do you know Andrei Zurov? Is he still with the troupe?"

Maria's heart beat fast as she waited for an answer.

"Andrei? Yes, he's in his dressing room. Door number

five." Polina gave the two of them a casual glance and walked off.

"Andrei," Maria whispered, grabbing Irina's hand. "I can't do this."

"Let's go. We're already here." Irina bristled and led her down the corridor. They stopped in front of a door with a large number five painted in red.

"I can't do this," Maria repeated, but Irina knocked. "It probably isn't him," Maria said.

"Come in." They heard a voice.

"Go in without me. I'll probably murder him if I see him. I'll go see if I can find Stanislavsky. I want to catch him before the show, so I don't have to mingle with the crowd of his admirers," Irina said and left before Maria could protest.

Maria stood in front of the door, unable to move.

"Come in," she heard again. Hands trembling, Maria pushed the door open.

Andrei was sitting in a chair in the middle of the dressing room. His shirt was unbuttoned and the first thing she noticed was the dark hair on his chest. She had an immediate flashback to their lovemaking and felt her heart rate accelerate.

"Andrei." She felt her lips move, but no sound came. "Andrei," she whispered. She leaned on the door frame and felt the room starting to move. The next moment, she felt his strong hands around her waist, and she would have fallen, but Andrei caught her and carried her to the couch.

"Masha." His voice reached her as if through a thick fog. "Masha."

Maria opened her eyes. Andrei's face was right in front of her. His deep, dark-gray eyes, the face that she'd had imprinted in her mind, the one she'd seen in her dreams. The face she'd pictured every day for five long years.

"You're here," Maria muttered.

"Masha, you've found me," Andrei said. "We arrived this morning, and I went to the church, trying to find you. But there wasn't enough time, and I came back." He spoke with urgency.

"Irina brought me here," Maria said. "Remember her? We're good friends now."

"Yes." Andrei's voice trailed off.

"Why didn't you come back?" Maria glared at Andrei.

She suddenly felt herself unable to withstand the emotions overwhelming her. Seeing Andrei after years of yearning and then, just as she had moved on, disrupting the delicate equilibrium she had reached.

"I couldn't." Andrei shook his head. "The theater was stuck, cut off by the Denikin troops, and you should have seen how he was welcomed. So the Kachalov team, it was as if they were glad of it. They sided with the White Army. It was like they didn't want to come back to Moscow, so they went south. And I left. I decided to do the right thing."

"So it was true? You'd joined the Red Army?" She clenched her fists.

"Yes." Andrei nodded. "I had to fight. Russia is a country of peasants, Masha. The land belongs to the people. I couldn't just stand by and watch."

"I see." Maria looked at Andrei and tears welled up in her eyes. "I waited for you. But there were no letters."

"What do you mean? I wrote to you, Masha."

"I never got your letters." Maria buried her face in her hands. "I didn't know. At the theater, they said the troupe went to Europe. But you never wrote. Not for six months. I thought you'd died."

"I should have known. I think it was Ivan." Andrei took her hands into his. "He must have intercepted them."

"Ivan?" Maria pulled her hands back. "Oh, God, I've been so stupid. I should have guessed. But why would he do that?"

"Ivan has this idea, he wants all of the Russian aristocrats to leave the country," Andrei said. "Masha, you know, Klava told me everything. She told me how much you suffered. About Avdotiya Timofeyevna." Andrei reached for her again.

"Yes. I buried her." Maria shook her head. "I just don't understand." She took a deep breath and rose. The room moved, and it took all of her strength to stay standing, but Maria held her head up high.

"Masha, please forgive me. Please come with me. I came to get you. Come back to Russia with me now. After the tour."

"Come back?" Maria muttered. "No. I can't."

"I love you." Andrei dropped to his knees. "I love you, Masha. I didn't know. I hoped you'd wait. I wrote to you, begging you to wait for me. I couldn't imagine you'd leave Moscow."

"You know I can't come back. My life is here now," Maria said. Her eyes were full of tears. "It's probably for the best I left when I did." Maria started to say. "I thought they were going to arrest me."

"Masha, I know. Klava told me."

"They took me to Lubyanka. The CheKa. Ivan did."

"Masha, please forgive me. I've told myself, if I see you in Paris, I won't come back without you. I've prepared everything, Masha."

"I can't go back."

"Masha." His voice cracked.

He reached for her. This time she didn't pull back.

His lips on hers felt just like she remembered. He kissed her face then her neck, gently, softly, discovering her all over again.

"This is crazy," Maria croaked, kissing him back. "Andrei, I'm engaged." She managed to say and he stopped.

"Tell me you want this?" He held her face in his hands and she drowned in his eyes. "I'll do anything, Masha."

She felt a yearning so strong, she reached for him.

"Yes," she said. "Just this once."

After they were done making love, and Andrei laid next to her, holding her, Maria was transported to a place of serenity and joy. They were together, and that was all that mattered. She nuzzled her face into his chest, as if for safety.

"Masha," he said. "Come back with me, please."

"And you? Can't you stay in Paris?"

"Masha, I've thought about it. I have. All the way here, I've thought of staying behind. But I'm a Russian actor. And I've fought for the Red Army. What future do I have in France? I won't be able to provide for you. What kind of husband will I be?"

"So this is the end." Maria pulled back and reached for her dress. "You know it is." Tears streamed down her face, as she slipped it on.

"No, please." He wiped her tears, kissing her face. "Please don't go like this. I love you. I don't want to live without you. Please come with me."

"I love you, too," Maria said. "I always have. I always will." Emotion overwhelmed her, and she looked at him one last time.

"My Masha." He kissed her.

"Adieu, Andrei," Maria said. "At least, this time, we know it's forever."

She didn't believe it was over, though, not until she closed the door behind her. And even then, it didn't seem real. She could still feel the heat of his body, his kiss, his lips on hers, and yet she knew she wouldn't go back for him.

CHAPTER 37

Maria ran out of Andrei's dressing room, through the long corridor, without stopping. It was as if her very survival depended on making it out of the theater as quickly as possible. She made it out into the vestibule and found Irina standing by the box office.

Seeing the expression on Maria's face, Irina muttered, "Oh, God. Come on, let's go." She led Maria outside, stuffing her into a taxi that was idling nearby. They drove to the Marais, and, once Maria was seated in her bed, wrapped in a heavy blanket and a cup of steaming hot chocolate in her hands, Irina quizzed her.

"Tell me what happened?"

"No." Maria shook her head, shame flooding over her. The momentary weakness that had nearly ruined the life she'd so carefully built in Paris. The betrayal of Sergei. "I don't think I can get married now."

"Darling, hold on." Irina sat down next to her. "Let's talk about it. I can't believe I did this. It was like I took you to slaughter with my own hands."

"It's better that I saw him. It's not your fault. I am to blame."

"No, no, no, I should have put an end to this insanity ages ago. When we first met. Or, better yet, I should have never introduced you to him." Irina huffed.

"No, I love him, Irina."

"You do not! He's in the past. Gone long ago. Forget about him."

"Irina, I slept with him!" Maria swallowed hard. "We made love."

"So what?"

"But I'm about to get married. I need to tell Sergei, and then, I guess I'll just be alone for the rest of my life," Maria cried out.

"Are you out of your mind?" Irina stared at her friend in disbelief. "What exactly is your plan?"

"Andrei asked me to go back with him."

"Alright, I assume you said no."

"I did, yes, and then, oh, then we just ended up making love."

"Okay, and then?"

"Well, how can I marry another man? And maybe Andrei will stay in Paris." Maria's voice trailed off.

"Another fantasy. Did he say he was staying in Paris?" Irina asked and then answered her own question. "Of course not. He would have never asked you to go back if he'd planned on staying in Paris. And I don't see it happening, not if he'd actually fought for the Red Army. Not if he's that much of an idealist." She sighed.

"He won't stay in Paris." Maria shook her head. She touched the ring hanging around her neck, the ring Andrei gave her years ago with a promise. "What am I doing? I want to be with him…"

"Forget about it, Maria. You're staying here and continuing with your life. And he goes back," Irina said coldly.

"But I was just with him, Irina."

"And in a week, you'll forget all about him. Once you and Sergei consummate your marriage."

"So I should just go through with it?" Maria stared at her friend blankly. Her mind was racing. Alternating between a life full of the unexpected with Andrei, who could disappear at any moment, just as he'd done before, and a life of stability with Sergei, who considered her his redemption.

"I can't believe we're even talking about it! It's not like Sergei expects you to be a virgin. For God's sake! And I'm so sick of these double standards. Is Sergei a virgin? I hope not. I'm sure he's had plenty of women."

"But Irina, it's not about that. I love Andrei. I always have," Maria said softly. "And he loves me just as much. It's like we're made for each other. Nothing else will ever compare."

Silence fell over the room as Irina contemplated her words.

"Darling," Irina said after a pause. "You must protect your heart. If you want to live."

"Protect my heart? How do I do that?"

"Forget Andrei and move on, darling. Live like he never existed. Learn to like being with Sergei. A good man who cares for you is more than many women only dream of."

"I think I should go back. See Andrei again." Maria tried to get up, but Irina gave her a cold stare.

"You're doing no such thing. You're staying right here, and I'm not letting you out of my sight until that theater leaves Paris. Got it?"

"But," Maria fidgeted on the bed, but Irina shook her head.

"I'm not letting you throw your life away. You've suffered

enough over that man. More than he, or any of the male species, deserves."

"Irina," Maria tried to plead, but she felt so tired.

Her eyelids flickered heavily and soon she fell into a troubled sleep. She woke up in the middle of the night, feeling the walls of the room move, as if collapsing one onto another. She'd just had the strangest dream. She was back in Moscow, next to her nanny's bed, and she was holding Dunya's hand. Her nanny was slipping away, she knew it, and she called Maria to come with her.

"Each moment in life is a blessing, but it's over now," Dunya was saying. "I'm waiting for you, Masha."

"Yes, Dunya, I brought you the Napoleon cake. Just like you asked." Maria gave Dunya a huge slice. It was large, creamy, and floated between them.

"It's too late, Masha. It's over now."

"No, no, please. It can't be over. Not yet. Please wait for me, Dunya," Maria mumbled. The next moment, she felt something pressing against her forehead.

"You're burning up," Irina said, pressing a cold compress on Maria's forehead. "I should have known. Darling, please, be strong. Your fever is about to break, and then you'll be fine."

"It's over now," Maria muttered.

"No, nothing is over." Irina knitted her brow. "I'll call the doctor in the morning. We just have to get you through the night. The darkest hour is right before dawn, that's what they say," Irina repeated as she brought Maria honey and forced her to swallow a spoonful of it.

Count Suvorov wrote off his daughter's sudden illness as nerves, although Antoinette came by with soup. Sergei, who had been working extra shifts ahead of the wedding, sat by her bed in silence, watching her intently and refused to leave, despite Irina's insistence. True to her word, Irina did not leave Maria's side until the day of the wedding. When Maria was well enough to move around the apartment on her own and tried to convince Irina to go, her friend shook her head.

She told her, only half-jokingly, "No, darling. You know what happens when I leave you by yourself."

Maria recovered just in time for the wedding.

Maria and Sergei got married as planned, on September 15th, 1923. She pushed down her feelings for Andrei and did what Irina had told her. She protected her heart.

Following Irina's advice, she tried to learn to love Sergei. But as much as she tried not to compare the two men, Maria couldn't get used to being with Sergei. With Andrei, it was as if their bodies had been made for each other. They were two pieces of the same puzzle, fitting together perfectly. She understood him. Felt him on a deep level.

This wasn't the case with Sergei. His ego fragile, Maria quickly learned to pretend she was satisfied with his love-making, but it left her frustrated and exhausted.

Maria tried hard to be a good wife. She cooked meals for the two of them, organized the apartment in such a way that Sergei had a separate place to study. She also helped him with his work, staying up late when he came home from his studies, and waking up at five in the morning if he worked the night shift to greet him with a hot breakfast.

In January 1924, Maria learned she was expecting. Her cycle had never been regular, and when she skipped her period right after the wedding, she didn't pay it much mind. A part of her, after being with Andrei for over a year without getting pregnant, even doubted she could get pregnant at all. Maria was thrilled, remembering her conversation with Klava and the advice to pray to Virgin Mary.

"I think it's a girl," Maria shared the news with Sergei. "I've always wanted a girl."

"Alright, if it's a girl, you can pick the name. And I'll name the boy. Deal?" Sergei kissed her.

"I know what I'll name her already."

"Oh yes? Tell me."

"Vera," Maria said. She didn't have one doubt in her mind: the little girl would be named Vera, or Faith in Russian. It was the name that would remind her of Moscow, of her youth. Of what had carried her all these years.

"Vera. Sure, I don't see why not." Sergei shrugged. "It has a nice ring to it."

CHAPTER 38

Maria's pregnancy was a difficult one, which, according to Antoinette and Yelena Yelagina, was a telltale sign Maria was carrying a girl.

"I had a beautiful pregnancy," Yelena shared. "With my Nikolai. It's because boys love their mother. Not so with the girls!"

"Oh, oui," Antoinette agreed. "Girls, zey just compete with ze Maman. Zis is what happens. I also loved being pregnant with Konstantin."

"Poor thing." Yelena looked over at Maria, as if Maria couldn't hear them. "But later on, girls are closer to the mother. Or so I hear."

"I still prefer boys." Antoinette looked over at Konstantin, who was absorbed in a book.

Maria knew her little brother was reading *The Count of Monte Cristo* for the third time. They'd been discussing the book, and Konstantin shared that his favorite part was the revenge.

Maria gave birth to a baby girl on June 6th, 1924.

"Just like Pushkin!" Irina exclaimed after learning the news.

"Well, maybe my daughter will be a great poet someday," Maria cooed at the baby.

"You should name her Alexandra, to honor the poet."

"Vera." Maria shook her head. "That's her name."

Motherhood fully consumed Maria. Vera was extremely smart, quick to react, and, Maria was certain, superior to all the other children. Everything Vera did was a source of fascination for Maria. Her first smile, her first tooth, the way Vera started crawling. The way she walked, toddling along, and much earlier than other children. Maria adored the little girl, sewed her countless outfits, and took her everywhere.

Though Sergei at first was against it, the little girl was baptized at the St. Alexander Nevsky church and was given the name Kseniya, chosen according to the Orthodox calendar. Irina became the baby's godmother.

"This is the best thing that could have happened to me," Maria told Irina one afternoon, putting little Vera on her lap. The little girl was about to turn three. Vera giggled and reached for Irina. The two of them had a game where Irina let Vera play with her necklace and told her stories about it.

"You see, and you didn't want to get married. Remember?" Irina said, turning to Maria.

"I suppose it happens to everyone, doesn't it?" Maria responded. "Having doubts is normal, right?"

"Of course, darling." Irina paused. "You know, Maria, I think it's the eyes."

"The eyes?" Maria raised her eyebrows.

"Yes. Vera's eyes. I haven't noticed before," Irina paused. "But Andrei had those incredible eyes, didn't he?"

"Irina." Maria let out a deep breath. Her hands trembled, and she bit her lip. "Please, you can't ever–"

"So you've noticed it, too?" Irina scanned her face for a reaction.

"I didn't think it was possible," Maria gulped. "It was just once. How could it be?"

"Oh, darling." Irina reached to give her a hug. Vera, who was observing them and assumed the game was about to start, whimpered.

"Let me look at you," Irina said to the little girl, and examined Vera's face closely. "Well," she said after a pause, "it is what it is."

"It is what it is!" Vera repeated and clapped. "It is what it is!"

"Irina, let's talk later, alright?" Maria rose from her seat. "Can you watch Vera for a moment? I'll go heat us up some lunch."

Without waiting for an answer, she went to the kitchen. There, she leaned on the counter. Her head was spinning. Maria had suspected Vera was Andrei's biological daughter, but she had brushed it off as nearly impossible. After all, Vera was born exactly nine months after her wedding. And the little girl had high cheekbones, just like Sergei. Even the hair color was Sergei's. But Irina was right. It was the eyes. They were just like Andrei's. Their color, dark-gray, almost black, an exact match, just as the shape.

I won't let this man haunt me forever. Maria balled her hands into fists. *I have moved on.*

But immediately the image of Andrei appeared in front of her. She felt his body pressed against hers. His lips. His face.

No. She shook her head. *No.* She didn't want it to be true and pushed the vision out of her mind.

But it wasn't just the eyes.

When Vera turned five years old, Maria took her to see a movie at a cinema on Champs-Élysées. Right away, the little girl became obsessed with acting. Vera decided she wanted to be an actress, dreamed of going to Hollywood and forced her mother to sign her up for English lessons, once she found out Hollywood was in America, where everyone spoke English.

Maria initially tried to ignore her daughter's obsession, hoping it would pass, but Vera loved to perform.

One occasion stuck in Maria's mind. They were visiting her father, the count's home filled with guests. As dinner was nearing the end, Maria watched, as if in slow motion, how Vera ran up to her grandfather and whispered something into his ear. He gave the little girl an indulgent smile, then nodded in agreement. Vera pulled out a chair and climbed on it, the count asked for the guests' attention, and the little girl proceeded to recite Tatiana's monologue from *Eugene Onegin* by Pushkin.

Maria sat, gripping the sides of her chair, frozen and uncertain, watching her daughter's performance and the guests' dazzled reactions. Her mouth went dry and the reality became more certain that she could not deny the truth about Vera's paternity.

Once Count Suvorov learned of his granddaughter's talent and unique abilities, he encouraged Vera's obsession with acting. Soon, Vera was taking acting lessons, performing in Russian and in French.

Watching her daughter on stage, Maria couldn't help but think of Andrei, but each time she thought of the actor, she told herself their love story was in the past. And even if Vera was Andrei's biological daughter, it wasn't important and played no role in their lives, current or future. Maria shut the knowledge down, burying it as she had always done, and continued to be the dutiful daughter and mother.

Maria kept herself busy at all times, not allowing herself to stop and think for even a moment. She did everything to keep Sergei happy, tried her best to be a good wife and a model mother. But she couldn't quite shake off the feeling that she was living someone else's life. She went through her daily chores, through the routine she'd so carefully put together, as if in a daze. She lived so she could be dutiful and good to others. Too busy to stop and ask herself whether she was happy.

The real her wasn't there.

* * *

1937 PROMISED to be a busy year. Paris was hosting the International Exposition of Art and Technology in Modern Life, which opened on May 25th – to much fanfare. Maria, through her job, got to visit the exposition before it opened, and was fascinated by the Soviet pavilion. She took Irina there days later, and the two of them walked past the enormous metal statue of a factory worker and a female peasant, holding hands, thrusting a hammer and a sickle upwards.

"It's terrifying, isn't it?" Maria noted, staring at the statue. "If this is what a Russian woman is supposed to look like."

"Do you mean the muscles? Or the utter lack of femininity?" Irina rolled her eyes.

"I just wonder. Do Russian women really look like this now?"

"Darling, don't take it so literally. It's art."

"Yes, of course." Maria sighed, "I just sometimes wonder. What would have happened to me had I stayed? Or if I'd gone back with Andrei? In 1923."

"Not that again," Irina huffed. They walked inside the pavilion and that's when Maria saw it. The poster for the Moscow Art Theater hung on the wall of the pavilion, right by the door.

"Irina," Maria said, walking up to it. "Take a look at this." She tried to keep her voice steady.

"What is it?" Irina asked.

"They're coming back to Paris. They will bring a production of *Anna Karenina*."

"Do you want to go?" Irina asked.

"I do." Maria nodded. "I think it's a sign we saw the poster here."

"Are you going to tell Sergei?" Irina asked.

"No. There's no need." Maria averted her eyes. Irina knew her better than anyone.

"But you remember what happened last time, Maria?"

"That was ages ago, Irina. No chance of that happening again."

"Alright. We'll go together. But only to the performance. We're not going backstage. Not this time."

"No, not this time."

CHAPTER 39

"Do you suppose Tolstoy hated women?" Irina stirred a sugar cube into her coffee. They were sitting at the Café de Flore, where they had agreed to meet before the performance. This was one tradition they wouldn't break. Posters for the performance of *Anna Karenina* by the famous Moscow Art Theater were all around Paris by then. The Russian beau-monde was expected to be there, and though the tour was in August, when Paris usually emptied out, all of the Moscow Art Theater performances were sold out.

"I am sure of it." Maria smiled, a sad smile. "Poor Anna. She never had a chance."

"She should have just waited it out. All her husband wanted was some decency. He wouldn't have cared if she was with Vronsky discreetly."

"I suppose so. But for some women, it's all or nothing."

"Darling, that's not real life. You know that, right?"

"I do." Maria nodded. "I wonder if Andrei will be performing."

"Remember, we aren't going backstage."

"No, my dear friend. We aren't."

* * *

MARIA WALKED into the theater dressed in her silk, navy-blue dress. She'd kept it all those years and it still fit her. She had put extra care into her appearance when getting ready.

There was no logic to what she was doing.

It had been fourteen years since she last saw Andrei. She was married, had a daughter, a great job, and a good life. She was just going to a performance with her friend. Only that.

The third bell rang, and she took a seat next to Irina. They were seated in the very center of the fifth row of orchestra, with a great view of the stage. Maria scanned the program right before the curtain came up, and noted, absent-mindedly, Andrei's name.

"Look," she whispered to Irina, "he's performing tonight."

"Maria, this is your chance to appreciate his artistic talents," Irina told her with a giggle, and a woman seated diagonally from them turned back, sneering.

The curtain rose and Maria watched the performance in fascination. She loved everything about the production. The costumes, the decor, everything had been done incredibly well. She'd made a mental note to mention this to Irina after the performance.

When suddenly, she felt as if the world stopped moving. It was the scene of Anna's first encounter with Vronsky.

"It's him," she whispered to Irina. "It's him."

Maria recognized Andrei, but the shock of recognition wasn't because she saw her former love. She remembered the man in uniform from her dream. The half-turned face. This was the image of her promised love, the one she saw as a young girl, when she did a divination by placing her comb under her pillow.

"It was always him," she muttered to herself.

Andrei-Vronsky was speaking, then the scene ended, and he left the stage, and Anna was left with Vronsky's elderly mother. But the image of Andrei in uniform, dressed as an officer, stayed before Maria's eyes.

"Irina, I have to leave. I have to get air." Maria rose.

"Darling, wait." Irina tried to stop her, but Maria, ignoring the murmur of the crowd, left the theater. She stood outside, alone in quiet contemplation, then waited in a nearby cafe for the performance to end to reconnect with Irina.

"I think I'm over him," Maria said. "I really think I am. You know, I sat there, thinking about it, and I've lived in a fantasy all this time."

"Well, good," Irina noted. "It's what I've been trying to tell you."

"I know. But it's seeing him on stage. It all just clicked. He's an actor. A good actor. And I fell for it. Head over heels."

"Maria, please give yourself some credit."

They were walking on the nearly empty Champs-Élysées, the summer air warm, the sound of a late-night taxi honking.

"Do you think he saw me? In the audience?" Maria asked.

"I doubt it. Back then, you know, when I was this great benefactress," Irina laughed, "I talked to actors a lot. And I've always been told they don't look at the crowd. Especially those who are in Stanislavsky's theater. They live the part. So when they're on stage, they are that person."

"Really? So, he didn't see me?"

"Does it matter, Maria?"

"No. I suppose not. And I should count my blessings, Irina."

"It's about time, darling." Irina squeezed her hand. "It's about time. And good that you never told Sergei."

"Yes. I agree." Maria nodded. She knew Irina meant Vera's paternity. "Besides, we don't know whether it's true."

PART V

CHAPTER 40

Count Suvorov had always prided himself on staying ahead of the game. On keeping his nose to the wind. And in September 1939, two days after Germany invaded Poland, he announced his decision to leave France for America.

"But Papa, this is so sudden!" Maria's teaspoon clanked, as she dropped it on the table.

"I'm not going through another war with the Germans," the count said. "I don't like where things are going. There's no time to waste. Come with us, Maria." He looked up at his daughter urgently, staring at her from across the dinner table.

"Papa, don't be so dramatic. We're going to be fine. And besides, I don't want to go anywhere. I've made Paris my home now."

"Think of Vera. I'm certainly thinking of Konstantin. I don't want my son to be drafted, to suffer whatever indignity men go through in a war."

"But Papa…" Maria clasped her hands.

"You would understand if you had a son."

"I'm sorry."

"Listen, send Vera with us."

"But Papa, she's only fifteen. I'm not sure. There's no need to go anywhere."

"Vera's wanted to go to America for ages, so now would be the perfect time."

"I'll think about it," Maria said vaguely, picking her spoon back up absentmindedly.

"Why don't you talk it over with Sergei and let me know?"

"We vill take great care of Vera," Antoinette interjected.

She'd been rushing around the living room, supervising the maid, who was packing her fine china. Antoinette appeared completely unfazed by the upcoming move, so complete was her trust in her husband.

Maria felt a sense of wonder. Having learned independence so young, she could not imagine herself to be so fully reliant on her husband to make all the decisions, even for a day, the way Antoinette did.

"And you know how much she wants to go to Hollywood. Ve vill take her zere." Antoinette insisted on speaking Russian, though her accent had gotten worse over the years of living in France.

By the time Maria left her father's apartment, she'd already made up her mind. She would send Vera to America. She considered it a mere formality when she mentioned the idea to Sergei, and Sergei agreed. Only on one condition.

"I'm going with her," Sergei said, staring at Maria blankly.

"What?"

"I'm leaving. I'm not doing this again."

"Doing what?"

"War. I'm not putting myself through war again. I want to live in peace."

"But Sergei, it won't be so bad—"

"It'll be bad. I've heard stories from the soldiers. The ones who fought the Germans first and came back to fight the Reds. They all said nothing in the world compared to their cruelty."

"But no one would expect you to fight."

"Do you realize what would happen if the Germans came here? To France?"

"To France? Sergei, what of the Maginot line!" Maria exclaimed, proud of her knowledge of military preparations France had made. "General Pétain says we're completely safe here."

"Safe? No. I don't think so. You know the French don't know how to fight," Sergei scoffed. "We should all go to America."

"No." Maria shook her head. "I'm not going anywhere. I ran away once and I'm not doing that again. Paris is my home now."

"But Maria. You could be in danger."

"No." Maria was categorical. She didn't know where this certainty came from, but she knew she would not be running away.

"I see. I suppose this is it then." The corners of Sergei's mouth curled down. He walked out of the room, ending the conversation.

Another certainty was that her marriage to Sergei was effectively over. They had not been intimate in years, and Maria was glad of it. She assumed Sergei had someone on the side, but never asked, as it relieved her of the marital duties that she despised. She'd forgotten when they last told each other they loved each other and wondered if they ever had.

She and Sergei had stayed together for Vera, putting up the pretense of stability, a common culture, a shared past tying them together. With Sergei's move to America, she would become a free woman again.

* * *

"Maman, this is so exciting!" Vera said, stuffing a dress into her suitcase.

Maria thought of her own mother, and how the two of them had packed for the Tula estate each summer.

"Remember, Vera, you only want to take the essentials," Maria said, repeating her mother's words.

"Maman, but I'm going for a whole year, maybe longer."

"I know, but still, don't overpack. And Vera, are you really sure you want to do this?"

"Yes, Maman, I am so sure. This is something I've wanted to do since that day you took me to the movies."

"Alright, then." Maria smiled at her daughter.

"Maman, can I take your bracelet? The garnet one?"

"The one from Russia?"

"Yes." Vera's eyes sparkled.

"Of course, Vera." Maria took off the bracelet and snapped it on Vera's wrist.

"Thank you, Maman. Please tell me about your first ball!"

"I was a little older than you. And your grandmother, my mother, told me how to behave. And I wore tiny earrings with diamonds. That was the only jewelry I was allowed to wear."

"Do you still have them, Maman?"

"No, they are back in Russia. I gave them to a friend. As a memento."

"So, were you like a real aristocrat?" Vera asked, eyes open wide.

"Yes, Vera, I was a countess. And so are you. Don't forget where you come from and your origins when you're in America."

"I won't, Maman. And what about your necklace? Did you have it then?" Vera pointed to Maria's neck, around which hung a golden chain with Andrei's emerald ring. Maria reached to feel the necklace and blushed.

"No, I got it later. It was a gift." She told her daughter.

"It's so pretty!" Vera said, kissed her on the cheek, and fluttered off.

After her family departed, Maria wandered the corridors of her father's apartment, where she would now stay, feeling nothing but relief. The only person she would miss was her daughter.

Life in Paris was stable at first. There weren't many changes, and Maria enjoyed her newfound independence. She loved living in a large, beautiful apartment, which was a welcome change from the Marais. Though she loved her neighborhood, she enjoyed living in the prestigious part of the city. She saw Irina regularly, always at the Café de Flore, the two of them reconnecting at least once a week. Irina, who never had children, was a recent widow. Count Kutuzov died in Monaco the previous winter.

"Maria, you wouldn't believe it. Two of his mistresses showed up to the funeral." Irina placed her coffee cup back on the saucer. "Now, you wonder what goes through those women's minds."

"Maybe they wanted to look at you?"

"Look at me? They must have seen me before." Irina shrugged and adjusted her curls. She'd recently started getting her hair dyed a platinum shade of blonde and looked even more striking.

"I'm so lucky to have a friend like you." Maria smiled at her friend.

"Listen, I recently met this adorable young man," Irina said. "Jean-Luc. He's an aspiring musician and is giving me vocal lessons."

"What? Irina, aren't you supposed to be in mourning?"

"I am. But who's to say a woman can't learn how to sing

while mourning her husband? Besides, you know what he told me?"

"The two of you talk?"

"Of course we do. Don't be so crass!" Irina giggled. "He told me that singing is great for curing a cold."

"I admire you," Maria said after a pause. "I sometimes wish I had someone."

"You should have gotten yourself a lover a long time ago." Irina raised her eyebrows.

"I can't do affairs. You know how I am."

"Well, it won't be an affair now. Sergei is gone."

"I suppose you're right. But I love being alone. I really do." Maria chuckled. "I think it was when my father had taken up with Antoinette, when I was eighteen. I was effectively all alone, only Dunya to keep me company."

"And me!"

"Yes, for a while. But then, I was alone in that big house. Taking care of things. And a part of me wants to go back to that."

"Well, I love male company." Irina shrugged. "So we agree to disagree."

CHAPTER 41

War came to Paris suddenly. The Maginot line, just as Sergei had predicted, couldn't withstand German attack, and German troops marched through Belgium, Luxembourg, the Netherlands, and parts of France in May 1940.

On June 3rd, Maria woke up to the sound of clanking and bells outside. She was used to rising early, when the city was quiet at dawn. But not that day. Something rolled down the street, and Maria peeked out of her window. Two women were pushing a cart loaded with household goods. Two suitcases, boots, an iron, and blankets stacked up high. Three children sat on top of the pile, their faces gaunt, observing. Maria stared after them in surprise.

They were walking westward, out of the city. She was about to have her morning tea when she heard the sound of hooves on the road. She looked out and saw a horse pulling a cart.

Maria got dressed and ran outside. A neighbor, a man in his eighties, whom she'd met when she first came to Paris and who was always polite, if reticent, was standing outside, smoking a cigarette. His dog was sitting next to him, just as polite and reserved as its owner.

"What is happening?" Maria asked, wide-eyed.

"Haven't you heard? The Parisians are fleeing."

"Where are they going?"

"No one knows." The man shrugged. "I'm too old to go," he said indifferently.

Over the next week, it was as if the whole city of Paris was on the move. Every day, Maria watched as crowds left the city. At first, it was a few people, but pretty soon, it turned into a steady stream. People fled on bicycles, horses, the few lucky ones drove away, but some cars had been abandoned on Champs-Élysées, as they ran out of gas and their passengers continued on foot.

Maria watched. She wasn't going anywhere. She waited, writing letters to her family in the United States.

I've been through the revolution before, she told herself; *I made it then, I'll make it now.*

* * *

ON JUNE 14TH, 1940, the Germans marched into Paris, the French government surrendering. German tanks rolled through Champs-Élysées, and Maria could hear them from her apartment. She stayed at home all day, refusing to believe the city she'd made her second home was now occupied by the Nazis.

Paris changed fast under Nazi occupation. German soldiers settled in apartments, took over offices and cafes. All of Parisian cinemas, including Vera's favorite movie theater on Champs-Élysées, became property of the Nazi regime. Posters warning the remaining Parisians against the dangers of communism hung across the city.

German soldiers were there to stay.

Café de Flore, too, had become a favorite Nazi spot, and a large swastika hung out front. Maria and Irina now saw each other at home, rather than risk going out in public.

"This is shameful. Utterly so. Doesn't it remind you of the abdication of the tsar?" Irina insisted, taking a seat in Maria's living room.

"Not at all! The tsar was hated by most of his people. But the French have a democracy."

"Exactly! It doesn't make any sense."

"I don't know. Who are we to judge? We're just immigrants here."

"Come on, you've lived here for twenty years. And I've been here for, well, twenty-five. I'm just not sure what to do next." Irina sighed.

"It's absurd, I agree. France needs us. But Sergei, I suppose he's too old to fight anyway, but it's like he knew this would happen."

"I suppose he did. I think they all listen to Denikin," Irina said. "You know he says Hitler will invade the Soviet Union next."

"Do you think that's possible?"

"Denikin is never wrong." Irina shrugged.

"He lost to the Soviets, Irina." Maria shook her head.

"Well, yes. But the Russian community sent ten thousand immigrants to fight for France just last year. What will happen to them now that France surrendered?" Irina ran her hand through her hair.

"You know, Antoinette told me I didn't want to leave France because I don't have a son. And now I understand. They were right to take Konstantin to America."

"Is Vera doing well?"

"Yes, she loves it in America. Not in Hollywood yet," Maria chuckled, "but soon enough, I'm sure of it."

"Will you move there?"

"It's too late now." Maria shook her head. "Even if I wanted to. I've made my choice."

"Do you think it's because you were trying to get away from Sergei? From your marriage?" Irina fixed her gaze on Maria.

"There must have been an easier way." Maria breathed out, balking at the question.

"Not for you, darling." Irina placed her hand over hers. "Not for you."

"I never thought I'd live through something like this again," Maria shared. "Feeling like an outsider in my own city. First, in Moscow, and now this."

"Listen, did you hear about de Gaulle's speech? He called for the French Resistance to the Nazis."

"He did? When?" Maria stared at her friend in amazement.

"Right after the surrender. Of course, since we're here, it wasn't exactly on the news. But I learned from a few of my friends. So, they've been organizing. And they need people."

"Really? What kind of people?"

"Like us, for example." Irina winked.

"Are you going to do it?" Maria opened her eyes wide. "Isn't it dangerous?"

"I suppose so." Irina shrugged. "But we need to do the right thing, darling."

For Irina, involvement with the French resistance was a natural continuation of combining her social skills with the desire to follow her conscience. Just like before the Russian Revolution, when Irina had turned her salon into a pro-revolution endeavor, she was compelled to fight injustice and oppression.

Maria was slower to start, but a few months later, she accompanied Irina to meet a man, whom the two of them knew only as Michel.

"Listen, I don't know much about him, but he's been living undercover. He is in charge of supplies, runs the cell in Paris. It might be a good idea to pick a fake name for yourself," Irina said. "So you aren't using your real credentials."

"That's easy. Did I ever tell you about Martha Goncharova?" Maria asked.

"You did!"

"Well, come to think of it, I might still have that passport somewhere."

"Great, so you can be Martha Goncharova then."

Her first task was to deliver a note from one end of Paris to the other.

On the way to pick up the note, Maria felt thrilled to be contributing to the Resistance. But, as soon as she stuffed the piece of paper into her purse, she felt her hands shaking. During the ride on the metro, she remained standing, and once she was out on the street, she checked frequently over her shoulder to make sure no one was following her and took the most round-about way to the drop-off location.

It wasn't until she delivered the note to the agreed site that Maria finally breathed a sigh of relief.

But she didn't quit. After the note, she was asked to transport a bag with supplies. The assignments seemed relatively easy and unimportant, but, Maria knew, helped the Resistance fighters in their cause, and she took each task seriously. Soon, she and Irina graduated to much riskier assignments, involving the maquis, the French resistance fighters.

Maria knew about the incredible people who'd made it their mission to disrupt the functioning of the Nazi regime in occupied France, who lived dangerous lives, hiding out in the woods, relying on the kindness of strangers, stealing weapons, engaging in sabotage. Each moment of their lives was full of danger. Maria soon met her first maquis.

Michel told her to meet a man, whom she would call Pierre, and hide him in Paris. She would need to house him in her apartment and accompany him across town after several days, when it was safe to do so.

She went to meet Pierre at Gare de Lyon. She was by herself, and Pierre arrived, dressed in an ill-fitting suit. He looked like a merchant who had come to Paris on business, and the only thing that could give him away were his shoes. Worn, dirty, those were the shoes of a man who'd been living rough in the forest. And wearing shoes like that in Paris was a risk. They could attract the attention of the Gestapo and lead to questioning and an arrest. So after Maria took Pierre to her apartment, she went to the Russian church, and got Pierre proper-fitting shoes he could safely wear in Paris. Then, she went to light a candle for Dunya, whose memory she treasured still.

Maria knew she had to be careful at the church, because informants were everywhere. So she had confided in one of the women who helped her get the shoes that she had a new lover.

"Irina, I'm sure the woman is writing to Antoinette with the news, and Sergei probably knows already," Maria shared with her friend.

"If that woman actually knew you, Maria, she would immediately know you were lying. No one would believe you've gotten yourself a lover."

"Come on!" Maria threw her hands up in mock indignation, but Irina was right. Love was the last thing on Maria's mind.

After the first maquis, Maria helped many others. Maria started to keep a supply of clean men's clothes at home. She took clothing donations and fixed them at home. Michel now considered her and Irina his most trusted assets in Paris.

"We have several Russian guerrilla fighters. They've come from Poland, to help the French resistance," he told Maria one day.

"Russian?" Maria gulped. "From the Soviet Union?"

"Yes. They have all taken an oath to fight against the Nazi Regime by joining the French Resistance. Some don't speak any French. So, you'll need to help them get around Paris. Translate, if needed."

"Of course. But how did they make it as far as Paris without speaking any French?"

Michel raised his eyebrows. He was a man of few words, but his facial expression said it all, and Maria understood: whoever these people were, their drive and sacrifice were such, it didn't matter what language they spoke. They navigated the terrain, relied on their intuition and luck, and made it across Europe with one goal: elimination of the Nazis.

Maria remembered the first Soviet maquis she met. He was a short man of an incredible athletic ability. An officer in the Soviet army who had volunteered to join the guerrilla fighters. The man went by the name Boris and shared he'd been captured as a prisoner of war but ran away.

"How did you get out?" Maria asked.

"I killed the guard and escaped one night," the man said simply. He didn't share what weapon he used or how he managed to do this, and Maria didn't press him for more information. "I stayed in the woods. That was the easy part. And then I found a few others, so we blew up the train tracks."

"Just like that?" Maria stared at Boris, wide-eyed.

"Just like that." He smirked.

Over time, Maria heard lots of stories from the maquis, and most of them were just like Boris'. Blown up trains, hijacked German vehicles, escapes from prisons, and each time, the men who shared the stories with her had the same glint in their eyes: they were proud of their accomplishments, but they were not done.

They would keep going until the Nazi regime was destroyed, fully and completely. These men lived for their mission. They had nothing else in their lives except for full and utter dedication to winning the war. They had chosen to fight as guerrilla fighters, knowing full well going into this, that they would be on the verge of death until the final day of the war.

It was a new breed of men. Maria wondered where they came from and, once the war ended, what would become of them.

CHAPTER 42

Over the three years of the Resistance movement, Maria had gotten used to always being on guard. She prided herself on keeping a low profile, in part thanks to her being a woman 'of a certain age', who was less likely to attract the attention of the Gestapo.

Now in her late-forties, Maria could easily blend in with the other French women, slim, dressed in all black, moving effortlessly through the crowd. She avoided eye contact and made the expression on her face as bland as possible. It was a skill, and she'd learned it well. She didn't want to be remembered. Maria usually wore a hat, a plain one, and dressed in clothes that were stylish about twenty years ago, projecting a look of faded glory, of a woman whose best days were behind her.

That day, she was to bring a newly arrived Russian maquis, whom Michel called Anton, to her apartment. Anton, as indicated by Michel, had recently arrived in Paris, and spoke French. Having gotten used to helping those resistance fighters who needed help with the translation, Maria asked why she in particular would be needed.

Michel shrugged. "He asked for you."

"For me?"

"Yes. He said he needed to see Martha Goncharova."

Before leaving her apartment, Maria checked herself in the mirror and, for the first time in months, decided to apply lipstick. With a sigh, she examined her face, seeing the small wrinkles under her eyes, and thought the years had been kind to her. If it weren't for her neck, she would look much younger than her forty-eight years.

Irina told her, half-jokingly, it was their limited diet and the hungry days of her youth, and Maria now smiled fondly, remembering her friend's words. Irina was in a relationship with a high-ranking Resistance fighter, who was half her age, and, despite the hardship of the war, their romance was blossoming.

Turning in front of the mirror, Maria decided to change. She got the navy-blue silk dress, the one she'd worn to the performance of *Anna Karenina*, out of the closet and put it on. The dress flowed beautifully and accentuated her waist. But the dress was too memorable, and Maria threw it off.

Another time. She couldn't risk attracting attention to her person.

She left the apartment dressed in all black, as usual, and made her way to the agreed location. It was a tiny storefront by the Place de la République. The store once belonged to a Jewish storeowner, but the woman had been arrested in 1941. Now it was operated by a former shop assistant and had been turned into an underground Resistance head-quarters.

In the back room, a small space, which, before the war, must have been a storage space, the Resistance fighters assembled. Maria knew they kept guns, clothes, and fake documents there, and if the Nazis ever discovered them, it would immediately lead to an arrest and an execution of those involved. But the Nazis never went to this store, where a seemingly bored assistant sat behind the dusty counter with a lonely jar of olives and stale cheese in the display case.

On the way there, Maria wondered who this man was and why he had asked for her, and how he knew her alias. She decided he must have gotten a recommendation from another maquis she'd helped over the years and was curious to ask him who had told him her name. Maria entered the store, examined the dusty jar of olives, and told the sleepy assistant she was looking for lemons.

This was the code to be let into the backroom, and each time Maria wondered what would happen if someone off the street walked in, and, by pure chance, asked for lemons. But the store front was such that no one in their right mind would ever expect it to have fresh lemons, or any other fruit. In the two years the Resistance had been operating there, the lemon code phrase worked well.

Hearing the code, the sleepy assistant rose from her seat and escorted Maria into the back room. The space was filled with smoke which made Maria cough. Michel sat at the table in the corner, facing her, and across from him sat the man who must have been Anton. His back was turned to Maria, but some sort of a primal instinct in her registered his presence in a way an animal reacts to danger in the woods.

She jerked back, her heart beating fast, as if it was about to jump out of her chest. Maria struggled to breathe and stood, staring at the man. He turned and fixed his gaze on her, staring at her with his dark-gray eyes that seemed almost black.

The spark of instant recognition shot through her. *Andrei.*

It had been almost twenty years since they last saw each other. He had aged, his hair now gray at the temples, and Maria noticed lines on his forehead, but his eyes had not changed.

"This is Anton," Michel introduced the stranger. Then, his face expressionless, Michel explained to Maria the assignment. He spoke in rapid French, and Maria wondered whether Andrei understood everything. When it was time to leave, it seemed Andrei had understood enough to follow her out of the store and onto the street.

They walked in silence next to each other, neither one daring to speak first. The memory of how the two of them used to go to the Moscow Art Theater together flashed in Maria's mind, and she felt a yearning for that feeling of closeness and togetherness. But she pushed it away. She would need to get through keeping Andrei in her home for several days. Then she could go back to living her regular life.

Maria wondered why he had asked for her. The man walked quietly beside her until she questioned if she had only imagined Andrei. The man was older and the room had been dark, and so, after walking in silence for several minutes, she decided she had made a mistake.

"It might be best to take the metro," Maria said to the man, and he nodded.

This is not Andrei. I'm just losing my mind, Maria concluded.

They were about to descend into the metro, when Maria saw the Nazi patrol walking down the street towards them. Maria didn't know what documents Anton had on him, for it wasn't discussed with Michel. The man must have noticed the Nazi patrol, too, for he stopped.

"Come here," he said to her quietly, in Russian. He pulled her towards him, and, before Maria could understand what was happening, he kissed her lightly. "Act like you're in love," he ordered and clasped his hands on her lower back.

Maria squealed, and he murmured into her ear, "Good girl."

She felt like she was falling. His lips on hers, the kiss, the feeling was back. The dam that had hidden her emotions, her feelings for Andrei, her love for this man had burst open. She could hear Irina's warning in her head, 'protect your heart', but it was too late.

"Andrei," she whispered into his ear.

"Masha."

The Nazi patrol walked by them. One of the Nazis whistled in approval. The sound of receding footsteps on the sidewalk. The danger had passed. Maria and Andrei pulled apart, reluctantly, and slowly walked to the metro.

"Is it you?" Maria asked quietly, after they got on the train.

"Yes," he said and took her hand into his.

"No. It can't be." Maria shook her head. "I think I've gone mad."

"Come here." Andrei leaned over and kissed her. A passionate kiss.

"It's the feeling of everything clicking into place."

"Yes." His eyes didn't leave her face.

"I won't be able to exist without you," Maria noted simply.

"Neither can I. Masha, I came to be with you."

Maria was in a daze. She didn't remember the ride to her stop, getting off the train, leaving the metro. It wasn't until they were walking up the steps to her flat, that she jerked back to reality. For the first time in three years since working with the Resistance, Maria felt fear.

She was exposed, completely at Andrei's mercy, and it happened without any warning, within mere seconds. Maria's hands shook as she fumbled for the keys and opened her apartment door. All the walls she'd built around herself, the safeguards she'd so carefully erected around her heart, had burst open.

"I can't," she squeezed out and rushed inside.

"Masha. What is it?" Andrei followed her.

"I can't. This isn't real." Tears flooded her eyes. "I'm not doing this again. You've come back to torture me. I'm not strong. I'm not. I can't."

Andrei let out a deep breath. He didn't react at first, but then walked over to her and hugged her. She felt small in his arms, protected from harm.

"Masha," he said, running his hand through her hair. "I never stopped loving you."

"I've waited for you. I want you to know that." She started crying again. "I've loved you all this time."

"I could feel it," Andrei said. "I saw you. Seven years ago, I saw you in the audience. Why did you leave? I had a letter for you, Masha."

"I couldn't," Maria said. "But I thought actors didn't see the audience."

"That's not true. We do. We just pretend like we don't. I saw you. You were wearing that navy-blue dress. You looked so beautiful, Masha. I've never wanted you so badly." He looked at her with a different expression now.

She read desire, raw animal desire, and felt the spark ignite in her body. The sadness, the fear she'd been feeling, gave way to passion, which bubbled to the surface and spread through her, like a fire. Blood pulsed through her veins, her heart beating fast. Her lips were throbbing with anticipation. She let out a deep breath, which would have been a moan had she not exercised all of her control.

"I have the dress," she croaked. "I'll put it on for you right now. You know, I was going to wear it this morning."

"Yes." The pupils of his eyes had dilated and his eyes looked pitch-black.

She hurried to change into the silk navy-blue dress, and when she came out and stood in front of the mirror, he didn't say a word. Andrei approached, and she saw his reflection. She saw him run his finger softly down her neck, then down her shoulder, and his touch felt like fire.

"Masha. I've found you." He breathed into her neck, and the next moment his lips were on hers. He moved to her neck, touching her breasts. His hands were on her hips, and he picked her up, carrying her to the bed.

It no longer mattered to her what came next. She wanted him then and now.

* * *

It was late in the afternoon, and the setting summer sun shone through the windows, casting long shadows on the walls. They sat together on the couch, holding each other, as if letting go would make their reunion less real.

"Some things are worth the wait," Andrei said. He reached for his coat, and Maria felt a knot form in her stomach, thinking he would get dressed to leave.

"Do you have any scissors?" Andrei asked, "I have something I brought from Moscow. For you."

"Let me do this," Maria said and carefully unstitched the lining.

Andrei took out a tiny pouch and handed it to her. She recognized the worn-out velvet sachet right away. Pulling apart the strings, Maria took out a pair of earrings. They were small, with little diamonds. The very ones she'd worn to her first ball and had given to Klava on her last day in Moscow.

"But how? Andrei, this can't be." Maria picked up the earrings and held them against the light. "Thank you."

"I told Klava I was going to find you. And she told Kira. Kira knew your story, our story. She thought we were the modern-day Romeo and Juliet, except very old." Andrei smirked. "How we're missing each other and never quite able to meet."

"Except we just did." Maria smiled at him and his whole face lit up. "Are they doing alright?"

"Yes, they're doing fine. They stayed in Moscow, didn't evacuate at the start of the war, and Gavrila, if you remember him, has risen through the ranks at the factory, so they've actually got two rooms in the mansion now."

"That's good to hear," Maria said. "And I've been wearing this." She lifted the necklace and showed Andrei the golden ring with the emeralds.

"The ring, your wedding ring." Andrei kissed her. "Oh, Masha."

"I've worn it every day since you gave it to me," Maria said simply.

"Does it fit? Can you wear it now? On your finger, I mean." Andrei scanned her face for a reaction.

"I haven't tried in years. Maybe." Maria unclasped the chain and the ring slid off. She held it up, the emeralds sparkling in the light.

"Let me." He took the band and slipped it onto her right ring finger. It fit perfectly. "I want us to get married, Masha," Andrei said emphatically. "I don't want to lose you now that I've found you again. I've learned my lesson."

When Maria didn't respond, he kissed her. "I didn't even ask if you were married. Of course, you must be married."

"We've been apart for several years now. He left before the war. He lives in America," Maria said. "And you?"

"I was married for a few years. She left me," Andrei said simply. "Right after I came back from Paris in 1937. You see, she found a letter I wrote for you."

"A letter? What letter?" Maria stared at Andrei.

"I wrote it before coming here on tour, with *Anna Karenina*. I never gave it to you. But I've kept it all these years." Out of his wallet, Andrei produced a neatly folded piece of paper, yellowed, creased on the edges. "It's been through a lot," he noted, handing it to Maria.

> *August 31st, 1937*
>
> *My darling Masha,*
>
> *I've thought of you every day since the day we parted. I think of you when I wake up and when I go to sleep. You are the first thing on my mind each day, your face, your smile. You made me once the happiest man alive, but I was too young and too foolish to understand my luck in having found you. I know that when I breathe my last breath, my life will not have been in vain, because I have loved you. I miss you every day, my dear Masha.*
>
> *Know that I will remain forever yours,*
> *Andrei*

"Andrei, I so wish you'd given me the letter back then," Maria gasped, looking up at him. "But then, seven years ago things would have been different…"

He ran his finger over her ring. "I've come to stay, Masha. I won't go back. Not this time."

"Oh, Andrei."

"I know, I sometimes think, maybe we had to suffer, to be apart, so we can appreciate the gift that is our love," Andrei noted. "It's been thirty years since we first met. Time is a strange thing."

"I have a daughter, called Vera," Maria said. "And I sometimes think, well…" Maria cleared her throat. "She's studying to be an actress. And her eyes. They look just like yours."

"You mean to say... But that's impossible. How old is she?"

"Twenty."

Andrei was quiet and then after a pause, asked, "Do you think I can meet her?"

"She lives in America. Studying to be an actress. I hope she can come back to Paris after the war. I miss her terribly."

"Vera. Faith," he said. "That's a beautiful name. That's what was uniting us all these years, wasn't it?"

"Yes," Maria said. "I never lost faith."

"Neither did I," Andrei said.

The End

* * *

Thank you for reading 'A Countess from Moscow'.

If you enjoyed my debut novel, I would love your honest review on Amazon and Goodreads. Why am I asking for reviews? For an indie author like myself, each review means I can get more books to other readers who enjoy stories written in the historical fiction genre. This is why every single review means a huge amount to me.

Thank you for your support. And above all, happy reading.

ABOUT THE AUTHOR

Alex Alvin grew up fascinated by history and felt connected to the past through stories of love and war. That fascination has translated into Alex's books that explore how world events impact people and their fates. Creating historically accurate books, where these stories come to life, is Alex's passion.

If you'd like to keep in touch, please subscribe to my newsletter. Or you can find me at any of the social media sites below.

facebook.com/AlexAlvinAuthor
instagram.com/alexalvinauthor
bookbub.com/authors/alex-alvin
amazon.com/author/alexalvin